SoBe Boatees

Kevon Andersen

V̲B

VONNIE BOOKS
MIAMI

Copyright © 2007
Kevon Andersen

This is a work of fiction. Names, characters and incidents are either invented by the author or are used fictitiously. Any resemblance to actual persons, living or dead, or events, is entirely coincidental. There actually was a fishing guide, ruler of his own island kingdom, named Sir Lancelot Jones. He lived in the Upper Keys for almost a century, and his story is based on information and news clips provided by the staff at Biscayne National Park.

Visit the author's website at: **www.vonniebooks.com**

Library of Congress Control Number: 2006911188

ISBN-13: 978-0-9791941-0-8
ISBN-10: 0-9791941-0-5

VB
VONNIE BOOKS
MIAMI

Cover photograph: A cruising cat in silhouette near the Featherbeds, Biscayne National Park, December of 2003. *Back cover photo:* A sloop leaving the harbor at Boca Chita Key in BNP, November of 2006. Photos by Kevon Andersen. Charts by the author.

Designed on *Ionia*
Printed in the U.S.A. by
Morris Publishing
3212 East Highway 30
Kearney, NE 68847

Dedication/Acknowledgements

To Debbie
For sharing the helm

The author would like to thank the staff at Biscayne National Park, especially the rangers on the water, who were always willing to field a question, send info, or just talk.   The author also thanks the sailors: Ken & Barbara Johnson, Gail & Steve Martin, Taft, Albert & Marta Gagnon, Mars & Mel Lawley, Bob Collins, Terry & Sue Green, Bob & Stephanie Lomnicky, George, Pat & Pete Walker, and all the wonderful boaters in Miami. And thank you to the landlubbers: Tony & Ana Fennema, Stephen & Jennifer Bailey, Dr. Mike Roman, J.J. Smith, Vic Baker and Lindy Benagh.   And a special thank you to **Chris Sekin** for his editing & advice and Paul Sekin for his support – since the age of three.   And a final acknowledgement to that aquaphobic non-boater Vonnie Green, for being the writer to emulate.

Index to Illustrations

Contents:

*Flotsam (discarded wine opener)
washed ashore on deserted Victory Cay, Bahamas.*

Preface

Using the GPS Coordinates

SoBe Boatees is fiction. Te Cuesta Isle, where these SoBe Boatees live, is a mythical place, dredged from the muck of upper Biscayne Bay and my imagination. But that doesn't mean I can't give you the exact GPS coordinates for it.

In today's world, we'd be helpless without our array of GPS receivers spitting out our position on the planet within a few meters – especially when it comes to boating. In discussions with boaters who cruised in the days before this invention, I was struck by the romantic theme throughout their discourse: *that we gave up some of the adventure of sailing when we lost the ability to get lost.*

The world is shrinking and there is nothing we can do but embrace it. Even the outdoor adventure magazines are getting into the act, proclaiming they are GPS-enabled. So I thought, since we boaters are dependent on these gizmos, why not make the novel GPS-enabled.

If you have a laptop, an electronic charting program and the charts for southeastern Florida and the western Bahamas, you can follow along on this modern sailing adventure. The goal is to provide a waypoint "route" through the novel and to feed the fixation that most boaters (and many readers) have with charts and maps.

Hope you enjoy this little feature. But remember this disclaimer: The GPS coordinates and the few maps in the book *are not to be used for navigation*. I mention this only because a few years ago Debbie (my wife) and I crewed on the delivery of a catamaran from Great Exuma to Grenada. My last-second assignment was to buy the missing chart of the waters from the Turks & Caicos to Puerto Rico before flying over to George Town, Bahamas. But *Blue Water Charts* was closed that Sunday, so I figured I could borrow or bum one from a northbound cruiser over in George Town. *Wrong*.

We ended up using a foldout map of the Caribbean in an old *National Geographic* found onboard to get from Grand Turk to San Juan. We only wandered into the Silver Bank's coral heads once, so I guess you could say it worked since we lived to tell the tale. But that did show me why they tag on those disclaimers.

-- K. A.

Note: If needed, there's a glossary of nautical terms in the appendix.

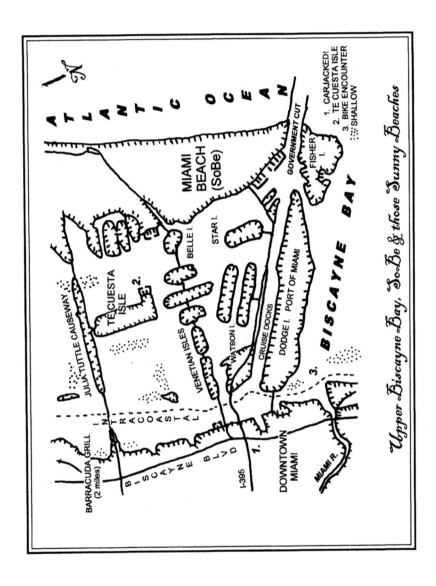

Upper Biscayne Bay, SoBe & those Sunny Beaches

Chapter 1:

Carjacked

On a February day in Miami in the recent past . . .

Blackie Petersen decelerated in the left-lane exit dumping him off of elevated I-395. No longer headed for Miami Beach, he descended to ground level and into the seething masses of downtown Miami. Blackie downshifted his Z3 Beamer twice to keep from hurtling through the intersection at the bottom of the ramp. Landing a 767 wasn't nearly as dangerous.

Taking this exit had been his fourth choice for a route home from Miami International Airport. His primary drive – Highway 112 – was closed again for endless landscaping. The first alternate was out since the west Venetian Causeway Bridge was still stuck in the up position after being rammed by a yachtee with many dollars and little sense. And a traffic alert – of another Royal Palm on the MacArthur Causeway median toppled by a distracted, but still speeding tourist – had turned this into his remaining route back to the boat from MIA.

Miami drivers were almost as bad as Miami boaters. Years ago he was near this spot that first time they held the Grand Prix in the park right off of I-395. He came upon a recently arrived islander stopped in the middle lane of the freeway, standing outside his car, leaning on the roof and watching the race. He recalled that was the year of the bad fatalities at the Miami Grand Prix – all of them occurring on the freeway running above the hairpin curve of the track.

Today, he was driving home on a gorgeous February afternoon, a day begun at Chicago O'Hare waiting on the tarmac for deicing before he could flee zero degrees Fahrenheit and a foot of snow. Winter layovers up north were awful, and the warm Miami weather had made him put the top down *and* his guard as well. He tried not to drive home without the protective top if there was any possibility of taking this alternate route through the homeless/arts district on Biscayne Boulevard, and here he was trapped at the long stoplight without protection.

Blackie was pleased with himself for having changed into "civvies" in Flight Ops back at the airport so that he wasn't broiling in his flight uniform in the subtropical sun. But he lost the smile as he looked up and a shadow passed over him. A tire thrown off the elevated expressway appeared headed straight for his face. But it passed in front of him, toward the passenger seat, shrinking. He realized that it was the sole of one of those old hippie sandals with a tire-tread bottom. The sandal was attached to a long, hairy leg and a lanky, cadaverous hulk of a body.

"Going my way?" asked the tall, but aging man as he slid the big foot to the floor and, with surprising ease, set his oversized frame into the tiny confines of the passenger seat.

"Depends on where you're going," Blackie replied, bewildered and even relieved that he would end up being hijacked on the ground, not in the air. "Just as long as you don't want me to drive you from Miami to Cuba."

"Funny, but dated," said the big man, not laughing. "I'm headin' north on Biscayne Boulevard, like you."

Blackie considered bolting from the Beamer and seeking help. But even if he could find a cop, he figured the Z3 would already be in a Hialeah chop shop or on a Colombian-bound freighter by the time he returned.

The light turned green, and in his millisecond of hesitation, Blackie was accosted by the pack of drivers behind him pounding on their horns. He turned left, swerving to avoid a homeless jaywalker in a makeshift chariot built from a grocery cart and being pulled by a Great Dane mix. Blackie glanced to his right so later he would have a description of his passenger. To Blackie he looked like the Marlboro Man, long retired and on his deathbed. He had been a rugged, good-looking man at one time, but now with all the scars, the broken nose and way too much sun those days were long gone.

The man reminded Blackie of an old, leather saddle he had seen as a kid in a Wild West Museum. Blackie could smell his parched, brown skin; it was a burning ozone smell. He also noticed that his hijacker held a fat, letter-sized manila envelope in his hands.

"You live around here?" Blackie asked, following the old book on establishing a rapport with one's hijacker.

"Used to live in Lauderdale," replied the man, who gave a glance his way and added, "You a pilot with a sailboat?"

Blackie paused, wondering where that had come from (had this guy been stalking him?) since he wasn't in uniform and was behind the wheel of his Beamer convertible, not the wheel of his cutter, a 38-foot Island Packet. "Yeah, how'd you know?"

"Way you sit in your seat and hold the yoke. Your Topsiders with the specks of Awlgrip paint on 'em – means you're a real boater and don't just bring the shoes out to go to Hooters. Those cuts on your knuckles probably came from working on an engine or generator in too small of an engine compartment. If you were a powerboater you'd probably have a diesel mechanic do the work.

"Oh yeah, and you got a Dade County airport decal next to the one for Te Cuesta Isle Marina," he added, pointing his immense, knarled finger at the windshield, "and a flight-crew uniform between the seats."

Suddenly Blackie felt that he wasn't quite outwitting his aging hijacker. "Yeah, so what's this all about?"

"I needed a ride. And in Miami, even those who do the carjackings have to be careful," the old man added, pausing to let out a sickening, almost dying cough. When he recovered he went on while still trying to get air. "I had a really nice houseboat once, slept on a half-acre of bed. Made a decent living self-employed. But these last few years I've had a run of bad luck, my health's gone – I've dropped almost 70 pounds. Life is catching up with me."

"A colorful life, no doubt," Blackie replied.

"I have a few stories I could tell. Listen, I know you have to turn up here for the Julia Tuttle Bridge – that's where you're headed, right? Only way to Te Cuesta Isle Marina from here. But can you drive up Biscayne to the next causeway – to the Barracuda Grill – and drop me off? I really don't want to be late."

"The Barracuda Grill? Yeah, I know where it is, at the turn up there near 79th Street."

They headed north in silence until Blackie pulled into the pot-holed lot and stopped. "This is all you wanted?"

"Unless you want to buy me a beer."

Blackie reached back to grab his wallet, a small handout being a cheap way out of a carjacking, but the old man grabbed him by the arm with surprising strength and said, "*Come in* and buy me a beer."

Blackie felt the old man might not let go if he didn't agree, so he nodded and turned off the ignition. He was intrigued by the old man and had all but dismissed him being a threat.

Although the place was on the west side of the Intracoastal, Blackie didn't have any trepidation about leaving the Beamer in the parking lot. For a short time the place had been his former hangout on his days off from flying.

The two-room, cinderblock building sat at the end of a short, squalid canal that spewed into Biscayne Bay, sort of an abbreviated version of the infamous Miami River. The grill's owner lived in an old Holiday Mansion houseboat parked in the debris floating beside the stone wall. When Blackie had first seen the houseboat he wondered why they didn't declare the unused outdrives artificial reefs. The place was a cheap dive with a small bar along one wall with a dirty grill tucked behind it. There were maybe six tables inside with a few more than that on the veranda. The deck overlooked the back entrance of an adult theater and two half-sunk hulks rotting in the canal. Definitely not bay-front at Turnberry Isle, but with Miami's condo-boom, maybe someday.

The food at the Barracuda Grill was incredibly cheap and a much better deal than the beer. On Wednesdays Blackie and a cheapskate neighbor, Yul Grant, would drive over the causeway and up Biscayne to get half-chicken dinners for $5 a piece. Blackie asked the owner why he didn't advertise or get the word out, since the place was always empty. The owner, who was probably the strangest character in the place, said, "If word gets out then I'd get way too busy and that would ruin it for me." Blackie never talked business with him after that.

The incident that made it a former hangout was the coral poisoning. It seemed that "Baha Fish Taco Night" (Thursdays) was such a good deal because the owner was using the grill's namesake, *barracuda*, for the fish tacos. He bought them cheap from a semi-pro Cubano fisherman who bottom fished at the end of the big sewer pipe five miles off Virginia Key (in a 12-foot skiff, no matter what the weather) and then peddled the Great Barracuda at the back doors of several less-than-reputable restaurants.

These weren't the small 'cuda that a few Crackers consider a delicacy, but the big monsters that had a good chance of having *ciguatera*, a potentially fatal form of food poisoning. They were saw-toothed revolvers in a gastronomic game of Russian roulette. Blackie had been off flying on a 3-day trip to Seattle and missed the "Baha Fish Taco Night" that sent a dozen patrons (including his marina neighbor, Yul) to Jackson

Memorial Hospital to have their stomachs pumped like a bunch of dirty bilges.   If the hospital hadn't misplaced the puke samples and bloodwork, the health inspectors might have had the evidence needed to shut down the place.

Today, Blackie figured he'd limit himself to beer.

Blackie and the old man found a table on the patio and the old man ordered them a couple of Buds. Blackie faced the canal, and gazing at the flotsam he saw a gargantuan manatee popping his head out amidst the trash and oil and slime. He remembered the manatee cow and calf he had seen a few months before as he motored to the boatyard far up in the filth of the Miami River. It was obvious why some of these poor creatures were in bad health.

None of the other patrons, regulars at the grill, took notice of the manatee.   Blackie thought that most of them probably considered it a competitor just slightly below them on the food chain.

"So what's your name?" Blackie asked with a smile, "I figure the FBI and NTSB will ask me when they investigate my hijacking."

"Name's Tr – ," he began, but paused. "You can call me *Skipper*. You a cap'n? Seem a little young to be one to me."

"Captain? In the air? No, still an F/O, a first officer. Almost made captain a few months ago, but they retired the last of the old Seven-two's a little early so I'm still stuck in the right seat for a while."

"Hang in there, you'll be a *cap'n* someday. What's your name?"

"You can call me Blackie."

"Blackie? What the hell kinda name is that? You look Scandinavian."

"I am – Blackie Petersen. How I got the surname is too long a story. So, is carjacking your preferred method of transport to Happy Hour? I'm your designated driver-under-duress?"

"No. Here to meet someone and I got a ride with you because it's real important that I make this meeting. Thanks to you I'm early. Gonna have a discussion about one of your marina neighbors. Guy named Ted," the old man replied in a hoarse whisper.

The name brought a strained smile to Blackie's face. Ted lived at the end of the T-head on Pier Three, one of only nine slips at Te Cuesta Isle big enough to fit an 89-foot Breakwater motor yacht. Rumors about Ted flowed like scotch on a Hatteras, and Ted's actions did nothing but fuel them.

"Ted Jones? On the big Breakwater? You're running with some wild company there, *Skipper*."

"I hardly know him. He's involved with one of my clients."

"*Clients*? You're still working? What are you, a down-on-his-luck attorney?"

"No, more of a PI. I help people recover things for a percentage."

"You have an office? But no car?"

"At this point in my life I have to freelance. I told you I was sick; it's the cancer. In my lungs, and nothing they can do. Even starting to affect my memory. Simply a matter of time."

"And you're still working? Where do you live?"

"The Camillus House. One of their shelters."

"You're doing PI work out of the Camillus House? A homeless shelter? How in the world –"

"I've got a cell phone."

"That doesn't bother the bum on the next cot, *Skipper*, when you get calls all hours of the night?"

"Bum? That's pretty insensitive there, Blackie, seeing as how I'm a current resident. I got one of those phones that ring or vibrate. And with Miami's homeless tax, the shelter even gives me an office the size of a broom closet to work out of."

"Sorry for the remark. But nobody's tried to roll you for the phone?"

"No, I'm pretty discreet. And why are *you* giving *me* the third degree here?"

"You've got to admit it's different. I see a TV show here. Get a James Garner type as an older, poorer Jim Rockford. He's lost the trailer in LA and retired to Florida, in the role of the '*Skipper*.' You have an agent?"

"Man, I would have to carjack a smart-ass."

Blackie felt a presence to his right and looked up. A bodybuilder in his mid-twenties with SoBe-model looks was standing there, staring at the *Skipper*. With the tan and the muscles and his spiked blonde hair he looked vaguely familiar.

"Say, don't I know you?" the bodybuilder asked the old man with a hint of a German accent.

The *Skipper* gave him a long look and asked, "Am I supposed to know you?"

"Guess not," he replied, a smile still plastered on his face.

The old man dismissed him with a wave and the words "So long then."

"Oh. Well, *sorry asshole*. Didn't mean to bother you," he said without meaning it, trying to hide the sarcasm in his voice. He turned and walked away. Blackie watched him leave and perform a SoBe ritual: he paused for a self-absorbed gaze at his reflection in the door pane, then pulled a cell phone from his shorts and punched in a call before disappearing into the dark interior of the grill.

Blackie and the *Skipper* had the hackneyed discussion about the pervasive rudeness in Miami. Blackie told the *Skipper* about a recent scene he had observed while getting gas at the Chevron near the airport. A rather large woman had pulled up to the air compressor and deposited her two quarters and filled a low rear tire before getting back in her car. Another motorist pulled up behind her, and finding the compressor still running, grabbed the hose to fill his tires. Blackie watched the woman pull her large frame from the car with surprising dexterity and scream, "Hey, you! That's my air! That's my air!"

"This place sure isn't like one of the old Coke ads, where the meltin' pot of humanity is singing in perfect harmony," the *Skipper* observed. "They do seem to scream and honk together to a perversely harmonious world beat," Blackie added.

Blackie finally flagged down the waiter for another beer and orderd a pair of *Presidentes*. He watched the old man's eyes glaze over as his impatience began to show.

Looking away toward the canal, Blackie saw a brand-new, center-console Mako 252 pull up to the stone pier. Onboard were what looked like a pair of Franciscan monks in long brown robes and beards – beards so long and bushy they almost appeared fake, a disguise. But he didn't give their outfits or their appearance a second thought. For more than a year a small waterborne religious sect had been anchored out on a pair of dilapidated sailboats just off his marina. They wore those identical outfits and beards even in mid-summer in Miami's sweltering heat – probably cult followers of both St. Francis and St. Peter. Blackie figured the two guys on the Mako were probably a power squadron offshoot.

He watched the monks turn the boat around so that it pointed back down the canal. One of them took the lines and tied them off on the cleats bolted to the decrepit dock.

Blackie felt an urge to pee, stood up and headed through the screen door inside. Returning, he rounded the corner coming out of the windowless bathroom, squinting in the bright light as the Barracuda Grill erupted into chaos.

The two monks on the Mako had stepped inside, turned, and ran back out onto the veranda. As they left each pulled an automatic weapon from under his heavy robe. Passing behind Blackie's carjacker at the table, they opened fire. The bullets tore into the worn fabric of the madras shirt of the *Skipper*, still seated with his back to them. Yet another slug pierced the back of the old man's head, exploding out of his forehead, spraying the wall behind where Blackie had been sitting with a splash of bright red.

Screams filled the room, then shouts and the sound of bar stools skidding across the floor. One of the monks patted down the corpse and yelled, "Not here!"

The gunmen both ran the few steps to the waiting Mako, but one tripped on his cassock and fell on the splintery deck, causing him to let loose with a long round of wild automatic fire. A few holes appeared in the screen door, followed by the sound of bullets whizzing past and ricocheting off the stuccoed walls. Blackie joined the others by diving to the concrete floor.

From there he could only hear the roar of the twin 150 Johnsons as the driver gunned the throttles and the boat sped away down the canal. The Barracuda Grill became unusually quiet but for the sound of a stream of beer hitting the hard floor, a bullet having pierced the line of a tap. Blackie and the others stood up. He followed the rest out through the screen door, and there was the *Skipper*, definitely on his way to Valhalla. It was a sickening sight. Blackie turned away, toward the canal, as the sliding door of the Holiday Mansion slowly opened. The faded Coleman air conditioning unit on the top deck of the houseboat hummed sinisterly. Blackie noticed a pattern of holes running diagonally up the chalky gel-coat of the cabin. The houseboat's faded curtains, billowing out of the open glass door, parted as the owner of the grill lurched out. On his face was a desperate, almost pathetic expression. He had his hands cupped over his barkeeper's apron, soaked a deep and shiny crimson. Blackie figured the owner must have been gut shot inside his houseboat by a wild slug from the monk's AK-47.

Blackie felt like he was at a dinner theater, watching a maudlin play. Holding everyone's attention, the owner took a few steps, and – ever the pessimist – said, "They've ruined it for me," before collapsing under the awning of the houseboat's front deck.

As Blackie and the crowd herded forward, he saw a brown blob surrounded by a murky, rust-colored cloud floating near the houseboat. At first Blackie thought that someone must have returned fire, killing one of the perpetrators in their escape

– or maybe the monk had shot himself accidentally
tripped. But slowly, like a polluted iceberg recently ca
brown blob rolled over. It wasn't a dead monk, but the
victim shot by the assassins. It was the manatee.

The growing crowd milled in and around the Barracud
Grill, and Blackie noticed most of the witnesses performing a
vanishing act, ducking out in the confusion. Blackie had a split
second to make a decision and he did what most any Miamian
would do – he headed straight for the door. He leapt into the
topless Z3 and made a hasty exit down Biscayne Boulevard
toward the Julia Tuttle Causeway and home. He could sort this
all out on the boat and decide at his own pace and on his own
terms when and what he would tell the police. As he turned
onto the causeway he glanced over to the passenger seat, where
just a few minutes ago the late *Skipper* had sat. Blackie saw the
corner of a manila envelope poking out from under the seat. He
reached down and pulled it out. A cell phone stashed inside
tumbled onto the floorboard. Blackie held the envelope up and
glanced at it. And he punched down harder on the accelerator.

when he
ved, the
third
a

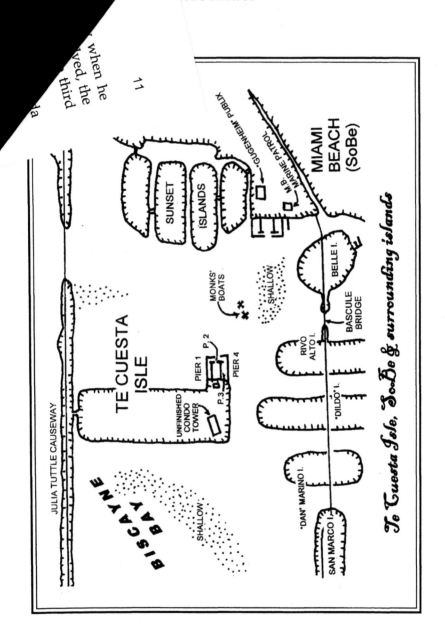

Te Cuesta Isle, SoBe & surrounding islands

Chapter 2:

The Marina

Blackie exited off the Julia Tuttle Causeway and drove over the short and amusingly named Meyer Lansky Bridge – after an early vacationing mobster – entering the inner sanctum of Te Cuesta Isle, one of the great long-running, boondoggles of the Beach. Passing the security gate, he gave a cursory wave to the dark-tint windows of the guard shack, knowing that the figure inside was only a mannequin dressed as a security guard. It was a cost saving measure implemented by the developers, since to date there weren't any condo-association members to hit up for a real security force. Blackie had grown to like the idea of a security dummy, and besides, he figured they wouldn't get that much more movement out of a $6-an-hour live one.

Like the mannequin, so much of Te Cuesta Isle had come to amuse Blackie. Such as the name. About 80 years ago, the island was planned to be the next and largest in a string of islands created by dredging and filling in vast areas of Biscayne Bay. Speculators dubbed their next island *Isola di Lolandoe*. After they dropped pilings in the muck outlining the future paradise, the '25 land bust and '26 hurricane stopped one of the last great bay fill-ins.

In the late '50's another developer had a vision to fill between the pilings for profit and bought the land from Miami Beach. And why not connect the new pile of muck with

Florida's past and name it for the Native American tribe that had been squeezed off their Gold Coast bay-front land? Despite the developer's dynamic vision he just couldn't spell. So the Tequesta tribe was improperly memorialized in his prospectus as Te Cuesta Isle Estates, Hotel, Nightclub, Marina *ad nauseum*. Unfortunately, in Spanish, Te Cuesta loosely translates as "It's Gonna Cost You!" which was a source of great amusement to Miami's Latin residents, who at the time (except for a few dictators in exile) would have been unofficially barred from buying in the upscale and overpriced Miami Beach development. It was still the "Whites-only" '50's.

The developer only needed to connect the dots with dredged muck to realize his vision, but the bureaucrats stopped him. He obviously didn't know whom to bribe, so he died with his lagoon unfilled and his dream unfulfilled. His vision of Te Cuesta Isle was simply noted as "fish haven" on nautical charts for almost three decades. But then came the late '80's and some crooked Colombians.

Their investment group hit town with plenty of laundered cash. They discovered the abandoned pilings and believed their territory had already been staked out for them. They proposed dredging the surrounding bay and using the tailings to create a spectacular palm-lined island holding a first-class marina, a condo high-rise, thirty half-acre bay-front estates, and lastly, a hotel-casino complex for the day that Miami Beach finally conceded to gambling.

As often happens when dealing with dirty money, things went wrong from the start. They had greased the right palms, but they learned that the dregs they used to fill most of Te Cuesta Isle contained a high level of toxic waste. That part of the bay had apparently been the sight of an early and very illegal Cold War dumpsite. Rather than hauling it the required distance offshore, an unscrupulous contractor had dumped the rusting drums in the bay. Soil tests proved that the entire north end of the island – to be the site of the bay-front estates – was uninhabitable. Removing the soil and finding a legal dumpsite 12 nautical miles offshore was too expensive. Development of the other, non-toxic areas on the isle went into full swing, with the first-class marina built and ready for occupancy. The marina, with the adjacent Olympic pool and four clay tennis courts, was logically the first to open because it was the lure, the trap, for the condo crowd who would buy the high-rise glass cracker-boxes simply for the proximity to nautical wealth. There was something special about waking up and looking down upon the view of rows of seldom-used, million-dollar yachts.

But the developers found that there weren't enough high-ticket yachts and sportfishing boats to fill the 80-slip marina. After abandoning the idea of constructing elaborate plywood facades of million-dollar Baias and Burgers to place in the empty slips, the developers opted to rent the remaining space to sailors and to people with Grady Whites and old Chris Crafts – even houseboats. *Commoners.* They were landlords to common boaters – some of them were even *liveaboards.* If only the condo-buyers wouldn't notice.

Construction began on the 50-story high-rise. Foundation piers were sunk. Artists' renderings appeared on every bus and billboard from Miami to West Palm Beach. Only then did the celebrity residents on the neighboring isles realize that a 50-story condo tower was about to peer down on their pools and backyards. They were able to get an injunction and save a little airborne privacy (having already lost their waterborne privacy to the Tour-Boats-to-the-Stars.) Construction came to a halt, suspended indefinitely. A few of the more belligerent condo-buyers were able to extract their deposits out of escrow. Rust began to form on the protruding rebar ribs of the condosaurus.

The Colombians were struck a final blow. Gambling lost again on another Beach referendum. Craps on the casino. The developers were left with nothing but a break-even marina and possibly a future nine-hole golf course, if they could convince the links crowd that it was perfectly safe to wear hazmat booties over their golf shoes. The developers hadn't wanted to spend the time and money to change the spelling of Te Cuesta Isle (the phrase, "it's gonna cost you!" actually found to be a positive marketing ploy for Argentine and Venezuelan expatriates wanting to flee to Miami to hide their wealth.) Blackie believed that for the Colombian developers, the place had more than lived up to its name.

Blackie wheeled the Beamer through the sandy glare of the island's northern end. A mini-Sahara. Nothing grew there. No grass, no weeds, not even Australian pines. Like an oasis in a desert, the marina shimmered in the distance through the heat waves rising off Te Cuesta Isle's inch of imported Bahamas sand. To the southwest rose the skeletal beginnings of an abandoned high-rise. The only sign of life on the island was at the southeast corner, at Te Cuesta Isle Marina, Blackie's home. He parked in his assigned spot in the lot between the abandoned high-rise and the marina pool. The vast lot was another joke, since Blackie had space 11 in a lot neatly painted and numbered to 140, yet there weren't ever more than a few dozen cars parked there.

Along with his uniform and flight bag, he grabbed the envelope and phone left in his car by the *Skipper* prior to his execution. Blackie walked quickly down the sidewalk toward his boat, anxious to open the manila packet, hoping it would give a clue to all the bizarre events that had followed his landing a Boeing 767 at MIA earlier that morning.

"Pssst. Hey, Blackie."

Blackie turned in all directions and saw no one.

"Hey! *Hey!* Come here."

Blackie recognized the voice but saw nothing. And his neighbor Yul Grant, even when he whispered, was not easy to miss.

A sharp metal bang startled Blackie, and he turned and looked at the dumpster, a 20-foot refuse container used at construction sites, a vestige of the abandoned high-rise project. Barely poking out of the top was the fat, shaved head of Yul.

"Damn you Blackie, don't make me scream. Get over here!"

Blackie thought that the sight of Yul, with his head poking out of the cobalt blue container, finally and irrevocably confirmed why everyone called him *The Human Manatee.*

"Doesn't your generator use a Racor 120R fuel filter?" Yul asked. "You've got a Northern Lights 5KW, right?"

"Yeah."

"Well, lookee here," Yul said, holding up two small cartons swallowed up by his meaty hand. "A brand new pair of 'em still in the box!"

"How'd you ever get yourself in there?"

"That wood pallet leaning on the dumpster. Come on in. I've found a gold mine!"

"Aren't you even slightly embarrassed going through other people's garbage?"

"Shit no. I could open up a shop with what these fools throw away. Look at this." Yul held up an engine's drive belt. "No wear. Still got the printing on it."

Blackie took a few steps up the slats of the pallet and peered inside. Besides a lot of garbage, there were boat parts, paint cans and what looked like an entire bow pulpit off of a large sportfisherman. He also saw a fresh stream of blood oozing out of Yul's knee, trickling down into his faded deck shoe.

"What did you do to your leg, Yul?"

"I kind of fell in, and that son-of-a-bitch - the one who just bought that Viking - threw away his old flag staff and it was sticking up in here. Had a perfectly good U.S. Yacht Ensign on it!"

"So you could say you were struck - or stuck - by Old Glory," Blackie said with a laugh.

Yul ignored him and rambled on, like a clerk doing the semi-annual inventory. "Check out all this one-inch stainless steel tubing. Must be 50 or 60 feet. These bastards kiss one dock and they replace their whole bow pulpit. I'm coming back with my hacksaw. Say, Blackie, you don't have a couple hundred-foot extension cords? I could use my jigsaw with a carbide blade."

"No, I got them in storage. Yul, I'm gonna let you carry on here, but when you get a chance stop by the boat for a talk. But it smells like you better take a shower first."

"It's a deal. You can nuke some popcorn for me. Remember, three bags at 3 minutes and 45 seconds each. Only the fat-free stuff."

"Yeah, like it matters."

"I'm trying to lose weight. Don't forget your filters."

Blackie stopped by the dockmaster's office for the mail and headed down the concrete dock to his slip out on Pier One.[1]

Walking the docks of the half-empty marina on a perfect February day, Blackie wanted to thank the developers who were going broke in the midst of another Miami condo boom. He wanted to thank them for providing him with such a wonderful place to live.   As a liveaboard, for $800 a month he had an island sanctuary off of South Beach almost to himself. An Olympic-sized pool to swim in and four clay courts to play tennis on. A workout room and spa. Free cable TV and even a paper delivered to his boat each morning. And as yet there were no condo residents complaining to the association board about him. No one bitching that Blackie had been standing on his own dock blocking their way on their evening stroll, preventing their obnoxious, little dog from taking a crap on his finger pier.

Blackie had been at Te Cuesta Isle Marina for almost four years, and no way was something this good going to last.

Blackie walked down his pier with one final thought on the Te Cuesta Isle situation.   One day it was going to get unbearable. The developers would pay off the right people and

---

[1] Blackie's slip, Te Cuesta Isle Marina, 25 47.93N, 80 09.43W.

get their permits. And they'd probably tack another ten floors on the high-rise to boot. Then he would wake up one morning to find a glass and concrete monolith blocking the sun. To find cigarette butts or chunks of Milky Way bars littering his decks, thrown off the 33rd floor by some rude and selfish bastard or his kid. And then there would be only one solution. He would have to step up to the cleats on the dock, untie the lines and sail away.

With a low tide, his Island Packet 38 sat almost hidden in the oversized slip. Like everything the developers did, it was done on a grand scale. Blackie had a 38-foot boat in a 70-foot slip – one of the smaller ones. He stepped down onto the gunwale, grabbed a stay and was aboard. He sat in the cockpit ready to tear open the envelope's seal. Whatever the old carjacker had left in Blackie's Beamer was bound to be a bombshell.

Chapter 3:

Nautical Neighbors

Sitting in his cockpit with the manila envelope in hand, Blackie unsheathed his "CIA Letter Opener," a razor-sharp polycarbonate blade given to him by former neighbors, two women on a battleship-gray Carver who both shared a fixation with all things paramilitary. He had once cleared their fouled prop of a ski-rope, and in return they had given him the lightweight, non-metallic blade, complete with a Velcro patch on the handle so he could wear it "to work in his sock" – and through airport x-ray machines without detection. They had ordered it just for him from *Brigade Quartermasters*, their favorite action-gear sourcebook. He had thanked them, but kept it in a cubbyhole in the cockpit of his Island Packet.

"Tally-ho there, Captain Blackie" shouted Reginald, an ancient Brit who lived on a wooden 48-foot Defever on Pier Four. "Permission to come aboard."

"Yeah, yeah, come on," Blackie replied to his surprise guest while he placed the envelope under the cockpit cushion.

"Reggie," as he insisted to be called, was half of the couple who lived on what some would call a classic wooden Defever, or what others might describe as a cosmetically maintained old trawler. Reggie had bought the boat after a successful career as a Boston-based executive for a British bank. Reggie had spent his entire adult life in America, but instead of adopting its ways, had become something of a die-hard Anglophile.

His wife, on the other hand, had her own fixation. Tina, a Bostonian originally from Texas, was maybe a half-dozen years Reggie's junior, yet still old enough to be deep into Social Security. Her interest was in fashion, *but only of the early '70s*. She was more than 70 and caught in a time warp. And what Blackie found interesting was that she could almost pull it off, because she had the body of a fit 35-year-old, thanks in part to her *Jane Mansfield* implants.

A great pastime at the marina was to observe a stranger, such as a diesel mechanic, watching her come onto the docks. She was usually dressed in an orange or lime-green miniskirt and white plastic boots, not retro, but original stuff. She looked much like those early photos of Southwest Airlines flight attendants – her long, bleached-blonde hair blowing in a light easterly wind. Then the stock reaction from the stranger. Usually a catcall or whistle or the elbowing of a colleague. This was always interrupted in mid-gesture with her approach, and the realization that she was easily old enough to be the man's grandmother. Blackie actually saw a varnisher from the Dominican Republic, on close inspection of her, bow and bless himself.

Blackie believed that she held a marina record of sorts. She was the only person ever seen walking the docks and stomping around on the deck of her boat wearing a pair of snakeskin cowboy boots. And that, while wearing polyester Cowboys Cheerleader hotpants with ultrasuede fringe. Reggie still had the black skid marks all over the deck of the Defever to prove it. Some things just weren't seen at a South Florida marina, and one was western wear.

Reggie put up with the scuff marks and her wardrobe because in truth he couldn't see them. His cataracts, despite two operations, were serious, and had prevented him from living his long-held dream: following in the wake of Sir Francis Chichester or Sir Eric Hiscock by roaming around the world on a boat. Reggie, like so many other would-be cruisers, had just waited too long to do it.

"If you could give me a hand here, Blackie," Reggie said, as he blindly grabbed the standing rigging – the wires holding the mast on Blackie's boat.

Blackie held out his hand, but had to turn away from viewing his guest's attire, fearing he might laugh. Reggie had raised the wearing of shorts, boat shoes and black socks into something of an art form. He was wearing a Guy Harvey polo shirt with a silk ascot in a nautique pattern around his neck. On his head was a Sahara cap, complete with a Velcro curtain in the back covering his neck. It was patterned after the cap that British officers wore when they fought Rommel in North Africa and amazingly in the same nautique print as his ascot.

"Reggie, step on the coaming, not the winch," Blackie said, trying to lead him aboard.

"How many of these *wenches* do you have onboard, you sly dog?"

"Counting the two self-tailing, seven."

"*Seven* wenches. My, you pilots are such *cocksmen*," Reggie said with a growl.

This was Blackie's third time to go through this verbal routine, letting Reggie repeat the joke with him like they were in the executive washroom. But Blackie tried not to let his weariness show. He enjoyed Reggie simply because Reggie, like many of his nautical neighbors, was such a unique character.

Blackie led Reggie to a cushion under the shade of the bimini and offered him a drink.

"Why, most kind of you, Blackie. The usual, please."

Blackie went below and made a Boodles Gin and Tonic for Reggie. Blackie never had to buy Boodles for Reggie. If there was any chance Reggie might come to visit a marina neighbor, that boater received, prior to a visit, the equivalent of an imperial gallon of the stuff along with an obscure brand of imported tonic water. To receive the gin was almost like receiving an announcement of Reggie and Tina's pending visit, because that couple did share one common interest besides boating; they loved to drink.

Making the G & T, Blackie mused that the couple's reputation for drinking even preceded them to the marina. Five months earlier Blackie had been roused from his sleep by the rumbling of twin diesels idling in the adjacent slip. He peered out of the companionway and saw for the first time the Defever, an aged, but classy wooden motor yacht that was missing both Reggie and Tina. That afternoon Blackie struck up a conversation with his new neighbor, whom he soon discovered was the delivery captain – the hired driver – for the yacht. The owners, said the captain, were believed to be in Bermuda.

Blackie recalled offering the delivery captain a beer and hearing, in the shade of the same cockpit in which Reggie now sat, his entire story of the trip, a story the man called *The Delivery from Hell.*

Reggie and Tina had bought the boat for their dream getaway in Boston. Cosmetically, the Defever was in excellent shape. The teak decks were sanded and regrouted, the wood railings and brightwork were "bristol," and the mahogany interior was oiled and buffed to a satin sheen. The boat even came with a few signed Michael Keane prints, tastefully framed, on the bulkhead walls of the salon. They instantly fell in love with its yachty feel. They made a few furtive looks into the dimly lit engine room and bilge, pushed a few buttons on the electronics at the helm, but decided to let a mechanic for the broker do a more thorough inspection. The survey said the boat was in "bristol" shape, although a few of the mechanical systems could use some attention and upgrading. The price was right, so Reggie and Tina took the plunge.

What Reggie didn't realize was that the essentials were all outdated junk. The autopilot was an old Benmar that looked more like an ancient Eureka canister vacuum cleaner than a piece of modern electronics. There were vacuum tubes in it. The boat had all kinds of museum-piece electronics, like the first model of a Loran receiver, a giant, old radio direction finder, even the VHF radio looked like something off a World War II PT boat.

Reggie's plan was to cruise the boat down the East Coast to Florida, then begin their worldwide trip to all other former British colonies, starting with the Bahamas.

The shakedown year in Boston was a great learning experience for them. Reggie discovered the hull of the Defever was virtually bulletproof, and that whatever came in contact with it was sure to suffer the damage. Sadly, he came to the realization that his eyesight was going to prevent him from ever captaining his vessel on a long voyage – Lloyds, after paying several of his claims, made sure of that. Undeterred, he still set his sights on at least living aboard the boat in Florida and the Bahamas. He hired the delivery captain to take it down the Intracoastal to Miami.

Listening intently to the story, Blackie offered another beer to that same captain, who proceeded to tell the story of *The Delivery from Hell* in his own words:

"You know, I like to do these deliveries on my own, with my own crew. Never with the owners. But Reggie and Tina seemed like such good folks. Anyway, they insisted on going, so I unfortunately agreed.

"I did have one rule for them. I had heard they were big drinkers so I demanded that there was to be no imbibing until we were in port or anchored for the night. They said sure, so early the next morning I took that old trawler out into Buzzards Bay."

"At first I thought they were some kind of health nuts, 'cause they always had a glass of water in their hands. By noon I knew it wasn't water, but gin, and they were both plastered and insisting that I join them. I wasn't about to jeopardize my Hundred-ton Master Coast Guard license for appearing unsociable, so I literally locked them in the master stateroom for most of the afternoon, until we were in port for the night.

"And it became a daily ritual. I never saw people who could drink like that. They maintained their composure, but I wouldn't trust either one of 'em behind a grocery cart.

"On the fifth afternoon we pulled into a marina at Hilton Head to refuel. I ran the high-volume fuel hose down the dock, unscrewed the cap on the portside deck fill, and started pumping. Reggie, ever the gentleman, insisted on helping. So I told him to top off the port tank and then fill the starboard one, while I went up to the pump and wrote down the amount of fuel the port tank had taken.

"I stood there and made small talk with the dockhand. When I finally walked back to the boat, I could see the distinctive gold color of diesel shooting in a long, fat stream out of the bilge pump through-hull.

"I ran aft to the cockpit, and there was Reggie, the boat owner, sticking the nozzle in a flush-deck fishing rod holder in the coaming, pumpin' away right into the bilge!

"It cost us ten grand to get out of Hilton Head. Had to pay a big fine. Pay for the hazardous materials team, and for the Coast Guard with their oil-spill booms. It wasn't cheap. And the first time my name ever made the front page of a newspaper.

"Needless to say, we sort of snuck out of Hilton Head. Right then I should have announced I was quitting and abandoned ship.

"South of Beaufort I was at the helm when Reggie came up, and in that calm and formal voice of his – like we're discussing the weather – says, 'Captain, I believe we've lost Tina.' I thought that he meant she had passed out for the day, but he literally meant she had gone overboard.

"I did the quickest 180 you can do in a Defever, but all I was finding were parts of her. First we found her red plastic hat with the big white polka-dots, then to starboard I spotted her long blond wig, a little further we dredged out the huge paisley top of her swimsuit. But no Tina. I yelled at Reggie, 'How long ago did she fall overboard?' He looked at me kind of blank and says, 'I noticed she was gone right before I called you.' So I figured it could have been anywhere in the last half-hour.

"I made sure both engines were in neutral, turned the boat over to Reggie and picked up the mike to call a 'Mayday' in to the Coast Guard. Then we both heard her shouting. We spotted Tina – half-naked mind you – coming up fast onboard a sportdeck Cobia filled with a pack of high school boys.

"When they pulled alongside it was a touching reunion. Tina smashing those huge bare breasts into Reggie's face, who was so happy that he was crying like a baby.

"She told us that she had been sunbathing on the aft upper deck when a barge passed. She had hopped up to wave at the skipper, who was just far enough away to be highly agitated. When the wake hit us she fell through a corroded lifeline gate and luckily didn't hit anything on the way to the water. She's a good swimmer, and headed over to a floating buoy and climbed aboard. She waved down the kids in the Cobia, who at first must have thought she was a mermaid or they had gone to heaven – until they got close. They set some sort of water speed record on the Intercoastal Waterway getting her back to our boat. Reggie gave them a hundred bucks each for saving her.

"When things calmed down and I had secured the lifeline gates with stainless steel seizing wire, I concluded that I had not only a derelict crew, but a vessel, too.

"Like I said, most of the stuff onboard was outdated junk. As a delivery captain, you always take chances because you never know the shape of the boat you've got to deliver. You end up spending more time repairing things than at the helm. But *The Prince of Whales* – that's the name Tina came up with and insisted Reggie name it – was like an ancient ship preserved in brine. I finally realized that prior to Reggie's tentative bashings on the bay the previous owners had probably never taken it out of its slip.

"When we got to Georgia, I knew it was true. The port engine had been smoking ever since we had left Boston. But it was the starboard that started to miss half way through the trip, probably from a cracked cylinder head. I told him we needed to shut it down, but Reggie had me keep going full-throttle on both engines – at least that's what I told him I was doing. Guess he was ready to get to Florida.

"Later that day I heard what sounded like the whine of a jet engine. We had a runaway diesel. I reached down and pulled on the starboard engine's emergency kill switch and raised it up to my face. The handle had come off in my hand. By this time it was a growing roar. I was backing away when it blew up. We limped into Savannah on the port engine, and it was another ten grand to replace the starboard one.

"At that point, I begged them to get off of their boat. Pleaded with them, and I think they got the message, because a few days later they were packed and had me drive them to the airport for a flight to Bermuda.

"When the new engine was installed, I got an out-of-work shrimper to crew and we headed on down here. Got a feeling you'll meet Reggie and Tina within a week."

With his story finished, the delivery captain asked Blackie to hold onto the keys to the Defever. Early the next morning Blackie gave him a ride to the airport for the flight back to Boston.

Climbing into the cockpit with the G&T, Blackie was surprised at how easily he had been taken in by the charm of Reggie and Tina. He handed the drink to one of his favorite guests.

"Why, thank you old boy. This does hit the spot. Makes me almost afraid of broaching the subject I've come to discuss, Blackie. Dreadful what it will do to the gin."

"So let's hear it."

"Do you know our neighbor on that big boat at the end of Pier Three, a Mr. Ted Jones," Reggie inquired.

"Sure, you can't miss him or his boat. That Breakwallet blocks out most of my view of the sunrise."

"Ah, *Breakwallet*, that's very good. Well. I'm tolerant of just about everybody. And Tina, of course, loves everyone, but even she has expressed concern."

"So what's he done?"

"He has had a long procession of wild people onboard, which we have tolerated. But just a short while ago I believe he crossed the line."

"Reggie, we've discussed this before. A wide latitude of behavior is permitted in a marina. And I never knew you to be intolerant of alternative lifestyles."

"I'm not. But Ted just had a powerboat of some kind come up to his stern, and on it were a few of those men in Franciscan robes."

Blackie, making the connection to the shooters at the grill, replied with a lie. "Reggie, those guys are some sailing sect of St. Francis communicating with the fishes. They've been anchored out there for more than a year. They're harmless."

"No. These men were in a new speedboat. And Tina swears – I really don't even want to say this, Blackie, since I have to admit she and I have both had a few Boodles already, but she swears she saw two men handing what looked like guns wrapped in beach towels to Ted before they left."

Blackie paused, wondering what to say. Finally he spoke. "Might have been spearguns. Hawaiian slings. Boat hooks. Our eyes can deceive us, Reggie. Let me get you another gin."

Blackie ducked down into his companionway, even more curious to find out what the envelope of the late *Skipper* contained.

Chapter 4:

Financing the Yacht

Blackie poured Reggie off the boat and onto the dock, sending him in the general direction of *The Prince of Whales*. Reggie had put a sizeable dent in the Boodles bottle and Blackie had polished off a liter of tonic. Finally alone, Blackie could examine the packet left in his car by the *Skipper*, the formerly homeless but now very dead PI. He retrieved the envelope from under the cockpit cushion, ducked below into the cabin and opened it. What spilled out were a half-dozen poorly composed photos, taken with a telephoto lens, of Blackie's increasingly notorious neighbor Ted Jones. The photos were taken from above looking down on Ted and his mighty Breakwater. Judging from the background they appeared to have been taken from the unfinished condo tower. He turned a few of them over and looked at the date stamped on the back by the photo lab. They were almost three years old, meaning the old PI had been following Ted for some time.

In one shot Ted was between two beautiful, scantily clad women, biting the neck of one while fondling the other. The blonde, facing the lens, had the most bored look on her face, if Blackie could remove his gaze from her exposed breasts. He couldn't make out much of the other, the dark-haired one, because of the angle of the shot. But there was something about her – even only seeing her back – that was oddly familiar. In the other photos Ted was in even more intimate contact with one or two men, who, although also bored, were doing a little better at feigning interest by pointing it out to Ted. The common denominators in all the photos were a naked Ted and a bottle of *Dom Perignon*. Until now, Blackie had been oblivious to what was going on aboard the Breakwater – the yacht was too far away and he didn't care, really. But from the photos Blackie saw why Reggie was concerned about his neighbor Ted on the nearby T-head.

Next in the stack of papers was a half-page ad taken from a ten-year-old issue of a *Yachting* magazine, describing the same 89-foot Breakwater at the end of Pier Three. Back then, the boat was named *Another Toy*. When it came into his possession, Ted had salvaged one word on the stern and had an artist paint the new boat name, *Ted's Toy*, a half-assed attempt at appeasing the superstition of not changing a boat's name to avoid bad luck.

The old ad described the boat. Four staterooms with en-suite baths, including a king master with an oval bed surrounded on all sides by mirrored walls. The countertops in the heads and galley were Italian marble, as was the master Jacuzzi. There were two forward cabins for the crew. A pair of Caterpillar 3412 diesel engines producing a whopping 1,250 horsepower each powered the yacht. Blackie's Island Packet 38 sailboat, in comparison, had a single Yanmar diesel producing a mere 80 horsepower. The Breakwater also had a pair of 55 kilowatt generators (compared to Blackie's generator, putting out a measly 5 kilowatts.) The yacht had a 6,000 gallon fuel tank. The ad concluded with a bullshit-boatee term stating that the Breakwater was in *Palm Beach Condition*, whatever the hell that meant. Blackie guessed that the phrase meant that the yacht, despite countless refits and renovations, still was a bit long on the tooth and destined one day for the scrap yard.

Blackie compared the photo in the ad with what was berthed out there on the T-head, and it was obvious that Ted had been adding on to his toy. On deck now was a 15-foot inflatable with remote steering, and also a pair of jetskis. Incredibly, Ted must have spent half a million or so in the boatyard refitting the yacht with a Euro-style back-end, or transom, complete with two sets of swim steps curving down to the water.   With an asking price in the old ad of $3.2 million, the yacht must now have been valued well over $4 million.

Finally, Blackie pulled a rather hefty report from the envelope, written by the *Skipper*, neatly typed, with surprisingly good spelling and grammar.   At first Blackie wondered how the old PI could have created such a professional report while living in a homeless shelter.   But then the date on the report caught his eye; it was almost a decade old.

Blackie scanned through the file, then started over to give it a more thorough read:

Subject: Ted Jones
Age: 35
Address: Sunset Harbor Marina, Miami Beach, FL
Occupation: Investor

Ted Jones currently is involved in the insurance business. More specifically, a small part of insurance known as the Viatical Settlement Industry, a business that gives terminally ill persons cash in exchange for the death benefits of their life insurance policies.

The "Industry" developed in tandem with the AIDS pandemic, providing the terminally ill or their families with a portion of the money that would later be distributed to the beneficiaries. The up-front money would help pay for the costs of health care while the terminally ill patient was still alive. It could help keep the patient off welfare, prevent bankruptcy and foreclosure proceedings, defray the exorbitant costs of health care, and give the patient a sense of dignity in their final days. For those reasons, some AIDS-advocacy groups have not been opposed to what many believe is a ghoulish way to make a profit.

Unscrupulous players attempting to maximize the profits at the cost of distraught and obviously weakened victims have plagued the business from the start. Players such as Ted Jones.

Mr. Jones had a checkered past prior to entering the Viatical arena. In the early '80s he was at the center of a series of home-

product pyramid schemes in the West. They were lucrative enough to provide him with a Laguna Beach address and his first taste of the boating world, a 50-foot SeaRay. But poor investing and a short-lived dip in the SoCal real estate market sent first the boat, then the home and finally Mr. Jones packing. He moved back East to New Jersey and worked for a time as a sales manger for an adjustable bed company under investigation by the SEC, and then came to South Florida to be a yacht broker just before Hurricane Andrew. His complicity in several fraudulent claims by yacht owners who had lost their boats in the storm was a factor in him being released by his employer, the yacht broker.

Next, he surfaced as the head of an investment group buying the life insurance policies of South Florida Persons Living With AIDS (or PLWA's.) The Industry was still in its infancy, and Mr. Jones was known as a rogue, an unlicensed viatical provider who set up shop on South Beach to profit off betting on the early death of a very select group of PLWAs, those with high-value life insurance policies.

From the start, Mr. Jones used every tool he had learned over the years in his various careers. To drum up investors, he conducted investment seminars each winter at hotel conference rooms from Fort Lauderdale to Fort Pierce. His prospectus predicted a return on investment of between 25 and 60 percent. He provided the investors with actual case histories of patients who died prior to their date of life expectancy, providing a true windfall for the investors, damned if it was a serious breach of privacy of the person whose death had triggered the windfall. But the disclosures were legal, because Mr. Jones was savvy enough to put a fine-print clause in the contracts allowing him to release information to the investors about the status of the viator (or seller.)

In those years, desperate PLWA's or their families were accepting as low as 25 cents on the dollar for the policies. Ted was paying $25,000 for a policy to be worth $100,000 when the viator died a few months later.

The investment groups were organized offshore in the Cayman Islands, and in the early '90s, Mr. Jones, and to a lesser extent his investors, reaped the grim profits from a national tragedy – and they reaped them virtually tax-free.

Mr. Jones went so far as to set up a 900-number for the investors, who could call, dial in a secret code, and learn of the current medical status of the person on whom they had invested. Macabre, yes, but still as exciting for a retired investor wintering in Boca Raton as a day at the Gulfstream racetrack or the Indian bingo hall – and Mr. Jones only charged them $9.95 for the call.

Like his money, Mr. Jones' boat bore the homeport of George Town, C.I. He had enough cash to afford the payments on a $4-million, Cayman-registered motor yacht.

But Mr. Jones' opulent lifestyle (and to a greater extent, his ever-increasing greed) has surpassed his income. New treatments, such as protease inhibitors, are extending the lives of PLWAs – bad news for the investors. Federal regulations are being proposed,including limits on how much viatical providers can low-ball their offers to the ill or distraught viators. And especially for Mr. Jones, it is increasingly difficult to satiate his need for more terminally ill insured. Simple fact: **Ted has to find more heavily insured people about to die.**

He has tried advertising in gay publications from Key West to West Palm Beach. Jones set up a direct-marketing phone bank in Pompano Beach, where his staff called the parents of the PLWA, often those who actually owned the policy, and used scare tactics to get them to sell.

Mr. Jones offered hefty "finders fees" for referrals of insured persons who were terminally ill, usually those with AIDS. He attempted to coerce doctors, health care providers, even clergy and those working with AIDS Advocacy programs, to divulge a confidential list of persons with the most severe cases of the disease. It was something of a lost cause, since those willing to get involved in the battle weren't about to be bribed. Even in Miami Beach, home to many a Medicare scam, few of those who were aware of his tactics would give him the time of day.

The above background info leads us to the death of Blaine Werner, who died in an apparent accident after falling off a ship on a weekend cruise to the Bahamas three months ago. Approximately six months before his death, Mr. Werner's family had sold his $160,000 life insurance policy to a funding firm represented by Mr. Jones. His *family was to be paid 40 percent of the value of the policy after a consulting physician determined that Blaine, with AIDS, had no more than 12 months to live. The contract had been signed for more than three months, yet no money was received by the family, who were paying for his mounting medical bills, his mortgage and other payments long overdue. That is until the day before Mr. Werner was to go on the cruise. His health, thanks to new treatments, was poor but steady. On that day, the investment group delivered a check by courier for the entire amount, about $75,000.*

Just before dawn of the following day, their son was dead, accidentally falling through a teak railing on the ship. It occurred less than a mile from the entrance to Government Cut off South Beach. It was dark, there were no witnesses, but investigators found a pin was missing from the railing's hinge.

Soon after, the family, in tidying up the deceased's estate, was going over the clauses in their copy of the multi-page viatical settlement contract. They were shocked to discover that in their haste and confusion, the family had signed a rider assigning the Accidental Death and Dismemberment benefit to the viatical providers. That group had made more than a third of a million dollars from the drowning of their son.

Although the family could sue the cruise line for the drowning, the settlement would be minimal, with documents showing that their son only had at most a year to live. Concerned about the possible involvement by the investment group that made a windfall over their son's death, they have retained this investigator to look into the circumstances surrounding the drowning, along with any connections to Jones and his investors.

This investigator, in searching for similar case histories, has discovered two recent deaths on South Beach, one a hit-and-run, another an apparent suicide, both surprisingly having a Ted Jones connection. In both cases, Mr. Jones and one of his investment groups have reaped the rewards of someone's early demise, and in both cases, the death was not the result of the viator's terminal illness.

And that was it. End of the old report, or at least all that the *Skipper* had gathered in preparation for his planned meeting with Jones at the Barracuda Grill. The material in the report obviously had done in the *Skipper*. What lay on Blackie's settee table, despite being a decade old, was still very dangerous.

Blackie grabbed his binoculars and pulled open the companionway hatch. He trained them on the big Breakwater out at the end of Pier Three, looking for an easy clue to prove the report of the *Skipper* was true. All he saw were two men in their mid-twenties, both blonde and muscular – twins, really. They were lounging at the yacht's bow, working on their tans on a built-in, wrap-around sofa of white vinyl. Focusing the binos, he finally made the connection. The blonde-on-steroids that spoke to the *Skipper* at the Barracuda Grill was one of those twins he saw in the binoculars.

Blackie watched Ted make his entrance, coming from the portside walk-around deck with a cellphone in hand. Call completed, Ted pointed it at the two and appeared to be shouting, as if he were scolding his pet dogs. They obediently loped inside, followed by the big Breakwater's owner.

Blackie set down the binoculars and pondered over a few obvious questions: Was Mr. Jones capable of killing the people whose life insurance policies he had bought, just so he could keep Ted and **Ted's Toy** afloat? He had read that the whole viatical business was long gone. So how was Ted generating income now? And finally, it was obvious why Ted wanted the PI's old report, but why now?

Chapter 5:

The Media & Manatees

Only ten hours before Blackie was snoozing under two blankets, safe in a warm hotel room protecting him from a foot of Chicago snow. Now at home, he was in the midst of a hot and sticky Miami Beach situation. He planned to discuss it thoroughly with Yul Grant, his neighbor, if he ever showed up at the boat.

Hoping to find out more about the shooting on the news, Blackie grabbed the remote and turned on his 20-inch LCD TV, hidden behind a pair of louvered teak doors on the forward bulkhead.

It was almost five o'clock and time for the local afternoon news. He surfed until he found Channel 11, since it was the worst of the "Blood & Guts" Miami stations and sure to give the shootings the most play.

He instantly recognized their frequently plugged "News Command Center," a cavernous sound stage at the station designed to give viewers the feeling they were getting their gore-fix from NASA's Mission Control. The set was another scam of the news director and nothing more than two walls of cheap TVs and a bunch of folding tables holding up rows of monitors. Low-paid interns manned the electronic equipment; they tapped on the keyboards, trying to look busy. On cue, one would pop up from his or her spot and run with a blank piece of paper to the bathroom.

On the catwalk above the troops were the expensive fixtures on which the news director had spent most of his money: the TV news personalities at their desks. And leading the pack was Pablo Ricardo Lopez, or P. Rick Lopez as he was called on TV, one of Miami's local media monsters.

Blackie distinctly remembered that face. A year earlier he had been in Nassau getting lightheaded on Kalik Golds at the bar at the Poop Deck. The place was packed and he was stuck on a barstool next to a big TV resting on a wall bracket. The walls were covered with faded framed celebrity photos – Brooke Shields and Burgess Meredith were two that he recalled. Unceremoniously placed *behind* the TV was an 8 by 10 framed glossy of Lopez, with that smug look plastered on his face, staring at him all through Happy Hour. By the end of the night Blackie loathed P. Rick and his creepy leer.

Blackie gazed at the news set shown in the two-minute promo and smiled. It looked uncannily like the interior of a dimly lit Brandsmart, a Miami-based discount warehouse appliance store. And P. Rick was planted right in the middle of Small Appliances.

After eight minutes of commercials, four of which plugged the station, they finally ran the lead story.

"Good afternoon, and I'm P. Rick Lopez. Today the new owners of Miami's professional basketball team announced that because of dropping attendance and the city's unwillingness to renegotiate their lease, they are relocating to Austin, Texas. They will leave behind a 15-year-old abandoned arena and a $200-million slightly used one on bay-front park land in downtown Miami."

"What?" Blackie screamed aloud. *"This* is the top news?"

Blackie surfed the other local stations, but as he expected, all of them were already into their first big block of commercials. He headed back to Eleven.

"And in breaking news," announced P. Rick as sirens and a wild graphic flashed on the screen, "tragedy has once again struck *our* beloved manatees. We go direct to our Environmental Reporter, Kukie Depew, at our Earth Watch Desk, with the latest."

The director cut to Kukie, standing in a corner of the studio, surrounded by a few potted palms and backed by a blue screen (with the viewers getting a scene of a swamp), all done to make her look like she was on a hammock in the Everglades. Neither Blackie nor the rest of the TV viewers knew what had qualified her as their "Environmental Reporter." Was she a marine biologist? Spent time in Alaska as a park ranger? No, her appointment came because she had helped clean up the beach at Bill Baggs State Park the previous Earth Day, and because she was in the Frequent Buyer Club of the *Whale Pals* catalogue.

"Yes, P. Rick, tragedy has again struck *our* manatees," read Kukie from her teleprompter, in a voice like she owned the sea mammals. A huge graphic appeared behind her reading, "MANATEES: Countdown to Zero."

This graphic brought instant warmth to the heart of the news director, seated invisibly in his remote booth. Ever since Channel 11 had begun their "MANATEES: Countdown to Zero" spots, ratings for environmental segments had increased by two points. And more importantly, three sponsors – an electric company, a pesticide maker and a flats-boat manufacturer – had been lined up to advertise between the spots.

It was simply brilliant, thought the director who had come up with the concept. He had combined a lovable, endangered species with brutal death, usually at the hands of a speeding powerboater. Clips of the mutilated and bloated corpses floating in the bay, often from Channel 11's Sky Captor, were powerful graphics. Combined with the excitement of an actual countdown of the last few of the creatures until they were extinct, the director had created tragedy, pathos and the excitement of a lotto drawing all rolled into one.

Channel 11 had gone so far as to introduce collectible bath toys, purple plastic replicas of manatees, called "Mannies." They sported a "Save Us" slogan and the Channel 11 logo, were produced by the thousands at a Yangtze River factory in China and given away with a kid's meal by a local fast-food chain.

Channel 11 even survived the fallout when, during an autopsy of one of the dead creatures, a purple Mannie was found lodged in its esophagus. Fortunately, hindgut blockage from ingesting the plastic bags of a Florida grocery chain – the bags bearing the sea cow's likeness – proved to be the manatee's cause of death.

"Incredible as it sounds, gunmen are the latest perpetrators in violence against manatees," claimed Kukie. "We now go live to Jeff Case, on the scene at the Barracuda Grill off Biscayne Boulevard between the bay and Little Haiti."

"Yes, Kukie, pointless tragedy once again has struck *our* endangered manatees," read Jeff from his notepad. The director quickly cut to the videotaped segment compiled an hour earlier.

With Jeff's voice-over, the clip showed aerial footage of the ballooned body of the young male manatee floating in the garbage of the canal. From ground level was more footage of the crime scene, including shots of the covered bodies of the grill's owner and the *Skipper*.

"The police have no idea why the gunmen – who interestingly were wearing some kind of costume capes – performed such a senseless act of violence against the manatee, a gentle creature, harmless to humans, that eats mostly sea grass," read Jeff in the voice-over. "Police originally speculated that the perpetrators shot the manatee as a diversion during a robbery attempt at the grill, but no money appears to have been taken.

"And in an interesting development, two more victims, apparently innocent bystanders, have been killed in the melee."

With the clip over, the news director cut back live to Jeff and prompted Kukie in her earpiece to ask the on-scene reporter a question.

"Jeff, you're still at the scene of this terrible tragedy," noted Kukie, looking at her blank, blue screen. "So tell me, is it possible those two persons killed were by bad luck at the dock?"

In the midst of live, rush-hour traffic, Jeff put his hand to his ear, paused and said, "I'm sorry Kukie, you're breaking up. You said two persons killed and you want to suck my *what*?"

"I said 'bad luck at the dock,'" repeated Kukie in a flustered voice.

"I'm having trouble hearing you. But, yes, this a tragic scene," said Jeff, who was now busy tromping on-camera through the crime scene, having been granted permission by the officer-in-charge in exchange for a 10-second cameo. Jeff was talking and walking and spinning as was the cameraman, which made Blackie, who never got seasick, dizzy from watching the acrobatic reporter on the 20-inch screen.

"One of the persons killed was the owner of the grill, who lived here on his houseboat," said Jeff, hopping down on its deck. "He was sitting inside watching TV when apparently a stray bullet entered his houseboat and killed him."

Jeff poked his head in through the curtain, peered around and came back out. "Kukie, he was watching Channel 11. If only he could have seen this report, he might still be alive now."

They cut to Kukie, who was speechless for a few seconds before responding, "Jeff, wouldn't he have needed to not be sitting there – ."

Ignoring her, Jeff broke in as he rambled through the patio's crime scene. "The other victim, seated over here, was an unidentified homeless man who was drinking a beer on the verandah when a wild spray of bullets ripped through him. Apparently random fire from the gunman's automatic weapon after they shot the manatee. Back to you, Kukie."

"Thanks, Jeff," replied Kukie. "And where does this terrible tragedy leave us, P. Rick?"

The news director cut to P. Rick Lopez. The anchorman was standing beside a blue wall, and the electronic graphic on the viewers' screens had the header, "MANATEES: Countdown to Zero," and below it the epic-sized number, "1,256", and in tiny letters to minimize the number, "pair." With a strange relish in his voice, P. Rick shouted over a siren, "Well Kukie, last week we had two deaths, a mother and her calf, during the filming of a water chase scene off Fisher Island for a Disney action film. So now we've lost eight of *our* manatees this month."

P. Rick insisted that they always tie his face and name with the graphic. He knew that when they got down to the last twenty or so of the sea cows, he would be at the center of the hysteria – especially important after he had seen the media, souvenir and enviro-charity industries that had grown up around the California Condor. The manatee could do for him what JFK's assassination in Dallas had done for his idol, Dan Rather.

The news director ran the graphic, a big, slashing red X through the number 1256 (and in tiny letters, "pair,") without giving a second thought to its impact. Yet already a University of Miami marine biologist studying the Florida manatee had said publicly that the Channel 11 marketing scheme was accelerating the demise of the species. Testosterne-charged young men with their hands pumping the throttles of their twin-250s were making kamikaze attacks on any dark shadow that they saw hovering below the surface. Like killer graffiti artists, they went home and watched the news, seeing if they had gotten 'some pub for their tag.' And with *no one* enforcing the manatee-zone boat speed laws, the end of the manatee was inevitable. Manatees were doomed despite the flood of boating industry propaganda that the manatee should be taken off the endangered species list.

Only a few, like boat dealers, Channel 11 and P. Rick, would profit from their demise. But those few were growing. Because of the Channel 11 coverage, local bookies were already taking bets on when the last wild manatee would go to Davie Jones locker. In a perverse way, it was like the "Last Wolf" stories that were fueled by the Montana newspapers in the 1930s – only now Floridians felt not hysterical fear, but media-induced sympathy for the manatees before they zoomed about on the waterways and killed them.

Channel 11's reported gore continued with the story of a deadly wreck involving two trucks, one loaded with Porsches and the other, a 50-foot palm tree. Besides snarling traffic on the Palmetto Expressway for five hours until the chain saws arrived, three of the Porsches were stripped clean before police were able to helicopter into the accident scene to stop the looting. Blackie hit the mute button and the cabin of his Island Packet was once again silent, save for a low squeak as the spring lines on the windward side rhythmically tightened. With all the recent events rolling around in his mind, and with the gentle rocking of the boat in a five-knot wind, Blackie put his head back on the settee and promptly fell asleep.

He was torn from his nap by a sudden lurch as the twenty tons of his Island Packet 38 dipped hard to starboard. He quickly regained his senses. Either Yul Grant had stepped onto the boat, or a tsunami had somehow snuck in through Government Cut and roared up the bay. Blackie rose and slid open the companionway hatch. It was Yul.

"Hey, Captain Blackie. I know this is bad etiquette, but I got tired of shouting for permission to come aboard," Yul said as he moved his heavy frame into the cockpit. Under his arm was his drink of choice, a 12-pack of an off-brand beer he bought at a local wholesale club for $8 a case. It had the unpleasant name of *Old Grogham Light*.

Unlike Reggie's gin, Blackie refused to keep any containers of Yul's brand of ration onboard. At one time he had kept a case of it in his bilge so Yul wouldn't have to make so many trips on and off the boat – they were putting a strain on the dock lines.

But returning from a 3-day transcon trip the past summer, Blackie had come aboard and opened the hatch to a smell that he could only describe over the phone to Animal Control officers as the spray of a dying skunk. The officers refused to come out to his boat, claiming not to have jurisdiction on water, but told him what to do. Blackie went to a spy shop on Biscayne Boulevard and bought a $50 high-tech disposable gas mask and a cheap, chemical-resistant jumpsuit, apparently popular apparel in Miami.

Decked out in proper attire and armed with a Maglight, he reentered the contaminated cabin. Despite the claims of the protective-mask maker, the skunky smell was getting through the charcoal filter and causing him to involuntarily gag. He searched the cabin, praying not to find the skunk alive, and found nothing. Next, he was down on his knees in the bilge. With the panel of the teak-and-holly sole removed, he searched the recesses under the floor. Definitely, the smell was coming from there. He poked a long piece of dowel in the space between the sole and the hull. The animal must have died behind Yul's beer. He pushed the empty cans away and again found nothing, and only then did he realize that the true culprit wasn't a stowaway skunk, but that awful beer. It must have overheated and exploded, causing quite a stink.

On later visits, if Yul left any *Old Grogham Light* aboard, Blackie carefully poured it into the head and pumped it into his holding tank for later disposal, not wanting to pollute Biscayne Bay.

"Come on down, Yul, but leave the 12-pack in the cooler up there," Blackie ordered. Yul lifted the lid of a cockpit locker, custom built to hold a small, top-loading Norcold refrigerator. He still felt guilty over the bad-beer incident, since Blackie wasn't able to move back aboard for three days.

As Yul lowered his rotund body down the companionway ladder, Blackie again said to himself Yul's nickname, the name he believed everyone knew but Yul: *The Human Manatee*. Blackie had made the connection the first time he had ever seen Yul, before he was told of the nickname. Blackie had just moved to Te Cuesta Isle and was walking the piers before signing in with the dockmaster. Yul was standing there, wearing only his size-46 boxer shorts and holding a running garden hose.   Blackie had stopped to observe. Wondering why the man would water the bay, he stepped over and looked down. There, holding the end of the hose by its cheeks or jowls, was the seabull version of Yul, the biggest manatee that Blackie had ever seen. Blackie walked over to the topside twin of the pair and introduced himself.

Yul Grant's blubbery body was burnt a walnut stain by the tropic sun. His shaved head and walrus mustache, and even the scar on his chest (from a quadruple-bypass, not from a propeller), made Blackie alternate his gaze from the creature in the water to the one on the pier.   Here was a reverse reincarnation, a manatee that had come back as an overweight, middle-aged boater.

Blackie recalled most of that first conversation.

"This here is my pet manatee."

"Pet? He's yours?"

"Just as well. I've got to water him most every day."

"How much does he drink?"

"I've timed him. Record is 12 minutes – two minutes less than to fill my water tanks when they're empty. And my boat with the extra tank holds 40 gallons."

"You mean to say he drinks that much? Where does it go?"

"Let's say that I make it a point not to jump in and scrub the prop for a couple hours after he's through."

Yul settled into the port-side settee with a big bowl of microwaved popcorn and a frosty mug of *Old Grogram Light*. Blackie glanced up at the brass clinometer on the bulkhead. The boat was listing three degrees port, or *three degrees Yul*.

"So why the invite, Blackie?" Yul inquired.

Blackie told his neighbor the story, beginning with the carjacking, and ending with the material from the packet spread out on the settee table. Yul listened intently, seldom speaking. He read through the report of the *Skipper* twice. Finished, he stuffed his face with popcorn and looked up at Blackie.

"You see when this report was written?" Yul asked.

"A long time ago."

"So why is all this happening now?"

"I have no idea. But the question remains, Yul. What do I do about it?" Blackie asked.

"Right now, nothing. Sit on it. See what develops. Keep an eye on Ted," Yul replied.

"Don't call the police?"

"I wouldn't yet. Read the papers tomorrow. See what a reporter with at least a journalism degree has to say."

"Well, you're a cop. That's why I came to you."

"An ex-cop, an ex-New York *transit* cop. Not a detective in either white-collar crime or homicide."

"Yeah, but you're always reading those mystery novels."

"So you're saying that being an ex-transit cop who reads Elmore Leonard and Kinky Friedman makes me a *goddamn expert*?"

"Better than me. I'm just a pilot living on a sailboat."

The silent TV flashed an aerial shot of the dead manatee, a promo for the news at six. Blackie hit the mute button.

"Check this out, Yul. It's the story about the shootings."

Yul and Blackie sat transfixed as an anchor or a promo teased them before every commercial break about the manatee shooting. Channel 11 obviously was giving most of their airtime to the defecting basketball team. The two sailors watched and watched.

"What the shit is this, Blackie? It's been 25 minutes, they've shown the weather and sports, yet they keep telling us the manatee thing is coming right up. Like bait and switch. Their investigative reporter should investigate *them*."

What Blackie and Yul as viewers didn't know was that in Miami, any sports story *not involving an actual game or score* was found in Channel 11 surveys to hold greater viewer interest than any murder story with less than three victims. But the exception was when the station could come up with an angle on one of the victims, be it naïve tourist, innocent child, or in this case, one of *their* manatees; hence it was shown last.

What Channel 11 viewers finally saw at 6:27 p.m. was an abbreviated version of the 5 o'clock story, since the director was running over on time but had still successfully manipulated the viewers into sitting through 18 minutes of the news show's commercials. Again the *Skipper* was only described as an unidentified homeless person in the report. Story over, the anchors reappeared to deliver their bouncy, parting drivel. Blackie hit the power button, the best way anyone could handle Channel 11.

"Crazy, huh? They're like a high school journalism class with a million-dollar budget," Yul joked.

"You're being way too kind," Blackie answered.

"Well, I guess the good news is that no one has ID'd you or the *Skipper*. You really think Ted Jones is behind this?" Yul inquired.

"Possibly – probably. You know him?"

"Spoke to him once, and from our brief conversation, I can tell you that Ted Jones is a jerk."

"Except for the Pet Shop Boys I saw on his yacht through the binos, who does like this guy?"

"After our meeting, not I. But he does have a few hangers on, including those two German muscleheads," Yul said, shoveling in a scoop of popcorn.

"I'll grab you another of your beers and you can tell me about your meeting," Blackie replied.

Chapter 6:

Yul Be Sorry!

Yul told Blackie about his dealings with his neighbor, Ted Jones. They were close neighbors only in proximity. The 31-foot trimaran on which Yul lived was on the Pier Two T-head and in the shadow of *Ted's Toy* on the end of Pier Three. Few liveaboards were out there since they didn't want to take such a long hike down the dock to go ashore. Yul was forced to berth his boat out there because the two amas or outriggers of his Corsair 31R gave it a 22-foot beam – too wide for a regular slip.

Yul had tolerated the late-night orgies on the nearby yacht because most of the noise was muffled by the Breakwater's superior insulation, and simply because the motoryacht's deck was so high up off the water. He put up with Ted's antics by ignoring them – until the past New Year's Eve.

On that night, Ted had an even larger party than usual. Yul had seen cartloads of Moet being hauled down the dock to *Ted's Toy* that afternoon. He figured Ted and company were going out for a bay cruise to bring in the New Year. But as the magic hour approached, the big Breakwater was still in its slip with the party in full swing. None of the marina neighbors were invited, since Ted had made it obvious that he considered the other liveaboards, especially the sailors, to be on a much lower strata of chic. Habitually, he ignored them when passing, refusing to even acknowledge a hello from his fellow boaters, although few of them cared and fewer ever repeated the futile gesture.

After the madness at midnight, a few of Ted's guests decided that their own fireworks would add to the fun. They began lighting and throwing bottle rockets off the bow of the Breakwater, damn the torpedoes *and* the other boats.

Yul, in a deep sleep, was awakened by the thump of a bottle rocket hitting his hull and exploding like a depth charge just under the surface. He pulled back the companionway hatch as another missile whooshed past like a meteor, exploding just off the starboard amas. Yul hoisted himself out into his cockpit to shout obscenities at his neighbors. The loud music, Ted's flush-mount, waterproof strobe lights, and the general din of the party kept Yul from being seen or heard. He climbed off his boat and headed over to *Ted's Toy* on Pier Three.

When Yul walked up to the gangway he was stopped by Ted's two identical muscle-bound crewmen; they were obviously relishing their role as bouncers that night.

"Where's your invite, papa," the first one – the one with the pierced nose – demanded, a snarl on his lips.

"I need to see Ted, the asshole that owns this boat," Yul replied.

"He's entertaining, can't you see," the other said, "and without an invite, you're sure not heading aboard."

"Yeah, well I live here, and you need to tell Ted to knock it off with the fireworks."

"Beat it, *fettsack*. Any damage, Ted'll pay."

"Yeah, so crawl back to your raft, blubber-butt. You – you *human manatee!*" the other added with a big laugh as he moved toward him, excited by the chance to earn his pay for his new role as bouncer.

Yul was outraged, but he realized that he was outmuscled and outmanned. The only thing to do was to leave. He went back to his boat, down into his cabin to consider a counterattack. Another rocket ricocheted into the cockpit. Yul opened the hatch and watched the dud fizzle out, burning a black patch in the fiberglass sole. Enough was enough.

Yul grabbed his marinized Mossberg shotgun, the barrel cut slightly longer than the Florida minimum, and pumped a 12-gauge flare shell into the chamber. He went out into his cockpit, pointed it at Ted's mirror-finish, stainless-steel anchor resting against the starboard bow, and fired. That got their attention. The flare hit just below the anchor's fluke with a loud, hull-rattling thud, exploding in a brilliant-red semicircular spray. Even Yul was impressed by the sight.

A few of the more sober revelers screamed, and a couple on deck rushed to the bow railing, *Titanic*-like, to see if they were sinking. For the first time, Yul saw Ted at the teak rail glaring down, apparently outraged, as his guests pointed to the trimaran. Ted turned and disappeared into the crowd. Yul went below for what he knew was the inevitable.

A couple minutes passed before Yul heard something wood cracking hard on the port outrigger, accompanied by the muffled shouts of The Twins. He waited, knowing that Ted's chumps-on-steroids wouldn't allow this chance for a confrontation to pass. Yul didn't come out, knowing that he might as well make it all legal.

The boat dipped as one of them came aboard. Yul waited halfway up his companionway ladder. When the bleached-blonde goon slammed back the hatch, Yul stuck the end of the shotgun hard into his throat.

"Alright, you pencil-dick musclehead," Yul said in a calm voice. "You move one fucking inch and you'll lose what little neck you have left."

The intruder, still holding his lead-filled bat, froze, since he knew it could well be over soon.

"Ted, you up there?" Yul shouted, keeping his eyes staring down the barrel at the intruder's larynx.

"Yeah, I'm here. So who do you think *you are* shooting flares at my boat?" Ted said in a voice of absolute-authority, knowing *he* was safe on the dock.

"Ted, look down at this asshole's feet. You'll see a burn mark from one of those rockets shot over here by some dumbshit on your boat."

Ted took a step forward and looked down. Trying to hold back a laugh, he said, "An accident. Looks cosmetic to me. No need to get carried away here."

"We both know I can take this guy out with a clear conscience. He's breakin' and enterin' my home here, Ted."

"I could really give a shit what you do to him. But since we have to be neighbors, here's for the repair," Ted replied, stepping up to the edge of the finger pier and removing a money clip from the pocket of his Armani white linen pants. He wadded up a handful of hundreds and threw them into the cockpit. "So we'll call it even."

With that, Ted motioned to the other, somewhat reluctant twin, and they headed off the fingerpier and down the dock, leaving the fate of the intruder up to Yul.

"I guess the lesson here, buddy, is that when you've got that much money, *life* – as long as it's not yours – *is cheap*," Yul observed.

"So I'm going to give you one option, one way to get out of this with your face still intact. Set down the little bat and take a leap to starboard, to the right. You can swim back. And you better not say one word to me until you're out of range. There's no flare in the chamber, it's shot the size of ball bearings – pretty much take your face away," Yul told him, bluffing.

The intruder dropped the bat, stumbled over to the amas, dove in and was gone.

That was a pleasant meeting," Blackie said. "Can't believe I've never heard it before."

"I don't think Ted or I have ever told anyone about our New Year's toast. Dockmaster wouldn't have liked it, probably would have kicked us both out of here. I've done my part to avoid Ted like the plague. Ever notice I don't go on Pier Three very often?"

Chapter 7:

The Marine SWAT Team

Blackie and Yul discussed the situation into the night and decided that wait-and-see was the best way to handle it. After Yul left, Blackie felt guilty about involving him in the shooting, but he had to tell someone he trusted to give him some good advice.

The next morning Blackie was up early, retrieving the *Miami Herald* off his fingerpier to see how the paper handled the shooting. Over a cup of espresso in the cockpit, Blackie examined Page One of the paper. The lead story was about the exodus of the pro basketball team, since abandoning the slightly-used arena right down the street from the *Herald* was bound to adversely affect the real estate holdings of the paper's corporate owner.

In the lower right-hand corner of the first page of the Metro section were a few paragraphs about the shooting at the Barracuda Grill, the story jumping to an inside page. The article made strong mention of the dead manatee angle, although it didn't go so far as to identify the victim as one of *their* manatees or suggest that the guys on the Mako were counter-eco-terrorists. At least the *Herald* had come up with a motive.

According to an unnamed source in the police department, the grill's owner had been identified as a former mob informant, relocated years ago to Florida with an altered face and identity. The manatee, reported the *Herald*, was an innocent casualty, like the unidentified homeless man, in a probable hit for revenge. The string of holes Blackie had seen up the side of the houseboat's cabin, according to the *Herald*, was carefully planned.

This new revelation gave Blackie time to ponder. The spotlight certainly wasn't pointing anywhere near the *Skipper*. He was probably going quietly to a pauper's grave. With the focus elsewhere, Blackie had time to decide what he was going to do – or not do.

About 10 a.m., Yul came over and helped Blackie replace the lightning dissipater on the top of his mast. Blackie's device was a variation of the $150-item found in most boater's catalogues, a fancy item of questionable scientific value that was supposed to avert a lightning strike. Blackie's was a $14 parody of the advertised item, but as he had proven, just as effective.

According to the literature for the $150-one, the bronze bristles on what looked like an oversized bottle-brush would dissipate the negative ions, preventing a bolt of lightning from being drawn to the mast top. Not one vessel with a dissipater had been hit, extolled the propaganda, which Blackie found an amusing claim. About a month after reading the pamphlet, Blackie had been in a kitchenwares shop at the mall in the Pittsburgh airport, looking to replace his rusted can opener ravaged by the salt air. There he spotted something called a kitchen witch, an ugly doll that was supposed to bring luck to those who cooked with one in the room. He bought it on the spot and once back on Miami Beach, went up the mast and installed the kitchen witch, strapping it on to the mast top with a safety belt of stainless steel wire.

Six months passed, and with the thunderstorm season over, Blackie went back up the mast and took a photo of the windblown and sunbeaten doll. He fired off a letter to *Practical Sailor*, the sailing world's equivalent of *Consumer Reports*. He claimed his kitchen witch, at less than a tenth the price of the advertised lightning dissipaters, also had a 100 per cent success rate of averting a lightning strike. Not a single boat with a kitchen witch on its mast had been struck by lightning – as good a claim as any similar product on the market.

His photo and letter caused quite a furor in the magazine – Blackie had even received a few veiled threats from a few readers on a blog for his sarcasm. A recent inspection showed him that his kitchen witch was deteriorating badly. A week later he was again between flights in the Pittsburgh airport, so he returned to the shop and bought three more of the dolls as replacements so that he could continue his grand experiment.

Yul manned the spinnaker halyard at the electric windlass, pulling Blackie in his bosun's chair fifty feet up to the mast top. Blackie loved it up there. An incredible 360-degree panorama of South Beach, the cruise port, downtown Miami and parts of Biscayne Bay. The Island Packet rolled gently from the shallow wakes of passing boats, and Blackie found the exaggerated swaying at the mast top thrilling. He always came up with his pair of Steiners to scope out the area. He trained the binos on Ted's boat, but saw no movement aboard. He examined the ten boats in the anchorage, including the two dilapidated sloops rafted to each other by the monk sailors, both apparently unoccupied.[2] The rest were transients, flying the Deutch flag mostly, Germans who had found an incredibly cheap way to be tourists on South Beach.

Blackie aimed the glasses at the Miami Beach Marine Patrol station, an elaborate stilt building near the end of the Venetian Causeway. Beneath it, penned behind 12-foot-high iron gates was a pair of fancy police boats, one a 35-foot Scarab Sport and the other a powerful inflatable.

---

[2] Anchorage of the monks' sailboats, 25 47.70N, 80 09.72W.

Yul was the one who said that he had never seen the boats leave the garage except to deliver Santa to a kids' party at a bayfront park.

Blackie remembered his marina neighbors' attempt last year to nab a thief preying on their boats, a kid on crack squatting on one of the vacant boats in the anchorage. They had followed the kid back to his boat, catching him loading Reggie's folding bike onboard, with another neighbor's missing kayak tied to the stern. Repeated calls to the Miami Beach Marine Patrol station about 100 yards away finally got a response: "Not our jurisdiction. Call the Florida Marine Patrol." So why were they there, other than to harass anchored and uninformed cruisers with Miami Beach's bogus one-week anchoring law?

Blackie focused on the pier in front of the station. Yul was about to be proven wrong, for both police boats were out of their pen and in the water. But he realized that at deck level, and without a pair of 7x 50 CAT-optics glasses, Yul couldn't see anything.

Blackie looked beyond the station, and noticed roadblocks had been set up where the Venetian Causeway entered the Beach. On the road behind the station, the street was filled with cops, police vans and what looked like a mobile command truck. He assumed they were practicing a hurricane or disaster drill. He let the binos hang and performed his task, replacing the kitchen witch that had served him so well. His plan was to display her in a Plexiglas case in the cabin for posterity.

Through with his task, he was about to shout down to Yul, who was sitting on the deck leaning back on a lifeline stanchion. Yul loosely held the halyard that was fortunately tied fast to the bollard, since he was sound asleep. Blackie paused, not wanting to disturb him.

He returned to his Steiners to see what was going on with the drill. A small flotilla of boats was assembled at the station's pier that also served as South Beach's public boat ramp. Blackie could see that even the Miami Beach SWAT team was in on this one. With the boats, including one borrowed from the Florida Marine Patrol, the team took off from the dock in the direction of Te Cuesta Isle.

Simultaneously, a chopper came in low from the north, so low that Blackie thought he was looking straight at it as it approached. Now *this* was a coordinated maneuver.

He focused on the lead boat, the inflatable. The SWAT team was in marine gear, and appeared to be better equipped than a SEAL team. They wore bimini-blue helmets, light-blue camo assault jumpsuits, and had their faces painted in shades of pale-blue and aquamarine. They must be taping this one, Blackie thought to himself from his perfect perch. In their hands were a variety of automatic assault weapons, and Blackie wondered what type of disaster drill would require that much fire power.

With incredible speed, the boats and the chopper converged on their target, the monks' two dilapidated sailboats rafted together and floating silently on their little patch of Biscayne Bay. With military precision, the SWAT team, guns trained, surrounded the sloops in a loose semicircle to the north, with the chopper overhead slightly to the south, covering that side. Over a bullhorn, the commander ordered the occupants to come out slowly, hands above their heads. No movement on the sloops. The police boats edged closer to the target and the order was repeated, this time from a speaker mounted on the chopper.

Through the Steiners, Blackie saw a small, bright flash at the transom or back of the port-side sloop. The explosion sent splinters of wood and smoke blasting out toward the nearest police boat, the inflatable. A young man in a brown robe emerged from the companionway holding something in his hands, not identifiable because of the smoke, unidentifiable even to Blackie through the high-powered binos. A brief but intense firefight followed.

The echo of the automatic weapons off the walls of Belle Isle's high-rise condos reverberated in every direction. No sooner had the shooting started than it was over. As the initial smoke cleared, the deadly accuracy of the SWAT team was evident. The sole monk who had emerged was sprawled over the wooden cockpit coaming, obviously dead from multiple gunshot wounds.

The inflatable was foundering, with large splinters of wood from the explosion having pierced two of its air chambers. One member of the SWAT team was down in the hypalon boat holding his neck, another casualty of the vicious blast. The Scarab came alongside to evacuate the rest of the team. The remaining boats cautiously approached the sloops. The port-side boat was still smoking out of the lazarette locker from the explosion.

From his vantage point, Blackie could see a flicker of flame in the midst of the smoke. The two remaining police boats drew alongside the starboard-side sloop. A cop leapt onboard, gun drawn, in what Blackie considered an incredible feat of bravery. He entered the cabin and emerged with two more occupants in monk's clothing, hands covering the shaved crowns of their heads. The mop-up had begun, the excitement apparently over. The Scarab, with throttles down, was racing for the pier with the injured cop.

Blackie looked back to the sloops in the instant of a stupendous flash. He felt the concussion at the top of the mast a split second later. First one, then the other sloop exploded in a ball of fire. The Steiners flew out of his hands, tumbling down, hitting the finger pier with a bounce ten feet up off the dock. Without the binoculars, Blackie watched a panoramic view of the disaster. Two orange fireballs rose up, one slightly ahead of the other.

What followed was total pandemonium. Pieces of people, of spars, of dark cloth showered down around the burning boats. Flotsam, on fire, bobbed on the bay. Sirens. More boats. Screams. More orders over the bullhorns. A few boaters ran down the Te Cuesta Isle dock to the T-heads. The whoop-whoop of the chopper overhead was joined by the mechanical vultures of Channel 11 and the rest of the electronic media. More sirens. Ambulances pulled into the deserted lot of the Te Cuesta Isle Marina to carry the casualties being ferried into the marina.

"Yul! Get me down from here!"

Yul, like Blackie, had been frozen in the role of spectator, watching the events unfold. He untied the halyard from the cleat and lowered Blackie down the mast.

"What in the hell is going on?" Blackie asked, once his feet had landed safely on deck.

"They wanted our frocked brothers for something serious," Yul replied. "Probably for what happened yesterday."

"What happened? What caused the explosions?"

"Must have been the fuel tank. The sloop probably had an old Atomic 4 in it – a gas engine, not a diesel. Or they could have had propane onboard."

"Sure, but what caused the first explosion?"

"What first explosion? I got woke up by automatic weapons being fired."

"No, they started shooting after the stern of the closer boat blew up."

"No idea," Yul replied. "Let's head down to my boat and see if we can help."

They stepped off Blackie's Island Packet and headed out Pier Two to the T-head. They weren't the first ones there. On the dock in front of Yul's boat was none other than P. Rick Lopez, with a cameraman and assistant, trying vainly to get his face connected to the disaster. P. Rick lived on nearby "Dan" Marino Island and had rushed over to the scene. The news anchor was about to swing a coupe – he was going live-on-the-scene at noon with the story, just like in the early days of his career. If only it had been raining to add to the effect.

P. Rick was obviously pissed about something, but Yul and Blackie ignored him, concentrating on the scene on the water. Out on the bay, police joined by firemen sprayed the smoldering hulks with fire extinguishers in an attempt to put out the flaming debris.

"Should we go out there? We could get my dinghy off the davits," Blackie shouted at Yul.

"No, looks like they got it under control."

They gazed out at the fire and didn't see the Channel 11 assistant untying the aft spring and stern lines to Yul's boat, carried out on the orders of P. Rick. The TV crew was trying to get an unobstructed shot of P. Rick with the smoking remains of the monks' sloops in the background.

A police boat raced into the marina with an injured cop. Yul's boat, held only by the forward lines, had swung out almost perpendicular to the T-head, blocking the entrance. The police boat couldn't get by to a waiting gurney. A cop screamed over the hailer, "Get that boat out of the way or we'll sink the bastard! We've got an injured officer here!"

Yul and Blackie turned simultaneously, their jaws dropping in horror. Blackie ran forward and jumped onto the port amas.

Yul stayed on the pier, yelling to Blackie, "The line's in the water! Throw it to me and I'll pull you back in!"

In less than a minute they had the aft end of the port outrigger against the piling. The cops motored by, cursing at them, unable to contain their disgust. Blackie threw a couple extra coils of line on the pier and jumped up on the dock.

"How did that happen?"

"I think those Channel 11 bastards untied me so that my boat wouldn't block their view."

"You've got to be kidding!"

They turned and looked at P. Rick, bathed in bright artificial light, doing what by now came to him as second nature, *ad libbing on-camera, live.*

"Yes, Sheila, I'm here at Te Cuesta Isle Marina, at an unfolding disaster. Just moments ago there was a tremendous explosion as SWAT members were boarding a pair of suspect boats out on Biscayne Bay. We have reports that they believed that onboard were the killers of a former Mafia informant and one of *our* manatees at a Miami bay-front restaurant yesterday.

"Early reports have at least five persons killed in the explosion, including one member of the Miami Beach Marine SWAT team and at least four of the water-borne terrorists. The police were securing the boats when the blasts went off, and total pandemonium ensued. Unsubstantiated rumors are that the explosion might have come from a suicide bomb on one of the boats.

"They are still bringing the injured in. And Sheila, just before we came on live, I witnessed just how chaotic the situation is here. Some boater, on this boat to my right, due to poor seamanship or just to go out there and gawk, had untied his boat and was blocking the police from bringing in an injured officer. We've got it on tape and will play it for you in a moment."

By internal cue, P. Rick moved down the dock toward the boat, leaning back, looking down at the stern. "I believe the name of the boat, a trimaran, is *The King 'n I*," P. Rick stated with just the right amount of chagrin. Once again, P. Rick was missing the big picture – the explosion on the water – and focusing instead on a tidbit that was connected to him. P. Rick stopped a few feet from Blackie, who just couldn't take it any more.

Blackie stepped up to him, still a foot off-camera, and shouted, "You *fucking* liar! *You* untied those lines!"

"This is P. Rick Lopez. Back to you, Sheila, in the studio."

The artificial light went out, and P. Rick turned to his accuser. "Listen, buddy, don't *ever, ever* get in my shot."

"You prick! You guys untied this boat."

"Like I told you, make sure your shit's not in my way when the light's on. Bernie, get this guy away from me."

Before the burly assistant could move Yul bent down and grabbed one of the lines Blackie had thrown on the dock. It snaked down the pier and under the cameraman's feet. Using his weight, Yul heaved on it with all his might. The video cameraman, already top-heavy from the Sony Betacam on his shoulder, had his feet pulled out from under him. The cameraman, with his $50,000 Sony toy, crashed into P. Rick and they both tumbled off the dock and into the salty water of Biscayne Bay.

Blackie and Yul went to the edge of the pier and watched the two news hounds treading water. Yul pointed down and said, "Live, from the depths of Biscayne Bay, its P. Rick!"

Later, back aboard the Island Packet, Blackie had a seltzer while Yul sipped an *Old Grogham Light*. They were watching the news (on a different channel out of principal), trying to find out what had happened that noon on the bay.

Unfortunately, up in Orlando, a washed-up sitcom star had taken his third wife and their two kids hostage on a new ride at Universal Studios, and that eclipsed any event on their bay, no matter how many had died.

Finally, the news switched from live national coverage of the amusement park standoff to the local story. According to the reports, Miami Beach police had been given an anonymous tip on where to find the Mako used in the attack at the grill. Stolen prior to the Barracuda Grill shootings, it had been abandoned on the north shore of Watson Island. Although thieves had beaten the cops to the boat and removed the outboards, seats and anything of value, investigators did find a brown robe onboard. Later, another anonymous caller said that the assassins could be found holed up in a pair of old sailboats rafted together off of Te Cuesta Isle. Not since Versace's killer hid out on a houseboat, not since the crazy waiter kidnapped the busload of kids and forced them to ride to Joe's Stone Crab, had the Miami Beach SWAT team been given such a perfect opportunity to try out their gear. And they could wear their new marine outfits out on the water. This was the stuff TV movies were made of (*surely, if the other two were*), and had every member of the team foaming at the mouth. Unfortunately, when there's that much firepower, something can go terribly wrong.

No one knew what caused the first explosion. The leading theory was that the suspects onboard set it off in an apparent suicide bombing, since the police vehemently denied opening fire prior to the initial explosion.

One thing for certain, the casualties were heavy. One policeman was killed, blown to bits when the wooden sloops exploded. One of the suspects had died prior to the second blast from gunfire, when he idiotically came up top holding a landing net fixed to an aluminum pole. In the midst of the smoke from that first explosion, police mistook it for a rifle.

Two other suspects, standing on the deck after their surrender, were killed instantly in the twin fireballs. The charred body of a fourth suspect, onboard the other sloop, was found dressed in a smoldering brown robe and curled up in the forward V-berth. Three policemen, all members of the SWAT team, were seriously injured. Four other cops had been treated and released.

Miami Beach officials were quick to condemn the suspects, whom they said bore ultimate responsibility for the mayhem. The mayor and officials from the Tourist Bureau and the Chamber of Commerce openly denounced the criminal transients living off South Beach, while secretly believing that they finally might have the solution for getting rid of cheap waterborne German and Canadian tourists who weren't paying their bed tax.

Blackie and Yul had their own trouble with the police after the incident. Fished from the water, P. Rick and the cameraman (minus his Betacam) attempted to press charges against Yul and Blackie. But in a bizarre twist, the assistant, finally fed up with P. Rick, sabotaged his own career in broadcast journalism by refusing to back P. Rick, the cameraman, and their bogus story.

The big guy, a news lackey with greasy hair and a beard, said he was fed up with covering for P. Rick, for helping create news when there was none, really for putting up with the abuse from vacuous, egotistical bastards like on-camera reporters and anchormen. He said that he had let loose the boat's lines on P. Rick's orders, and that he would testify that he saw the cameraman himself trip on the lines, causing the two TV journalists to hit the bay.

With that revelation, Yul took the offensive and asked the police to arrest P. Rick for trying to steal his boat. The police, caught in the middle, worked out a compromise: if everyone would stop yelling and P. Rick and his news crew got off the Te Cuesta Isle docks, all could carry on with their lives. Their precious camera, after all, was heavily insured. It was a deal.

P. Rick knew that this wasn't to be the reporting event of his life, since all the media attention was on some TV-sitcom has-been holed up and holding hostages on a brand-new ride at a theme park in Orlando. For this to be his Signature Piece, his stepping stone to the networks, he would have needed the luck of it happening on a slow news day. Channel 11 packed up and headed home. The assistant, having confessed his sins and given as penance his termination via cell phone by the news director, wandered off into the desert at the north end of Te Cuesta Isle.

Sitting in the cabin, news over, Blackie and Yul mulled over another day's wild events. They came up with one thing for certain about the Anchor/Betacam dunking. Jerks like P. Rick should never put too much trust in low-level employees being both grossly abused and underpaid.

And as the evening concluded, they tried to figure out what role Ted Jones might have played in the conflagration.

Chapter 8:

Dani, A Modern Sailor

Blackie woke up early the following day with what he thought was a hangover. Although Yul had polished off almost a 12-pack of that god-awful beer, Blackie had stuck to mineral water with a squeeze of lime. It was all the excitement affecting him, wearing him out. He almost wished he was back flying, but he was through with his trips for the rest of the month.

Blackie picked up the phone on the second ring, heard her familiar, but muffled voice.

"Blackie? Can you hear me?"

"Yeah, barely. Where are you?"

"Kennedy. My flight from Milan got in about 5 a.m. so I'll be back in Miami about 10. Can you come get me?"

"Yeah, sure. Your flight empty?"

"Maybe 30 people. How'd you know?" she asked.

"Good guess. You got anything going when you get back?"

"No. I thought I would take it easy for a few days."

"Great. We can finally talk to each other *in person*."

"That would be different."

"See you out front by the Dolphin Garage. Have a good flight."

"Okay. Ciao."

Blackie hung up the phone and crawled off the foam mattress of his Island Packet. He sat on the edge of the bunk with the fiddle, the wooden slat that held in the mattress, cutting off the circulation to the back of his thighs. Random thoughts floated through his mind. Had he said he'd meet her at the Dolphin garage? Or was it the Manatee? And why did Alpha Airlines have a flight from Milan to JFK that left Milan at midnight and seldom had more than 30 people on it? And how did he ever get involved with Dani Parma?

Blackie made his cup of espresso and drank it in silence. He was sick of news. With no paper, no TV, he could plod on in ignorant bliss.

Skipping a shower, he left his boat to head over to Pier Two, where Daniella Parma kept her 42-foot catamaran, a Fountaine Pajot Venezia with the overused name *Carpe Diem*. He stopped at one of his three dock boxes and retrieved a bucket, long-handled brush, and soap. A clean boat would be a good homecoming for Dani. She had been on a grueling job in Milan, earning her keep as a well-paid SoBe model in the twilight of her career.

With their divergent schedules – opposite lives, really – the two of them in Miami together for a few days would be a welcome break from all craziness. Walking down the dock, he thought about their bizarre relationship, if one could even call it that.

Dani was seven years younger than Blackie, yet the two of them were a generation apart. At one time he amusingly called her his "Post-Gen-X Sailor," which she had told him was a bit dated. She had called him, after one too many glasses of Barolo, "my tight-assed pilot."

He wasn't that far chronologically from her and her friends. But heading from college into the confines of a cockpit with ex-military flyers, then under the corporate umbrella of Alpha Airlines, had insulated him from ever developing the sarcastic contempt, even despair, he saw in her and so many of her contemporaries.

Yet he often felt he was stereotyping, especially when it came to Dani. She was a dichotomy. She talked the trash of her generation, and talked it well enough to get him thinking. But she herself didn't fit into the mold the marketing firms had created for her and her kind. Restless? Yes. Disaffected? Yes. But she lived on a $300,000 sailboat. Was she the heiress to Newport yachtees? No, just the recent orphan to well-insured upper-middle-class parents from a Dallas suburb.

How could she ridicule life and still be a high-paid, jet-setting SoBe model? Because she had a brain, a degree in advertising, but had rejected the corporate culture for what she considered a McJob: living without thinking off her extremely good looks by standing there on South Beach, gyrating in a shoot for a German sportswear catalogue. It was a McJob, but one for which only a few could apply.

Blackie uncoiled the water hose on the dock and pulled it down the finger pier. He squirted some Joy into the bucket, filled it with water and began the mindless task of scrubbing, removing the film of dirt and jet fuel that had settled on the white hulls of the Venezia and all the other boats in the marina. The vaporized fuel had spewed out the previous week from a passing, sputtering Super DC-8, overloaded with garment fragments bound for Santo Domingo.

Te Cuesta Isle was in the flight path of Runway 9L at MIA, used by the fleet of cargo planes that ferried clothing fragments out of or Colombian flowers into Miami. This particular DC-8 had taken off for the Dominican Republic with an unlatched aft cargo door, seen by the controllers in the tower banging away as the jet went into its rotation halfway down the runway. The pilot of the old bird had to dump fuel so he could circle and land back at MIA. Visualizing that scene of that rear door pounding away as the pilot started his approach made Blackie remember an early conversation he had as a rookie in an Alpha Airlines cockpit. A senior captain, about to retire, made an interesting observation while they waited on the runway at MIA for a '50s-era, triple-tailed Constellation to take off ahead of them.

"The guy flying that Connie – looks like a Starliner to me – probably has flown for Bravo, then Echo, then a bankrupt charter outfit before taking that job," the $200K-a-year captain observed. "You know, partner, I think pilots are like seagulls. Some of us soar to the heights, like in that book from the '70s, *Jonathan Livingston Seagull*. And others, unfortunately, spend their lives circling over the dump, pecking the flesh off old chicken bones."

Periodically, one of the old planes would fall from the sky as it left MIA or another South Florida airport. Blackie remembered seeing on TV the eyewitness account of one high-rise condo resident on Miami Beach. The elderly woman described the sight of an old DC-7 as it flew low between two buildings on its way to ditching in the surf. She said that as it passed she saw the pilot was wearing Rayban aviator sunglasses and had a terrified look on his face.

What were these guys risking their lives for? To fly obviously, but their cargo was fabric being sent south so grossly underpaid seamstresses in Santo Domingo sweatshops could craft them into designer sportswear. The finished product, marked up outrageously when compared to the costs in producing it, was then airfreighted back to Miami to be distributed in designer boutiques throughout America before its fashion-freshness date expired. That's how designers – really former designers, since they had turned into figureheads at large corporations – could reside in mansions or high-rise penthouses on South Beach. And applying trickle-down economics, that's how Dani, too, paid her rent, wearing copies of those outfits in a catalogue shoot.

Blackie shook his head. He had stepped onboard her boat, and suddenly he was thinking like her and the rest of them.

She held nothing sacred. She knew she had started late and her modeling career was fleeting, so then what would she do? Blackie thought of the overused name for her boat, *Carpe Diem* – "Seize the Day." Was that her motto?

It could be. She was born a suburbanite and raised in the banality of a North Dallas suburb, a strikingly beautiful child from the pictures he had seen. Her parents had met in Hawaii, and her mother was half-Japanese. They had moved to Dallas after he left the military to work for a weapons systems manufacturer. They weren't part of the Texas evangelical-church-going scene, so Dani like many her age was raised without religion. Her parents, career-driven Dallasites, divorced when she was five. (Later, to everyone's shock, they had reconciled and remarried each other after she had gone off to college.) Shuttled between two homes of oft-absent parents, she like so many other kids was forced to develop her moral code based on TV-sitcom values or what she read. Fortunately, she read voraciously.

In high school, she flirted with the post-punk movement, thriving in Deep Elum near downtown Big D, but had enough sense not to pierce or tattoo anything, or her later modeling career might have been over before it started.

Her only connection emotionally with her parents was with her father, whose one diversion from work was to sail a J-24 on summer weekends on Lake Dallas. She often was his crew, and they had won quite a few races, even placing near the top in the Texas finals for that class. That explained the sailing, but what about the rest?

She attended college at the University of Texas at Austin, majoring in advertising. She came back reluctantly to Big D and landed a job at a big agency. Dani toiled endlessly at her tiny workstation, mostly cranking out copy for products made at third-world factories and sold in the malls of America.

She felt she was going nowhere fast, and she developed a strong case of Boomer envy. She despised her bosses. They were former hippies, unlike her father's friends who had been conservative youth with their lives mapped out by the time they were 15. But her bosses in advertising and marketing had always considered themselves counter-cultural and always cutting-edge cool. And had they ever sold out, she had told Blackie more than once. They were the Baby Boomers who once had protested in their youth for causes closely tied to their megalomania, and now they had surreptitiously taken over the world. They sat in the big corner offices on inflated salaries while she and her young colleagues did all of their creative work.

One gray and miserable winter day, driving down Central Expressway in another evening of horrible traffic, she snapped. She was fed up with Dallas and its seasons of Too Much. Too cold in winter, too hot in summer, too windy in spring and too much football in fall. It was time to move on. She went home and called up her boss's voice mail and resigned. She packed up and drove to South Beach.

To survive, she succumbed to a "career" she had dabbled in during college but despised, modeling. She had a portfolio, given to her a few months earlier by a friend in Dallas, who used her to create his own workbook. She walked it down the row of agencies on Ocean Drive and slowly the work had begun to trickle in. She lived in a tiny efficiency on Euclid Avenue with no goals, no cares, and a hodge-podge of evolving "adultescent" values.

Blackie hadn't been able to pry much from her about that era. She alluded to it being hedonistic, bordering on nihilistic, a time when what little sleep she caught was soon after sunrise. She had been a classic, albeit shortterm SoBe party girl.

A personal tragedy changed all that. Her parents were killed in Dallas when they ran their Lexus into the back of a stalled semi. Both were killed instantly. She went back to Texas for the funeral filled with grief and anger. Her parents, both Boomers, had deprived her of a family during her childhood by their personal pettiness. With her off to college, they became a couple again. And now they had died together, leaving her once again an only child alone. She definitely had some issues to address, Blackie thought.

With the estate liquidated and the generous insurance money in the bank, as sole executor and beneficiary Dani no longer had to work. She could move to a fancy condo on Fisher

Island if she wanted. But Dani didn't touch the money, feeling it was tainted with her anger. She stayed on Euclid and continued to model.

When the big boat show came to town a year ago, Dani wandered over to the Convention Center. She took the shuttle to Bayside to see the sailboats. She strolled out on a finger pier and stepped aboard a cruising catamaran. Within a month she had found and bought a previously owned Venezia 42 and berthed it in an oversized 70-foot slip at Te Cuesta Isle.

Blackie wasn't sure if the boat was a step forward or a step back. It had given her a purpose. She threw herself headlong into sailing, working on her Captain's license and becoming familiar with her boat.

But now Dani had mobility and the ultimate escape vehicle. If she sickened of the scene on South Beach (and who eventually wouldn't?), she could untie the lines and sail away. Blackie's secret hope was that she would take him with her.

But in viewing their relationship, Blackie knew that she definitely wasn't looking for any long-term commitment – that phrase wasn't even in her vocabulary. And besides, she had once commented, "Me with you, a man named Blackie? Who's going to be with a guy called Cap'n Blackie? Sounds like a comic strip character. Don't think it's going to happen."

Still, whatever they had was better than nothing. To be around her was to feel a fresh breeze out of the northeast, coming in off the Atlantic after thousands of miles, unpolluted and exhilarating. And no small factor was that Dani was the most beautiful woman he had ever met.

She had certainly had an effect on him. He had been so insulated in his pilot cocoon, living a materialistic life and blaming the oft-used "missing gene of pilots" as his failure in the past to commit to anyone or anything – except maybe flying or sailing. She had lured him to go with her to Sierra Club beer nights and "Hold the Line," meetings to limit urban growth toward agricultural land and the Everglades. She dragged him to film festivals and author's nights at Books & Books. She had used her beauty and her charm to break him out of the superficial shell in which he lived and to start thinking – and caring.

Finished with cleaning her boat, Blackie wrapped her hose in a perfect circular coil, an obsession of his with all lines and hose. His fixation had elicited more than one comment from her. He doubted that she would change him, or he change her. He headed over to his boat to shower so that he wouldn't be late picking her up at Miami International Airport.

Blackie drove around the Departures loop at chaotic MIA for the third time, still not spotting Dani. They both knew never to meet at Arrivals, since the trapped and noxious auto-exhaust fumes in the lower level were enough to shorten one's lifespan during the wait.

Blackie often thought that MIA was the "best-landscaped, poorest organized" airport in the world. And with the endless construction, now only the latter applied. The place had more in common with the marketplace in Karachi than with a modern transportation center. Traffic was stopped in front of him by a monster pickup pulling a 35-foot Donzi speedboat, trailered to the airport only to impress. It blocked three lanes of traffic while the occupants pitched a half-dozen oversized suitcases out of the boat onto the curb. Twenty yards away three oblivious traffic cops argued over the previous night's Heats game.

Dani had arrived at "complex" time, before a bank of flights left to all points north and south, and on a Monday, when half a dozen cruise ships disembarked 10,000 passengers off their abbreviated 3-day cruises, before embarking an equal number of folks for the 4-day ones. Finally Blackie spotted her in front of the Flamingo garage.

"I couldn't remember if the garage was fish or fowl," Dani apologized as she hopped into the Beamer.

"Neither. Sea mammal. Dolphin," he replied, feeling like an idiot for trusting MIA's confusing signage. "You drive around here a few times and you realize that the only possible safe place at this airport is in the locked cockpit of an airplane."

"A zoo alright. Last month after my flight from London to Miami, I got in line behind an elderly man in Customs with two monstrous suitcases of smelly cheese."

"Where was he from?"

"I think his flight was from El Salvador, and he was going to Washington, D.C."

"Smuggling cheese into our nation's capital? They've got a cheese shortage up there?"

"Not smuggling, I guess. The bored-looking Customs agent put a handkerchief to his face and waved him right through."

"So how was your trip?"

"Exhausting. But I was able to get away for a few days to Siena."

"Tuscany. Well, I know how you love their wine."

"How about you? You're through flying for the month, aren't you?"

"Finished," he replied.

"Just hanging out under the bimini top?"

"No, nothing like that. Probably the two wildest days of my life."

Driving back, he told her about the recent events, starting with the carjacking and ending with the marine SWAT assault off Te Cuesta Isle. They were at the marina parking lot when he finished his story. Dani was aghast.

"What are you going to do?" she asked.

"I don't know enough yet to do anything. Even Yul says I shouldn't go to the cops yet."

"A dilemma, Blackie."

"You don't know that jerk, do you?"

"Who?"

"Ted."

"A little."

"How?"

"From a party or two a while back."

"Oh."

"I'm trying to think how I can help. I'll make some calls to some people on the Beach and see if they know anything more about Mr. Jones."

"Any info will help."

Sitting in the car, not having seen her for almost a month, Blackie was quickly losing his concentration. He studied her in the harsh light. She didn't have a bit of makeup on, was coming off 13 hours of flying, yet she had a look of child-like innocence. Even in the light of midday she was flawless. He tried not to stare, because he knew that it bothered her, since so many people did. All her adult life it had bothered her.

"What do you say we go for a sail?" he asked.

"Where?"

"Down the Bay to the Park, off Elliot Key. Just for a couple days. We can talk things over. Relax. Swim."

"Midweek? We'd have the anchorage all to ourselves. Your boat or mine?" Dani inquired a hint of excitement in her voice.

"I don't care. I'm just glad you didn't say you'd meet me down there."

"Since I didn't, we'll take mine."

"Sounds good," Blackie replied, making the assumption, yet still not comfortable enough to say it – that they would both be sleeping in the same hull of her catamaran.

Back in the marina, Blackie carted her bags down Pier Two, helping stow them aboard the Venezia. They agreed to be ready for a 1 p.m. departure, more than enough time to get to the anchorage by dusk. He headed back to his boat to grab his gear and lock up.

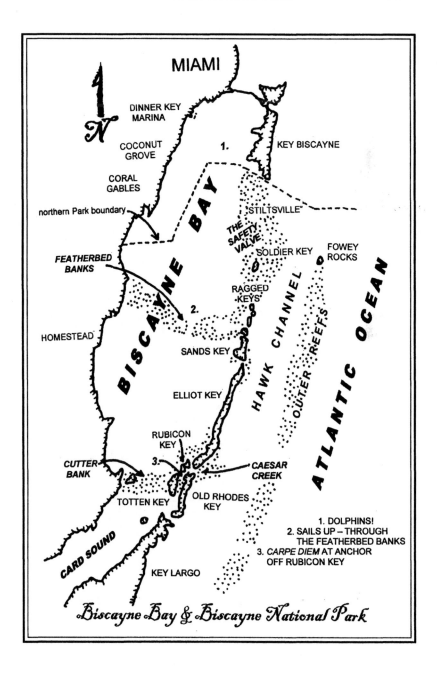

Biscayne Bay & Biscayne National Park

Chapter 9:

The Bay

At a little past one, Blackie threw the bow lines off the
Venezia. He stepped back and grabbed the aft port spring line
and removed it from the cleat. He pitched it on the finger pier
as Daniella pulled down on the throttles, putting the twin
Yanmar diesels to work. The cat backed, clearing the outer
pilings by a foot on each side. She spun the wheel
counterclockwise, and *Carpe Diem* swung her stern toward
land. Dani pushed the throttles up, rotated the wheel back, and
they were off between the piers toward the marina entrance and
the bay.

She took the boat west, through the channel north of the
Venetian Isles, as Blackie brought in the fenders and stowed
them in the large anchor/storage locker aft of the trampoline.
He methodically, almost absentmindedly, coiled the lines
perfectly, only to look over the coach-house roof to see Dani at
the helm, obviously laughing at him for his obsession with
shipshape lines.

They stopped to wait for the spans to lift on the western
bascule bridge on the Venetian Causeway. Once through, they
had somewhat clear sailing, since the drawbridges between
them and the great expanse of Biscayne Bay had been replaced
over the years by high, fixed bridges.

Out from under the MacArthur Causeway bridge,
Blackie scoped out the horizon to the north and west. Sure
enough, an amphibious airplane was looping around behind the

Marriott high-rise, on its final approach for a sea landing in Government Cut. Blackie walked aft, grabbed the stainless steel tube of the bimini top overhead, and swung himself into the cockpit.[3]

"You've got traffic at 3 o'clock. A Grumman Mallard off the starboard beam."

She looked over the water and saw nothing, especially not a duck. "A what?"

"A plane about to land in front of you."

She stepped to starboard and saw the flashing landing lights of the Grumman seaplane as it began to settle down, pelican-like, on the bay.

"A seaplane! It's got the right-of-way?"

"He'll clear your mast – I think."

"Thanks for the assurance," she said, throttling back for it to pass.

Blackie went forward and watched two locals in a skiff in the midst of the "runway," their fishing poles out, ignoring the commotion. They probably wouldn't have moved if the pilot had raked them with machine-gun fire.

Blackie stepped out of the cockpit and grabbed a lifeline, looking up. The seaplane momentarily blocked the sun, hurtling by overhead a short distance above the VHF antenna at the mast top. The plane lumbered down onto the bay, kissing the water of the channel used by the big cruise ships mostly on weekends. Only two of the huge ships were berthed there today. Once the flying boat was on the water, it reversed its props and kicked up a big salt spray. A beautiful Miami sight. But one that – because of the hi-rise construction – probably wouldn't be allowed to last.

They motored under the Dodge Island bridge, alongside the big guitar at Bayside, and skirted the imposing wall of new condo high-rises downtown. Dani slowed at what could only be described as an aquatic intersection, where the Intercoastal

---

[3] Seaplane's runway, 25 47.12N, 80 10.87W.

Waterway crossed the Miami River entrance. She put the throttles in neutral as a tugboat towed a Haiti-bound tramp steamer out of the river toward the cut. Loaded to the gunwales, the freighter had a mound of twisted metal piled thirty feet high on the forward deck. Blackie, at the bow, ran back to the cockpit shouting.

"My bike! My folding BMW mountain bike! I see it!"

Dani laughed, for she, like most Miamians, had also lost a couple of bikes to Haiti since she had moved to the Beach.

She throttled up, setting her course for the distant Rickenbacker Causeway. They passed the tiny marina at the Four Ambassadors and the ever-growing collection of high-rise condos on Brickell, and finally reached the high bridge marking the point of freedom, the open waters of Biscayne Bay.

Blackie had only sailed with her in the role of captain a few times, when she was just learning to handle her cruising cat, yet even then he was impressed by her innate sailing skills. As the elevated roadway of the Rickenbacher Causeway to Key Biscayne passed overhead, they made their cursory wave to the kids fishing from the old bulwarks where the spans of the draw bridge, long since removed, had once pivoted.

"Hey, Cabin Boy," she said from the helm, "you ready to go to work?"

"Aye, aye, Cap'n. What's the sail plan?"

"You said the cold front was through two days ago, and the winds are slowly clocking around to the north-northeast at between 10 to 12 knots," she said. "So I thought we'd go with the main and the cruising spinnaker."

"Cruising spinnaker? So that's what's in the striped bag in the locker."

"I got it two months ago. You just haven't been around."

"Yeah, I'm your fair-weather friend."

"So we'll raise the main, then the sock for the spinnaker, run downwind and set it in the lee of the main. Then head at

197 degrees straight for the cut through the middle of the Featherbed Banks."

"Sounds good."

"And we'll accompany that with some calamati hummus, sliced French bread and raspberry sparkling water on the rocks."

"I can go with that," Blackie replied with a smile. He knew she loved to sip good wine as much as to sail, yet on each of their respective boats, they had a no-imbibing rule for the captain until at anchor.

He pulled out the cruising spinnaker, kept in its "turtle bag," and hooked the bag to the starboard lifelines. He attached the halyard and ran the sheets back to their respective snatch blocks aft. He hooked the point of the gennaker to a Tacker, a device that wrapped around the furled headsail, then returned to the cockpit to raise the mainsail.

"Ready with the main," he reported.

She swung the boat hard to port and into the wind. "Belay," was her reply.

The mainsail halyard – the heavy line that pulled up the sail -- led to the cockpit. Blackie pulled it in, then wrapped it on a winch and cranked the handle to raise the head of the fully-battened sail the last few inches up to the mast top.

"It's up."

"Falling off," she replied, and the boat swung around, the sail caught the wind, but on the cat the heel was negligible. He moved the mainsheet traveler to starboard and set it before winching down on the line.

Dani grabbed a headset hung on a hook at the helm and handed it to him, one of a pair of electronic toys she had just bought at a South Beach spy gear/wireless phone store. They were remote mikes, used mostly by touring bikers on Harleys or Gold Wings to communicate on the highways. He put his set on and went forward to the bow.

"Ready with the headsail," he whispered into the mike.

"You can pull it up whenever you want," she replied into his earphones.

Blackie grabbed the spinnaker halyard and repeated the hoisting, raising the cruising spinnaker as it poured out of the bag snakelike – but still doused in its sock – all the way to the mast top. With the halyard cleated, he grabbed the line running through a second pocket sewn against the 50 feet of nylon sock. "Ready to hoist."

Dani turned her boat 20 degrees to starboard, blocking the wind from the sock with the mainsail. "Bring her up, Cabin Boy."

The sock rose, and the huge chute filled. Slowly Dani returned to course as the sock finished folding on itself accordion-like up to the masthead. Blackie cleated the line off at the base of the mast. He turned and looked. In the golden light of a sub-tropical February day, the cruising spinnaker billowed out in front of the boat in a pattern of triangles, each in alternating shades of iridescent turquoise and sparkling coral pink. Dani set the autopilot and joined him on the trampoline.

"Where did you get this thing?" he asked her.

"I had it specially made. You like it?"

"It's spectacular. I've never seen those colors before."

"Neither had the sailmaker. But I thought it would be tropical. Real SoBe."

"That it is. I really like your new toy – or toys. These headsets are the greatest."

"They're really for when we set and raise the anchor. No more confused hand signals and shouting."

"Makes sense."

"And they're just a few of my new toys you'll like."

Blackie paused. Toys for the sail or after they anchored? He let it pass. "What's our speed?"

"I was seeing a 12-knot wind true on the wind instrument, and the GPS shows us having a speed–over-ground of 8 knots. The speed log shows 7.8. Ready to see the next toy?"

"What?"

"Just stay there and be the lookout. I'll be back in a minute."

Dani checked the autopilot, removed her headset and went into the cabin. She returned a minute later with a soft canvas wine bucket, a pair of acrylic rocks glasses and two remote controls, one with a lanyard and the other with a short coiled cord. Blackie took the paraphernalia while Dani unscrewed the cap off a waterproof plug high up on the inner hull of the port pontoon and plugged in the cord. She returned to him at the middle of the trampoline and sat down.

"So what is that?" he asked pointing to the tethered remote in her hands.

"I had them wire an autopilot remote up here, so I could steer from the trampoline. Water, please."

As he poured the sparkling water, he nodded toward the other remote, its lanyard around her left wrist. "And that?"

She didn't answer, instead setting it in her palm and tapping on its controls. Immediately they heard a familiar voice singing a cover version of an old Marilyn Monroe lounge-song over the two tiny, high-end waterproof speakers. They were mounted above and behind them in the recesses of the overhang of the coach roof.

"Who's that singing?" Blackie asked.

"Sineád O'Connor. Attempting yet another comeback. She never recovered from that pope-bashing thing."

Dani grabbed her glass and toasted him, their plastic glasses touching with a clack, and said, "Let the show begin."

They were in the upper reaches of the bay heading almost due south, with the Vizcaya mansion off the starboard beam and the entrance to Crandon Marina on Key Biscayne off to port. Blackie sipped and looked at her, wondering what she had up her sleeve next.

A minute later they heard an exhale, long and deep, below them, followed by a warm, moist fish-bait smell.

"See."

Daniella pointed down through the netting of the trampoline. Below them, riding in the two converging bow waves of the Venezia, were three dolphins.[4]

A family. The largest, leading, zipped from bow to bow ahead of the pack and would turn intermittently on its side to peer at them with its all-knowing eye.

"I've yet to be right here that the dolphins haven't come to see me," she said.

"They're a good judge of character."

"That's a nice thing to say. I think they know that I care about them and won't do anything to hurt them."

"And it helps that your boat is under sail with no obnoxious propeller going, you're cruising at a perfect 8 knots, and that the twin bow waves create their own Six Flags ride between the hulls?"

"I liked what you said first better."

"Well, go with that then, Dani."

"Look at the little one."

The baby, only a yard long, was an aquatic child in ecstasy. And never with a parent more than a few feet away.

The boat-bound pair was silent for a long time. The sun reflected in warm shimmers off the water, and the only noise the splashing of the dolphins in the bow waves, their high "tick-tick-tick" the only conversation. Idyllic. Blackie glanced off over his shoulder and watched the high-rises of Miami fading in the soft February light. He thought of his hackneyed saying made at this point on the water with the skyline shrinking in their wake: *Miami was a beautiful city – but only from one's stern.*

Finally tiring of the ride, the dolphins headed off to port, toward the channel past No Name Harbor on Key Biscayne. The low, flat profiles of the houses on pilings known as Stiltsville marched past to the east.

The mid-channel marker at the northern boundary of Biscayne Bay National Park appeared dead ahead.

---

[4] Dolphins, Biscayne Bay, 25 43.90N, 80 11.06W.

"Look! One of the big problems with a GPS," Blackie said, pointing at the approaching I-beam with a reflective marker poking ten feet out of the water.

"That's my waypoint," Dani said, grabbing the autopilot remote control.

"Right. But these things are so accurate, you can run down a marker or buoy unless you purposely enter a waypoint that's *next to* the object," Blackie replied.

Daniella clicked a green button twice, and the boat swung two degrees to starboard to clear the planted I-beam. Once past, she returned the boat to its original course, and headed for the cockpit, returning with a blanket to share, a cushion between them and the heavy 3/8-inch netting of the trampoline. Blackie stretched out while she went below to change. The afternoon sun was fighting a losing battle with the cool sea breeze out of the northeast.

Blackie realized that this was one of life's special moments. Something to die for. To be onboard an incredible boat on a glorious afternoon while a frigid Alberta Clipper swept over most of America - and he hadn't even gotten to the best part yet. He was with a woman who had taken it upon herself to be a proficient sailor - and not onboard as crew or cook or charter agent. She was out here as captain, on her own boat, heading down to the Keys. This was *her* deal. All he had to do was kick back and relax.

For a hardened woman in her late-twenties in the twilight of - of all things - a modeling career, she did at times surprise him with her acts of kindness and so little preoccupation with herself.

He reclined on the trampoline and gazed at the high cirrostratus clouds streaking in from the southwest. Staring at the wisps of clouds, he recalled her attempt to involve him in her current, somewhat dubious profession. He worked hard to suppress a laugh as the memory came into focus.

The previous summer she had called him to see if he had any interest in a modeling job.

"What?" he had asked. "Why would I ever want to do that?"

She said that she had a friend, a German photographer, who needed a model for a product shoot. He wasn't happy with what the agency had sent him, looking more for a buff dad than an underaged Apollo. He was desperate because the shoot was the next day and they needed the photo in Taiwan to put on the product packaging in just a few weeks. Daniella and the photographer gave each other a great pitch; the only one left to convince was Blackie.

"You're perfect. They want some All-American-type guy in a swimsuit in a sports-equipment action shot. You're always running and working out. Why not put it to some use?"

He didn't give in until she begged him. He reported for the shoot the following day, to a big motor home parked off Ocean Drive on South Beach. The account exec for the ad agency and the photographer looked him over like a piece of meat before huddling in a whispered two-minute discussion. He would do fine.

Blackie had taken her advice and kept his mouth shut, not letting on that he was a rookie; he did his best imitation of being blasé. After dealing with wardrobe and makeup, he was ready to hit the beach. He was led out to the location at 7:30 a.m., the sand off the lifeguard station near 11th Street.

The shoot consisted of Blackie spiking a tetherball with an ecstatic grin on his face. It was to go on every carton of a million tetherball sets that they were mass-producing at that moment in a Yangtze River factory, a probable Christmas-gift hit after it was prominently featured in the made-for-TV-movie, *Bay Watch, The Golden Years*, a sleazy rehash of TV drivel. Blackie was too far in it, with his surreptitious agent Daniella on the set like an overwrought stage mother, to back out. For almost fifty spikes he gave it his best, hitting the ball-on-a-string while showing as many teeth as possible. Finally the photographer was satisfied with the morning's shoot. A few weeks later Blackie got the check in the mail, and he figured that the whole episode was over. It wasn't.

Months later, just before Christmas, he was in the right seat of the 767 from LAX to MIA. It was a half-full red-eye flight that left long before midnight and arrived in Miami at seven the following morning. The flight was smooth and uneventful, the type that brought the crew out of the cockpit to say goodbye 85 times to the disembarking passengers. Halfway through deplaning a mother and her six-year-old son were heading for the door when the kid stopped dead in his tracks.

"Mommy, it's him!"

The line came to a halt.

"Keep moving, Kenny."

"No, Mommy, it's him. I saw his balls. I saw him playing with his balls last night!"

The woman's mouth dropped open. She was speechless. The Captain and two flight attendants turned and looked at him in shock.

His mind raced. He did remember going aft to get an Evian water from a flight attendant in the mid-cabin galley somewhere over Texas. And he recalled that all the cabin lights were out. But exposing himself to any kids?

"What are you saying, Kenny?" his mother asked, as a few passengers further back shouted to move on. But the kid wouldn't budge.

"I saw him playing with his pole and balls and he was real happy."

No one spoke.

"Look, Mommy." The kid grabbed the bag out of her hands and pulled out the box. There was Blackie in a swimsuit, feet in the air, spiking a multi-image tetherball that through some stop-action special effect was shown looping around the pole. On Blackie's face was an absurdly happy, toothy grin.

The crew couldn't be restrained, even under captain's orders. They howled as the remaining passengers walked past, causing many to wonder if the crew hadn't been hitting spiked eggnog on their Holiday flight. Somehow the story had made it all the way to Flight Ops before he made it up there after the trip.

On his next flight, just prior to pushback, a ramp crew chief had come into the cockpit with a bewildered look on his face.

Ignoring Blackie, he turned and said, "Sorry Cap'n, but I was told you have to sign off on this." In the man's hand was a carton with a dangerous goods form attached. "Don't know why you have to sign off for a tetherball set."

Blackie had taken it in stride, although only an oblivious landing at the wrong airport could have caused him more ribbing from his peers. Yet he had never mentioned it to Daniella. He wasn't sure she'd understand.

Dani covered a second blanket around them, and leaned against Blackie as she steered the Venezia from the bow. Soldier Key, the first visible island south of Key Biscayne, appeared, marching slowly by to the east. Far off behind it was the Fowey Rocks Light, marking a shoaling area on the outer reef. When Soldier Key passed in front of the light station, it was time to look for the cut through the shoal that extended across Biscayne Bay.

Chapter 10:

To Rubicon Key

They approached the western cut in the Featherbed Banks, a narrow channel through the shoal marked by six Intracoastal I-beams. Blackie, a bit nervous, asked her if she wanted to take down the spinnaker.

"No, Cabin Boy, it's a *cruising* spinnaker, a giant balloon jib. Just stay back here and get ready to pull in on the starboard jib sheet."

They shot through the channel, encountering no traffic, the bay as usual vacant on a mid-winter weekday. They cleared the final marker, a green "5" on their port side. It was striped with the white poop of four resident Florida cormorants sitting atop the sign.[5] The snake-like birds – better swimmers than fliers – uttered their bullfrog croaks as the shadow of the giant chute passed over them. Dani turned the boat to port, on a heading of 178 degrees and set the autopilot, sending *Carpe Diem* toward the southern tip of Elliot Key.

They were in the midst of Biscayne National Park, one of the country's newest (1980) and least appreciated parks. Blackie, on the trampoline, peered east toward Elliot through the binoculars at what he knew could have been another urban blight like the new South Beach. Instead, he saw a low, verdant jungle of mangroves and tropical hardwood trees, somehow

---

[5] Featherbeds, western cut, 25 30.95N, 80 14.36W.

saved from overpriced condo towers and strip centers by a miracle.

Elliot Key, and the other 32 islands that make up the Northern Keys, had a brief but bitter history. Native Americans had been replaced a century ago by a few pioneers who grew pineapples, raised hogs, or planted key lime trees, with each attempt at agriculture cut short by a devastating hurricane. In the late 1950s, those who had primitive getaway cabins on the island saw development as the next get-rich-quick scheme. But a burgeoning environmental movement, led by Herbert Hoover Jr., scion to the vacuum cleaner empire, was clamoring for the bay and its keys – or what was left of them – to be saved. Elliot's landowners were alarmed, because they had yet to put in even the first of several causeways to link "Islandia," their name for the city to arise on Elliot, with the mainland. They planned to pave over the Featherbed and Cutter Banks with causeways, even pave over America's northernmost living coral reefs, the "Safety Valve," leading north to Key Biscayne, as well as a highway rolling south to Key Largo.

In early 1968, the Islandians secretly ferried over on a barge a bulldozer and work crew. They began plowing an unauthorized road down the center of Elliot Key. Their hope was that the road would ruin the pristine character of the Northern Keys, causing the federal government to lose interest in making it a national monument or park. But their scheme backfired, because they bulldozed right through a small parcel of Dade County park land. A lawsuit followed and public sentiment swung toward the environmentalists. Later that year Congress passed a law creating a national monument. The Islandians had been done in by their own destructive greed.

"What are you looking at?" Dani asked as she returned to the trampoline beside Blackie.

"Elliot Key. You've got me thinking what might have happened if the developers had come to South Florida 30 years earlier – if they had been born a generation earlier."

"Developers?" she asked as she ran her hand down his back.

"Yeah, the SoBe developers you say are largely responsible for the manhattanization of South Beach."

"They're a powerful group. I've met a few of them at parties on South Beach. They've certainly had their way."

"I wonder if Hoover's foundation could have battled them on Biscayne Bay, if they were around in the '60s and had their eyes set on Elliot Key. I have a feeling they wouldn't have bulldozed a road, they would have bulldozed the people that got in the way."

Off the port hull, in the clear, shoal water off Elliot, a large spotted eagle ray leapt out of the water, revealing its pale belly turned golden by the reflecting rays of the winter sun. It landed on the bay with a loud splat, startling them.

"Incredible! I wonder why they do that." Blackie pondered.

"To get a better view," Dani replied.

"So where do you want to anchor your boat?"

"I just checked the electronic chart and it's an hour before a really high tide, so I thought we'd go into Caesar Creek."

"You sure? It's real skinny there at the first marker. I was about to try it at high tide once and the Sea Tow guy coming out of the cut got on the radio and said don't even think about it. I kicked up some mud with my prop just turning around."

"Well, that was nice of the man, since he could have charged you dearly if he had let you get stuck. Our boats draw the same, *and* I've done it before."

"When?"

"I told you that you're not around enough."

"Skipper, I'll do whatever you say."

"There's the red marker dead ahead. Why don't you pull down the sock on the spinnaker and I'll start the engines. We'll motorsail with the main up to the anchorage."

"You're a brave captain."

"And you're a tight-assed pilot, as I've often said."

With the spinnaker doused and in its bag on deck, the Venezia turned east past the first marker and into Caesar Creek, not really a creek, but one of many channels of water allowing the tidal flow to pass around the Northern Keys and into Biscayne Bay. Dani turned the boat south, skirting Adams Key, the water deepening in the cut. The wind dropped, blocked by the island, as Blackie let out on the mainsheet.

At a fork in the channel, Dani turned the wheel and *Carpe Diem* headed southwest. The mainsail contemplated jibing, but was stopped by a preventer she had rigged to a block on the starboard hull's track. The depth sounder read 22 feet, the most water under the boat since the turning basin near Miami's cruise docks.

She piloted the boat up the channel between Rubicon and Reid Keys, surrounded in almost every direction by mangroves. The impression was that of complete solitude.

"Prepare to drop the main," Dani said quietly into her headset mike.

"Aye, Cap'n."

She turned the wheel and the Venezia swung around, pointing to the northeast into what little wind remained.

"Drop it," she said, noting the depth was 10 feet.

The mainsail fell, folding upon itself, contained by the lazyjack lines on each side of the boom. Blackie turned his attention to the Delta anchor ready to release at the bow.

"Drop anchor," she whispered into the mike.

The anchor hit the water with a loud splash, and he watched it settle on a patch of sand, visible in the clear water despite the waning light.[6]

"Reverse," he murmured back, not wanting his voice to disturb the quiet scene.

---

[6] At anchor off Rubicon Key, 25 23.51N, 80.14.78W.

She pulled back on the throttles. The chain rode out of the locker and over the toothed wheel on the windlass – called the gypsy – snaking into the water as the boat slowly backed. Blackie saw the three paint marks on the chain – ten fathoms or 60 feet – pass the windlass and said, "Neutral," before tightening the clutch on the gypsy and securing the chain around the . . . the – what was it called, he thought – the "samson post."

Blackie took off his headset and pulled a snorkel and fins from the anchor locker. Shedding his clothes and donning the gear, he jumped in and swam to the anchor. Hovering over it, he gave a hand signal back to Dani, and she again put the throttles in reverse. The chain went taut as the toe of the anchor dug into the sand.

Blackie gave the okay and swam back to the stern of the starboard hull. Dani had released the aluminum ladder, so Blackie climbed aboard and sat on steps that were molded into the sterns of both hulls. The water was cold for South Florida, but at 74 degrees Fahrenheit he knew it was still warmer than the Pacific on the hottest August day in San Diego.

He pulled out the sprayer housed in a small locker on the steps, rinsing off the salt with the engine-warmed water. The spray reflected the golden light of the sun setting to the west. Dani handed him a beach towel as he surveyed their domain in all directions. They appeared to be alone at their anchorage, with not a single sign of civilization visible from where they stood.

As he dried himself, Blackie recalled his earlier, sickening thought. What if those SoBe developers had gone back in time and pushed through the development of Islandia? Where they floated now could have been land – or landfill – and this serene spot could have been the asphalt parking lot of a Discount Auto Parts store, since they probably would have had Rubicon Key slated for retail development.

Where *Carpe Diem* rested, there could have been an old Honda Civic, hood up, its owner pouring two quarts of Valvoline into the crankcase before chucking the empty plastic containers at the foot of an ignored and unenforced sign. The trash littered the asphalt around the base of a sign saying "City of Islandia Ordinance: NO WORKING ON CARS IN PARKING LOT."

Thank god for miracles.

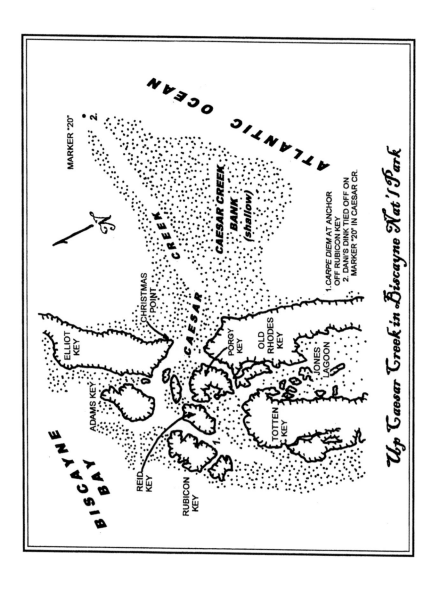

MARKER "20"

ATLANTIC OCEAN

CAESAR CREEK BANK (shallow)

CREEK

CAESAR

CHRISTMAS POINT

ELLIOT KEY

ADAMS KEY

PORGY KEY

OLD RHODES KEY

JONES LAGOON

TOTTEN KEY

REID KEY

RUBICON KEY

BISCAYNE BAY

1. CARPE DIEM AT ANCHOR OFF RUBICON KEY
2. DANI'S DINK TIED OFF ON MARKER "20" IN CAESAR CR.

Up Caesar Creek in Biscayne Nat'l Park

Chapter 11:

Cap'n Dick

Carpe Diem, at anchor, pointed to the northeast, since the tide was still coming in from the Atlantic. The two retired to the cockpit to catch the last rays of the afternoon sun. Dani stepped into the cabin, and emerged with a bottle, two stemless Riedel "O" line wineglasses, and a melamine plate with crackers and Brie.

"What's this?" he asked, pointing at the red wine.

"*Rosso di Montepulciano*. Kid brother of the great *Vino Nobile de Montepulciano*. I picked it up at the winery when I went down to Siena."

The label had a small watercolor print of the sun setting on rolling hills. It was a burnt orange orb above layers of lightening shades of lavender.

"What did you think of Montepulciano?"

"A fantastic hilltop town. There is a view from a churchyard there, overlooking a panorama of rolling vineyards below as far as you can see. Just like that painting on the label."

Dani cut the foil cap off the top of the bottle with a knife and picked up a black plastic contraption in her hand. She pulled off its sheath, revealing a heavy two-inch needle poking out of one end.

"What's that, Dani? A high-tech sewing awl?" Blackie asked.

"Sewing awl?"

"Old salts use it with wax thread to repair sails."

"I've got one of those, but it has a hardwood handle," Dani noted. "No, this has a much more important purpose. Watch."

She deftly poked the needle down into the cork and hit the button on the handle; the cork popped out in a millisecond.

"You've got that down. How does it work?"

"It shoots a blast of nitrogen in the bottle and the pressure pushes the cork out. I've had this one for years, stuck in the back of a drawer. I just found some replacement gas cartridges at a kitchen store on Lincoln Road. The newer versions of this thing have a protective cylinder around the needle that slips over the bottle neck," Dani said, pouring the red wine in each of their glasses. "I never go anywhere without it – except on airplanes."

"No, I don't think we want those onboard," Blackie observed, as he watched her resheath the needle.

They swirled the wine in their bowls and sipped.

"Is it Cabernet? Merlot?" he asked.

"My god, Blackie, what's the grape in the great *Montepulcianos*? It's a clone of the Sangiovese grape. Under the new DOC rules they can only add in a little Cabernet or Merlot."

Blackie knew his question would get a response from Dani, who wasn't a wine snob or aficionado, but more of a wine scholar. She had said that wine was what made her trips to Milan tolerable, for she was able to carry on her research.

"I was able to taste a couple of the Super-Tuscans at the wine center in Siena. They've got quite a bit of Cab in them. And they're awesome."

"Dani, why don't you get a job at a winery? Or move to California or Oregon and start your own?"

"They'd stick me in a tasting room. And I sure wouldn't get back into advertising for a big producer. As a rule, quantity is inversely proportional to quality."

"So start your own."

"No, the capital outlay is way too much. I could only have a basement operation," she said with a sigh.

"I guess vineyards and cruising grounds for a sailboat don't tend to mix."

"Not necessarily true. Several winemakers or winery owners in Napa and Sonoma have their boats on San Francisco Bay. You've seen those beautiful sailing labels on bottles of Dry Creek Vineyards. I read that the owner has a boat at Alameda."

"Tough life."

"And there are half a dozen wineries on islands in Puget Sound."

"They grow grapes near Seattle? Is there enough sun?"

"No, they truck them in from Yakima or even the Columbia River Valley. But I believe they do have a few vineyards on the Olympic peninsula, in the rain shadow on the eastern shore."

"So, there's your answer."

"No, I think I'd rather go south."

"South? A winery in the Caribbean? It's too humid, unless you made mango wine."

"No, further south. As in Chilé."

"Sail your boat there? Around Cape Horn? Are you crazy?"

"No. Through the Canal and then south."

"So you've been giving this some thought, Dani?"

"Yes. Why do you think I've been taking Spanish lessons?"

"Because you moved to Miami from somewhere else like everyone else?"

"I have even nobler motives."

An extra-loud hail on the marine radio interrupted the conversation.

"*Carpe Diem* Miami Beach, *Carpe Diem* Miami Beach, this is *Flying Fortress*."

"Damn, Dani, that's Captain Dick. I told him a couple days ago we might be out sailing on your boat," Blackie said as he headed for the helm.

"Isn't that a bit presumptuous? Since we hadn't even talked about sailing – on *my* boat?"

"Sorry, but I was hoping."

Blackie picked up the mike to the VHF radio and looked up in the sky to the east. A contrail was streaking south, 38,000 feet above the Gulf Stream.

"*Flying Fortress, Flying Fortress*, this is *Carpe Diem*."

"Switch to six-niner."

"To Six-nine."

Blackie twirled the knob on the ICOM radio.

"*Carpe Diem*, this is *Flying Fortress*. Hey, how's it going?"

"Fine. We just anchored in Caesar Creek."

"Jeez. I started hailing you a little while ago and there must be three *Carpe Diems* in every port down the coast of Florida. That's why I stuck in the 'Miami Beach.' She's gotta do something about that name."

"No need for me to tell, her, Cap'n, she's standing right here and hearing every word you say."

"Uh-oh. Well, tell her I'll come up with something better – something unique – for her to rename that old tub."

"More like twin tubs, Cap'n. Where you headed?"

"We're sailing south from New York for Providenciales, Turks & Caicos Islands."

"Yeah, I think I can see you with your sails up, headin' south due east of us." Blackie pointed to the contrail making a beeline for the southern Bahamas. Dani looked at him in disbelief before focusing her binoculars on the shiny speck creating the white streak.

"Yeah, we're gonna be losing you soon. But I can probably get you again in two days in the early morning."

"Got a layover in Provo?"

"Watch your words there, buddy."

"Sorry. Gotcha. Will keep our ears up."

"Last thing. Tell your friend she can rename her catamaran the *Carpe Corpora Cavernosa*." That's *Carpe Corpora Cavernosa*."

"Yeah, sure. Have a good sail."

"*Flying Fortress* back to 16."

"*Carpe Diem* back to 16."

And they – the voice and the jet making the contrail – were gone.

Dani set down the binoculars and looked inquisitively at Blackie. "Don't tell me," she said pointing skyward, "that *that* was him?"

"Yeah, the son-of-a-bitch is crazy."

"He can get you on the plane's radio?"

"No. He has a tricked-out, hand-held VHF in his flight bag. He pulls it out in-flight to communicate with me and a couple other boaters when he's flying JFK-Provo or JFK-San Juan. It's not legal."

"Why?"

"It's a marine radio. You're supposed to be on the water, not above it."

"I don't see how it can hurt."

"VHF radios work by line of sight. Remember that from your sailing school? Normal range is maybe 15 miles because the antenna is only about 50 feet off the water. Combine that with the curvature of the earth, and that's as far as a signal can be picked up in a straight line. But with his radio at 35,000 feet he is being heard on every VHF in South Florida and the western Bahamas."

So the Coast Guard doesn't approve."

"They don't. Nor does the FCC. That's why we go quick to a working channel and try to be careful what we say. I kind of blew it asking about his layover."

"I would think so, unless he has a really fast sailboat."

"No, he was into go-fast powerboats. But he's got a Hatteras motor yacht now. He had a 45-foot Bahia named appropriately *Floating Fortress* at Te Cuesta Isle about the time you got your boat."

"Oh my god, not *that* Dick. *The Floating Fortress* Dick. *The Sunken Fortress* Dick."

"That's him."

Dani had met him at her first of the quarterly marina parties at Te Cuesta Isle. He was the classic cocky pilot, or as Reggie would say, "such a cocksman." Cap'n Dick had a wife and two kids at the Trophy Club, a sprawling suburb of palatial homes north of DFW owned mostly by Alpha Airlines captains and corporate executives. Dani, when she once lived in Dallas, wondered if those younger, second wives to so many of the pilots had their own luncheon sorority called *The Trophy Wives of Trophy Club Club.*

Somehow, Captain Dick had been able to hide an incredible amount of his assets from what was then his second wife, and he continually bemoaned to the woman that the only way he could remain a Triple-Seven captain and maintain their lifestyle was to be based in Miami. He rented a squalid studio apartment adjacent to the Miami Airport employee parking lot, and had actually taken photos of the place to show her before he sublet it to a half-dozen Salvadorans working as janitors at MIA. Dick's real crash pad was an Italian go-fast boat, an oversized speedboat. It had to have monstrous engines and big bronze props to get all those marble countertops up on a plane to go fast, since, well, it was a go-fast boat.

But the thing sucked fuel, a point Dick often lamented to Blackie on his sailboat. Dick hadn't factored in fuel in maintaining a second, parallel life, so he seldom took out the boat. But then he seldom had to spend the night alone with the Bahia at the dock. In the shallow social scene of South Beach, to any beautiful woman on ecstasy, one Bahia was worth a hundred Bohemians. There was a point where Dani wondered if Cap'n Dick didn't walk down Ocean Drive with one of those sandwich boards plastered with photos of his *Floating Fortress,* because so many of the models she worked with were on and quickly off the Bahia. But she realized that Dick, although "older" – for he was making at least $200 grand a year then as a 777 Captain – was a very attractive man with a very good line of cocky bullshit, as they would say in Texas.

Dani paused in her recollection of him, to ponder that he wasn't that different from Ted on *Ted's Toy*. Both a couple of lying, hedonistic megalomaniacs, just that Dick wasn't so very, very evil.

Dani thought of how Cap'n Dick floated along with his double life until he hit his personal coral reef. Cap'n Dick screwed up. Dani believed that when men think only with their dicks they can get sloppy, and Cap'n Dick broke his own cardinal rule; he ended his abstinence of dating co-workers in the back of the plane, and he started fucking a flight attendant – a sure way to get caught. No matter that the flight attendant was born and still based in Peru, or that she had never been to Dallas outside of the recurrent training campus at DFW. Word still got back to the wife at the Trophy Club somehow.

Blackie had told Dani the best version of the story, relating an eyewitness account of the confrontation by a Miami-based flight attendant.

The wife, with the two kids in tow, had flown to Miami to ambush him in the wee hours of the morning. The woman had to lie to get past the porters and agents in the connecting room outside of the exit of Customs, saying it was the final retirement flight of her returning husband, a Captain with Alpha Airlines. She stood there, just her and the two kids, one holding flowers and the other a bunch of balloons. Behind them was a glass wall, holding back the crowd of people pressed to the thick panes as they searched for their friends and relatives coming in on the bank of Deep South flights.

Cap'n Dick, having breezed through Immigrations in the crew line on his flight from Rio and having no bags checked, marched past the Customs agents and out into the connecting room. He was hand-in-hand with his Peruvian goddess. They were oblivious, their eyes locked on each other since they were in the final countdown phase before having sex on the Bahia. The older of his kids immediately spotted him and cried out, "Daddy! Daddy!" To which his wife hysterically screamed, "And the bitch he's been fucking!" before taking a swing at her with the bottle of champagne in hand. The flight attendant – conditioned from years of dealing with Shining Path terrorists – ducked, the wife missed, but did land the bottle squarely on Dick's arm and something shattered, but it wasn't the champagne. Dick bent over in excruciating pain and watched as his wife – in some sort of perverted Texas tradition – attacked the mistress instead of the piece-of-shit husband. A fight ensued, with skycaps and the crowd behind the glass starting to cheer. The eyewitness who related the event swears bets were being taken, with most of the skycaps riding on the wife from Texas, and the greeters pulling for the goddess from Peru.

Dade County airport police finally arrived, after cleaning crews from concourses as far away as A and H had steered their carts there to view the spectacle. The cops sauntered up after the flight attendant had fled back through the exit and into the safety of Customs agents armed with Glocks. The cops appeared long after the wife had grabbed the kids and was lost in the throng of onlookers in the greeters lobby. That left only Dick, his crushed arm hanging limply at his side, shaking his head no to the cops who were inquiring whether he wanted to file charges. He repeatedly said no, that what he needed was medical help, and he was taken by ambulance to Doctor's Hospital in Coral Gables.

But it still wasn't over, and Dani and Blackie both witnessed the final act of revenge. Late that night after the confrontation, well after midnight, they were both torn from their sleep on their own boats by the wails of a man in terrible, terrible pain.

They rushed down the dock with a few of their neighbors to find Dick kneeling at his slip. He had a fresh, white cast holding his right arm out from his body.

"Shit, Dick, what happened to you?"

"Me? My boat, Blackie, my boat!"

Everyone turned and there wasn't the Bahia, just a few closed-cell foam cushions bobbing in the slip, hung up on an antenna barely piercing the surface. Dani knew Dick's wife may have been a fool for love, but she was a fool from Texas who knew how to disconnect a bilge pump and take the hose off her husband's seacock.

"So where did Dick go after they refloated his boat?" Dani asked, as she held the *Montepulciano* up and watched the legs streak down the inside of the glass.

"Insurance covered everything. And they never pinned it on his ex-wife. She had an airtight alibi provided by one of the parking-ticket cops at the airport. She was sleeping with him in a suite at the Hotel MIA the night the boat sank."

"She's not as dumb as I thought."

"Dick took his Bahia to the yard, cleaned it up and sold it. He traded it in for an old Hatteras that he's got up at Aventura now. Living on it full-time. Back to one life, and flying a 737 now."

"So what was he saying I should rename my boat? It was Latin, right?"

"Yeah. You don't know?"

"No. I'm studying Spanish, not Latin."

"He said call it **Carpe Corpora Cavernosa.**"

"And?"

"I think you can literally translate it, Dani, as "**Seize the Dick.**"

"Son-of-a-bitch."

"That's what I told you."

Chapter 12:

Up Caesar Creek

"What do you say we go explore before it gets dark?" Dani asked, her face bathed in the pink light reflecting off the cirrus overhead.

"You're the skipper. Let's go."

They set down their stemless wineglasses on the cockpit table, and Dani disappeared into the cabin. She stopped at the nav station to flip on the switch for the anchor light. Blackie lowered the inflatable, a 10-foot AB with a 15-horsepower Yamaha outboard. The dinghy was suspended from davits aft of the cockpit between the hulls.

The inflatable settled in the water, and he lowered himself into it to release the davit lines. Dani followed him onboard.

"You okay with one anchor out?" he asked her.

"We're at slack tide, and we have enough room to not have to Bahamian moor," she replied.

"So let's go."

Blackie pulled on the starter cord and the engine sputtered to life. Dani uncleated the painter and the dinghy headed past Rubicon Key for Caesar Creek.

They headed east, and Blackie stopped the boat at the ruins of a pier at the tip of Adams Key.

"This is something of an infamous spot, Dani."

"Looks like there was a dock here. And a foundation of some kind over there."

"Before Hurricane Andrew, that was a nice dock with a house behind it.   When the hurricane was approaching, everyone was scrambling for a protected place to ride out the storm.   Three guys that spent years restoring a sportfish boat decided this creek was a safe spot, so they brought their boat out here and anchored it in Caesar Creek, right about here.

"They hid inside the cabin of their boat as the storm got worse and worse. The older guy went out to check the lines and was blown off the boat and never found. The other two clung to each other inside on the sole, when the house and pier started disintegrating. Two-by-fours and two-by-sixes were being torn off and sent hurtling through the cabin walls.   One came through and decapitated one of the guys while the other still had a grip on him. He finally had to let him go and he crawled into a big baitwell, like crawling into a coffin, but it saved him. They spotted him from a helicopter a couple days later barely alive but still in that box resting on top of the mangroves."

"Are you trying to scare me?"

"I'm sorry. It's the most horrific of all those Andrew stories and is burned in my memory."

"On that pleasant note let's move on."

They dinghied around Meigs Key, then up Hurricane Creek between Porgy Key and Old Rhodes Key. Blackie slowed so they could watch a great blue heron, in its white phase, search for dinner by twilight in the mangroves. Dani spotted the twin fins of a giant tarpon pierce the smooth surface as it fed in the flats.

The silence of the moment became even more silent when the engine died. Blackie tried a few pulls on the cord to no avail. The tide, now turned, was going out.

"First time it's ever done that," she said.

"No big deal. Engine's almost new."

Blackie tried a few more tugs, adjusted the throttle, pulled out the choke, then more pulls, but the engine was still not cooperating. The inflatable was back in Caesar Creek, floating east toward the Gulf Stream. Blackie fiddled with the engine while Dani picked up her 8-pound mushroom anchor and heaved it over the side. She watched in horror as the bitter end snaked over the tube and disappeared in the dark water.

"Blackie! It wasn't tied off! I know I tied it off!" she cried.

He stood, ready to dive in after it, but reconsidered and sat down. There were way too many stories of people diving in the dark to retrieve something and never being seen again. In this current, a small mushroom anchor just wasn't worth it.

"Dani, I took everything out of here when I washed your boat this morning. I forgot to retie the anchor line."

"That's okay. I see you put the oars back in."

"Yeah, and it looks like I better get busy."

By the time he assembled the high-tech paddles and fitted them into their even higher-tech oarlocks, the dinghy was well out into Caesar Creek Bank heading for Hawk Channel. The day's final light was fading in the western sky.

Battling the current, Blackie rowed like hell in a losing skirmish with the tide. Despite his best efforts, he saw that they were actually moving toward the marker at the far end of Caesar Creek. He was able to steer the inflatable toward the I-beam, with its red "20" appearing briefly when the solar-powered light atop it flashed every four seconds.

The aft end of the port tube bumped the I-beam, and Dani reached out and tied the dinghy's painter around the rusty post, before pushing the dinghy away from the marker. The painter line went tight from the current, and the jerk almost knocked Dani overboard.[7]

"Careful. This is a hell of an outgoing tide."

"Let me sit next to you," she said moving in close, "What a mess we're in."

"How'd we get into this predicament. One minute we're having a glass of Tuscan red wine snug on your catamaran, and

---

[7] Out to sea, 25 23.11N, 80 11.51W.

the next we're adrift in this tiny damn thing heading for the Gulf Stream."

"I can think of a couple reasons why."

He searched the gloom of the horizon, but the only light to be seen was a tanker far off in the Stream, going south. They had already discussed the missing ditty bag, forgotten in their haste. It held the portable VHF, the flare gun, two flashlights and a small amount of provisions – all of which they needed at the moment. Not having it aboard was a first for Dani.

"Blackie, what in the world is that? A fire?" she asked, pointing east.

They watched a crimson glow grow over the Gulf Stream.

"Maybe a ship on fire," Blackie guessed, "Out in the Stream."

"It's getting brighter."

"They could be trying to beach their ship," Blackie said, remembering a scene in Hemingway's *Islands in the Stream*, when Nazi U-boats sank a freighter in the deep water off Bimini.

As they watched, a crimson flame rose up into a pillar on the horizon and spread out on top, turning into a glowing mushroom on the eastern horizon.

"An explosion."

"A nuclear explosion."

"My god! They've nuked a cruise ship."

"Or Nassau."

"What a place to be for the end."

"I'm just glad I'm here with you."

"And I'm with you."

As they waited for the shock wave to reach them, the mushroom transformed itself into an octagon, then a ball.

"The moon!"

"It's the moon! We're not going to die!"

"Are we stupid or what?"

They hugged each other and laughed hysterically for what seemed forever.

"The moon. Dani, we have to make a pact. I will never tell anyone if you don't about what we *thought* we just saw."

"It's a deal, Ancient Mariner."

"It was the moon."

They sat in silence, actually relishing their string of errors. Finally Dani spoke.

"So we've got another five hours before the current changes and we can drift back in?" she asked, not able to hide the dejection in her voice.

"Yeah. At least we're not going anywhere tied to this post."

The words were barely from his lips when the marker, still flashing red every four seconds, drifted from overhead and began to shrink.

"What the hell?"

Dani reached over the bow and found the painter. She pulled on the line attached to the dinghy's bow until she reached the end; it was frayed like it had been cut.

"Sliced right through, Blackie."

"That rusty I-beam must have had a flaky piece of metal on it. And the current pulling on it was enough pressure to cut it. Time for me to row."

Blackie used the moon to help him maintain a course as he rhythmically sculled.

"Talk about stupid. I just realized that this is just like a rip current in the surf, Dani, we've got to get out of the current, so I'm heading north and out of the channel. If we get on the other side of Caesar Bank, we should be able to row back to Elliot."

An hour later they were just off Christmas point, both sore from taking turns on the oars. They rested before their attempt to cross the channel and head back into Hurricane Creek. Surrounded again by mangroves, Dani wondered aloud how they would have found their way without the full moon providing them with at least shadows to navigate by.

Blackie fought the outgoing tide as they worked their way across the cut. He knew that if they kept to starboard at some point they should come into a shallow bay and spot *Carpe Diem's* anchor light atop the mast, somewhere off to the west.

Another hour of rowing and they were in a narrow cut, a box canyon of mangroves. They were obviously lost.

"Dani, maybe we should tie up to a mangrove and wait until morning. We made a wrong turn somewhere. With all these creeks we might never get back in the dark."

"I feel like I'm in a scene from *African Queen*."

"Dani, the leeches! The leeches!"

"Stop it. You know I saw the boat they used to film it down in Key Largo."

"Yeah?"

"I couldn't believe it was so small."

"So let's tie up and take a break. At least the bugs aren't too bad."

"Thank god it's February. Only now could we possibly be here without being eaten alive."

Blackie rowed to the nearest mangrove, and Dani tied what was left of the painter around a stout mangrove root curving into the water. Blackie removed the seat from between the inflatable's tubes and they laid down together on the sole to keep warm. Despite the occasional buzz of a mosquito, they both drifted into a deep sleep.

"Blackie! Blackie! I hear something."

"Wha – "

"Wake up. I hear an outboard."

Blackie sat up and could hear the distinct sputtering of a Seagull, an ancient English outboard that his grandfather used on an old skiff when Blackie was a kid.

"I can't see shit but I recognize the sound of that engine."

"You know them?"

"No, but I know that engine."

Out of the shadows a figure appeared in an ancient wooden skiff, slowly puttering toward them. At first the skiff appeared incredibly small, then the man incredibly big. He was in silhouette, backlit by the moon, as he approached.

"Hey, there," he uttered in a deep baritone. Alongside in the dark, Blackie still had trouble seeing him, although he made the immediate mental note that he was the first black man he had ever seen in a Tilley hat.

"Are we glad to see you."

"You two into ultralight aqua-camping or something?"

"No, the engine died and we kind of . . . we kind of drifted out to sea."

"You're a long way from the mainland."

"The mothership's at anchor just west of here, by Rubicon Key."

"So why don't I give you a tow to find it."

"It would be appreciated."

He threw them a line that Dani tied to the frayed painter, and their savior revved up the Seagull for what it was worth. They snaked through the mangroves until *Carpe Diem*, her white plastic hulls bathed in moonlight, came into view.

"Dani, are you okay? You haven't said a word."

"No. I'm – I'm fine. I am just glad to be saved again."

The big man pulled his skiff alongside and they grabbed the stern of the port hull and clambered aboard. Their savior, standing in his dink with his hands on the Venezia's port lifelines, almost looked over the top wire. The man was huge.

"Hey listen, you have to come aboard and have a drink, a beer," Blackie said, as he glanced at his watch; it was 3 a.m.

"No thanks. I'm gonna get in a little more fishin'. Snappers are bitin'."

"Well can we pay you for your help? Pay for the gas?"

"No," the man said with a laugh. "Okay, you owe me 34 cents for the fuel for this Seagull. Forget it. I would hope you'd do the same for me if the roles were reversed."

Blackie hoped he didn't see him blush from guilt in the moonlight, and plodded on. "I'm sorry, but I gotta ask you. What are *you* doing out here?"

"Like I said, fishin'. My granddaddy used to have a place here, over on Porgy Key. In fact, my great granddaddy had a place here. Family was on Elliot and Totten and Porgy for more than a hundred years. They took my granddaddy off days before Andrew."

"But you never lived here?"

"No, I was raised on the mainland."

"So what's your name?"

"What's yours?"

"I'm Blackie. And this is Dani."

"Hi, Dani. What kinda name is Blackie?"

"Long story. I spent a summer during college on the North Shore. In Hawaii. Not wearing any clothes. Ah, forget it. So does your family still own land here? It's all a park now."

"They paid my granddaddy dearly for it, and let him live out his final days here – until Andrew."

"So you come out to kinda get back to the land – or water."

"Something like that. Well, I gotta be going."

"So you haven't told me your name."

"No need to. You take care now."

"Thanks – thanks for rescuing us."

"One thing I want to tell you before I go, Dani," the man said turning his gaze toward her.

"Yes," Dani replied, finally speaking.

"You be careful now. Real careful."

"Okay."

"Sure," Blackie added.

Their savior shoved off, started the Seagull and motored away. They listened to the hum of the engine until the dinghy vanished behind a stand of mangroves, and the boat and the sound disappeared.

"Can you believe that?"

"What?"

"That he appeared out of no where and saved us."

"Saved us?"

"Yeah, gave us a tow back to the boat."

"Blackie, we couldn't have been 300 yards from *Carpe Diem* when we fell asleep. I think we could have found our way back, probably wading, at daylight."

"Okay, so he didn't save us. But he did a really nice thing."

"He was a very nice man. But Blackie, he didn't come by for the tow, but to warn us."

"Warn us?"

"Warn me. To be careful. Real careful."

Chapter 13:

Sir Lancelot

Blackie woke to a lemon-yellow sun flashing through the low clouds hanging behind Reid and Elliot Keys. The warm Gulf Stream water meeting the cool air of a weak Florida norther created the clouds, the only ones in the sky. But the breeze had all but died in the early morning hours, and the boat was motionless in the cut between Rubicon and Reid Keys. The anchor rode hung limply by its bridle when he went forward to check it. Looking around, Blackie saw that *Carpe Diem* was still alone in her anchorage.

At the mast-top the windex – the sailboat's high-tech weathervane – rotated lazily around in a clockwise revolution. "What they mean by variable winds," he muttered to himself as he stepped back into the cabin and over to the galley. He stopped at the electrical panel to turn off the anchor light. He held his finger on the glow switch before pushing on the generator starter. It came to life in the aft part of the port hull, the corner opposite of Dani's cabin. Most boaters – especially sailboaters – could at least get a hot pot of coffee off the inverter, but then most boaters didn't have a copper-and-brass, Jules Verne-inspired espresso maker bolted to the galley countertop. Daniella did have some nice toys on her boat.

Blackie filled a demitasse cup with the thick, ebony liquid, skipping the frothing milk routine; if firing up the generator hadn't woken her, he wasn't going to push his luck. He grabbed a beach towel and headed out to the trampoline, the heavy netting between the bows of the hulls. The water, a greener shade of tourmaline, was perfectly clear. He watched a southern stingray bury itself in the sand beneath the boat. A bright red starfish, the size of a small pizza, lay in the sea grass to starboard. A dozen yellow and blue striped grunts loitered in the shadow of the port hull, awaiting post-breakfast handouts. Another day in paradise had begun.

He heard the espresso-maker re-awaken in the galley, meaning Dani was up. He turned looking aft, awaiting her entrance to the day. The previous night's bizarre events seemed so removed, almost dreamlike. He wondered how they couldn't have made love, but realized that they were exhausted when they finally came back aboard at 3 a.m. He did manage to fall asleep in her arms, if that was a consolation. What was wrong with him?

She stepped from the cockpit out on the port hull, grabbing the bimini rail. She came forward but stopped at the stays and grabbed a wire. She gazed off toward the sun suspended over the Stream. He wondered if she was ignoring him, or was she truly unaware of his presence?

Dani wore a hunter-green silk kimono, a natural choice since her grandmother was from Guam. She had told him that almost every photographer she had worked with told her that they were fascinated with her "Eurasian" looks, yet she was neither European, nor Asian. She had called herself, in a tone of self-deprecation, "Texanese." That was only somewhat accurate.

Her kimono was untied, open, providing him with a heart-racing view. With the cup of espresso to her lips, the steam rising in front of her face in a veil of pale saffron mist, she was so . . .

He felt like a voyeur, but surely she saw him. Yet she stood transfixed, looking into the sunrise, one foot firmly planted on deck, the other atop it, her knee out in front through the parted kimono. Observing her, he could hear himself exhale with each breath audible.

He just couldn't label her. She wasn't Japanese, or Anglo-Texan. She was a dark-haired raven, not the least bit petite. Tall, at least five-eleven, thin, but with a muscular hardness. Her hair was long and lustrous. Tahitian? No, that exotic quality was but an undertone. She was so . . .

He couldn't bear to stare at her any longer. He turned to face the stage of another day. She came and sat beside him.

"Quite the sunrise, Blackie."

"Glad you're up to see it."

"The sculling wore you out last night," she said, caressing his back.

"Sorry. How could I? Or more succinctly, how couldn't I?"

"Couldn't what?"

"Have made love to you?"

"You got us back. We could have been half-way to West End on Grand Bahama by now in that dinghy."

"I just can't believe we weren't better prepared when we headed out last night. I'm a pilot. I run through a checklist before every flight."

"Dinking around isn't exactly flying," Dani said.

"It can be just as dangerous. And don't think I haven't heard over the years the chiding comments that most pilots are lousy sailors," Blackie added.

"Lousy sailors? I haven't heard that," Dani lied.

"There's something to it. I was berthed for a year next to a 757 captain with an old wooden sloop. Every time he would take it out there'd be a disaster."

"Disaster?"

"His boat wouldn't steer worth a damn in reverse – or forward for that matter. He hit three of my neighbors just leaving his slip. He took out two of my stanchions with his bowsprit coming in one day. Couldn't take the boat out of gear. And that concrete pier didn't give when he hit it. But his bowsprit did."

"I would have moved," Dani observed.

"I couldn't. I ran netting between our slips, sort of like a U-boat barricade. And helped him put a bridle of lines he could ram on re-entry to his slip. Worked fine until he sold the boat."

"He got out of boating?"

"His final 'incident' was a factor in that. He took his wife out on the sloop on a perfect spring day. They were heading under the Dodge Island Bridge and somehow he hooked a stay on the wooden barricade that protects the bridge pilings. Pulled the hardware right out of the deck and it shot straight at his wife. Barely grazed her head before taking out a chunk of the wooden mast. Two inches over and she'd have been dead. As it was she only needed 30 stitches in her scalp."

"That'll get you out of boating."

"That, and not being able to get insurance."

"How was he in the cockpit of an airplane?"

"Never flew with him, but from the F/Os I talked with who did, he was an excellent pilot."

"That's assuring for us passengers."

"Sometimes I think us pilots are a little too fixated with the gizmos. The electronics. The variables of boating are a little too much for some of us."

"Such as?"

"Know that Amas 53 over on Pier One at Te Cuesta Isle? Cost more than a half million dollars. Always someone on it polishing something, or under it scrubbing the hull. Ever seen it go out?"

"Never. But I've seen many a sunset party in the cockpit."

"In truth, I think it has been out twice in three years. A Captain for Central American Charter Airlines owns it. The man flies a Scarebus 340 for CACA, yet he's afraid to take that boat out."

"That's a shame," Dani replied. She ran her slender fingers through his hair and down his neck. "So before I came out here, what were you sitting here thinking about?"

"About how you can't be labeled."

He turned and put the back of his hand to her face, running his fingers lightly down her cheek. Blackie took their cups and set them on the bow seat on the port hull. Alone at anchor off Rubicon Key, the sun sending warm beams into their little cove, it was the perfect setting to be holding her, to make love to her.

They rolled on the trampoline in a long embrace. They were falling together into the – "the abliss." Ha! He would have to remember to tell her that one. But the buzz in his ears was distracting – yet this wasn't the season. Louder still. Bug spray would do the trick, but to get it and then the smell would ruin the mood. Yet the noise was everywhere. Finally, it came to him. Outboards, not mosquitoes. He lifted up and turned to see a Park Service boat approaching.

"We've got company."

"This isn't illegal, is it, like lobstering?"

"Just get out your ruler and make sure that what you've got in your hand is legal."

"No, I don't think I have to throw it back."

"I could probably hang a dive flag from it. Let's hope that I can just sit here and talk to him with a beach towel over me. I better not have to get up."

With total professionalism, the Park Ranger throttled down, cut her engines and glided the boat parallel with the Venezia. Trying to hide his embarrassment, Blackie read the name Rosella Diaz on the shiny brass badge pinned to her kakhi uniform shirt.

"Morning. I'm a ranger with Biscayne National Park. I'm coming by to inform you that you must have a holding tank onboard. No discharging within the Park boundaries, or within three miles of land for that matter."

"Yes, I'm aware of the law," Dani replied. "I own the boat and it has all that. And I assure you that the 'Y-valve' was locked before we left Miami Beach."

"Great. Unfortunately, you're one of the few who even know what a holding tank or a 'Y-valve' is. And we appreciate your knowing." Aware that she was interrupting something, the ranger started her outboards to leave when Blackie waved her down.

"Listen, I've got to tell you what happened to us last night. We went dinkin' around and the outboard died, and some guy that must be living out here gave us a tow back to the boat."

"Living out here?" she said, killing the engines. "No one lives out here except the rangers on Elliot and a couple on one of the Ragged Keys."

"He was this huge guy, about 30, in a little skiff with a Seagull."

The ranger looked at him quizzically.

"You don't know what a Seagull is?" Blackie asked.

"A rather common bird of the *Laridae* family known for their webbed feet and hooked bills –"

"No, the engine. The old English outboard. They made it 50 years ago and now it's a collector's item. He had one. No way he came across the bay from Black Point in that."

"I haven't seen him or his Seagull. Did he say he lived here?"

"No. He said his family lived here for generations, for more than a hundred years."

"What did he look like?" She grabbed a pad of paper and pen from the console to take a few notes.

"He was huge. It was dark out but he was a giant black man and he wore one of those Tilley hats."

"Tilley hats?"

"An essential part of most every middle-aged white man's sailing wardrobe. I think it comes from Canada. Worn by pale sailors who go out in the sun but wear the hat to get out of the sun. Never seen a black man in one."

"Thank you. Now I know more about that hat than I'd ever want to know."

"I do remember, in the moonlight, seeing a scar, a horizontal scar under his left – no his right eye. Right, Dani?"

She didn't speak.

"Dani, did you see it?" the ranger inquired.

"Yes, his right eye," she replied.

"Did you see anything else, Dani?"

"No. That's about it."

"And what is your name, sir?"

"Blackie Petersen."

"Blackie? What kind of name is that for a blonde man who's probably of Scandinavian descent?"

"Long story. I spent a summer on the North Shore in Hawaii – forget it."

"No, this is interesting."

"And I didn't wear any clothes. I was in college. So when I went back the next semester, I got the nickname Blackie. I mean, because, you know, it was black."

"Oh, I see."

"And later I legally changed my name – I didn't like my given one."

"I see, *Blackie.*"

"So officer – that's what they call you gun-toting rangers – you don't think that man lives out here."

"No. But years ago I guess his grandfather did. You've never heard of Sir Lancelot?"

"No."

"I usually have a desk job at the Park on the mainland, and only do these rounds in the boat on occasion – because I can. I've done a little research on the man called Sir Lancelot."

"Now that's a name. You've got to tell us more about him."

Ranger Rosella told them about Sir Lancelot and the pioneer black family that once owned all of Porgy and Totten and parts of Old Rhodes Keys.

The patriarch was Israel Lafayette Jones, known as Parson Jones, born just before the Civil War in Raleigh, North Carolina. He was a stevedore in Wilmington before venturing south to Florida, where he worked for Ralph Munroe,

Commodore of the Biscayne Bay Yacht Club. Parson Jones saved his money and bought, for $5 an acre, Porgy Key. He moved there with his wife Mozelle, who was from Harbour Island in the Bahamas and later head cook at a Coconut Grove hotel before they moved to Porgy. They cleared the hardwood trees and grew pineapples on the island until the devastating 1906 hurricane wiped out their plantation. During that time two sons were born, King Arthur in 1897, and Sir Lancelot, about 1900. Legend has it that Sir Lancelot was born in an open boat on Biscayne Bay as Parson Jones tried to take Mozelle to the doctor in Miami.

The Jones's next grew key limes, and they became the largest producer in the Northern Keys, with 300 acres of island-turf under their domain. Parson Jones operated a small horse-drawn railroad on Elliot bringing produce to barges waiting to sail for Key West. They lived in a two-story, four bedroom home built in 1912 on Porgy Key.

The value of the key lime was directly linked to the popularity of the Gin Rickey cocktail made famous in the Roaring Twenties. The key lime industry on the islands was wiped out by the double whammy of the 1926 hurricane and Prohibition.

Parson Jones died in 1932, seven years after his wife. His sons became fishing guides, their profession for the next three decades. Their clients were the rich and famous and included four presidents. Arthur passed away in 1966.

Sir Lancelot lived alone, and when legislation enabled the Interior Department to buy the land for the park, Jones agreed to sell his homestead for $1.2 million, as long as he was given a life-estate on Porgy.

He lived "alone but not lonesome," as he often said, and the Park rangers worked hard to protect the privacy of the old man they called Lance. In 1984, a propane tank exploded and burned down the old family home. Jones and friends built a small shack on stilts beside the old foundation in which he continued to live.

In 1992, at age 94, Sir Lancelot was evacuated just before the arrival of Hurricane Andrew that destroyed his stilt home. He couldn't bear to go back and stayed on the mainland. Jones died in December of 1997.

"Blackie," the ranger observed, "what doesn't fit in your savior's story is that Sir Lancelot had no children. He did say he was married for 12 years – when, we've never learned – but he supposedly didn't have any kids or grandkids. So I don't know who that man is – or thinks he is."

"Well, it was nice of him to come along."

"I've taken up enough of your time. Your encounter with that mystery man will make a good story back at Park Headquarters. We'll keep an eye out for him. If he is as big as you say, we should be able to spot him."

"He was a really nice guy."

"We get rotated around the Park Service, so many of the rangers who knew Sir Lancelot are gone. But I guess we could say his legacy lives on."

"Appears to be."

"Enjoy your cruise," she replied, hitting the starter, bringing the pair of 150-horsepower outboards to life. She turned the wheel with one finger, gunned the throttles, and the open-bow powerboat raced for Caesar Creek.

"That was an interesting story," Dani observed.

"But I don't think she believes he's Sir Lancelot's grandson."

"Do you?" she asked.

"He could be. Do you?"

"No. I don't, Blackie. What do you say we weigh anchor and head up to Sands Key. We've got just enough water under us to get out of Caesar Creek and back in the Bay."

"Aye, aye, Skipper."

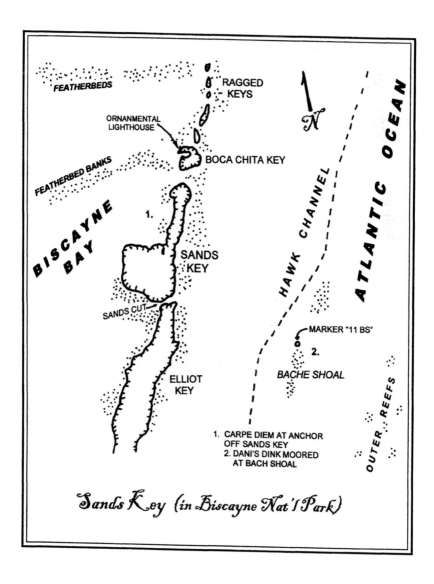

Sands Key (in Biscayne Nat'l Park)

Chapter 14:

Bache Shoal

Dani and Blackie repeated the anchoring ritual in seven feet of water off the lee of Sands Key. [8]

"Sands Key, just no sand," Dani said to herself gazing at the shoreline shrouded in mangroves.

Blackie jumped overboard to check the set of the anchor.

"What they should have called this place was 'Cock 'n Balls Key,'" she mused to no one, studying the island's shape on her electronic chart. "Nice head, but the shaft could be a little thicker for me."

Back onboard, Blackie announced that his next project was to determine what was wrong with her outboard.

"I already did."

"You found the problem? When?"

"While you were out there swimming around. No gas."

"No gas? Shit! I never checked the bow tank. It's hidden under that canvas cover."

"When you cleaned the dinghy yesterday, you took out the reserve gas can and put it in the lazarette."

"Oh my god! It was all my fault. Dani, I'm sorry."

"Don't worry. I can't disrate you lower than Cabin Boy."

"Why didn't you tell me last night?"

---

[8] At anchor, Sands Key, 25 30.40N, 80 11.09W.

"Because some men can have fragile egos, especially when being swept out to sea."

"Thanks for not getting upset," he said as he let her words soak in before trying a different tack. "Now that we have the outboard fixed – now that we have *gas* – what's on the agenda, Skipper?"

"Look at the tailtells," she said, pointing up at the flourescent streamers hanging limply on the stays. "Dead calm. We've got to go dive when it's like this. And Yul told me there's good snorkeling at Bache Shoal just out the cut. Let's go."

"You know how to get there?"

"Yul gave me the waypoint. The tripod marker for Bache Shoal is easy to spot. Let's get going before the sea breeze kicks up."

They loaded up her Rigid Inflatable Boat, in tow since Caesar Creek, but only after Dani made the Cabin Boy pour the reserve fuel into the empty bow tank. They loaded in two net bags of masks and fins, a pair of aluminum SCUBA tanks, as well as a bag of new toys foisted on them by Yul – a pair of hookah hoses and regulators.

Yul, in one of his marina dumpster-assaults, had found 150-feet of almost new hookah hose pitched in the refuse container. Only later did Yul learn that the hose had been deposited there by the heirs of a boater formerly at Te Cuesta Isle. The deceased had wanted to dive, but not with all that gear on his back.

The man had attached the hose and regulator to an oil-less, ¾-horsepower paint compressor. It worked fine when he scrubbed his hull. But he ran into trouble when he went down a hundred feet for an hour on a wreck off Fowey Rocks. Knowing something about dive tables would have helped. Even the life-flight chopper and a recompression chamber couldn't save him from a fatal attack of the bends. The heirs trashed the hookah paraphernalia before selling the boat and tidying up his estate.

Yul had cut the salvaged hose into three 50-foot pieces and had the guys at Amazon Hose patch in brass quick-release fittings and attach three refurbished, heavy-duty regulators he had found at the Dania Nautical Flea Market. His two spares were Christmas presents to Dani and Blackie.

To demonstrate that they were safe, on New Years Day Yul had cannonballed into the water at the marina to frolic with his new friend, a calf-less female manatee that they all had nicknamed Jewel. Yul dove and bobbed, cavorting with the unusually friendly sea cow; he was as free as her but for a 5/8-inch rubber tether. The scene had the dockside crowd whispering that they had trouble telling Yul from Jewel.

Dani's plan was to give the hookahs a tentative try after snorkeling on the reef at Bache Shoal. With the waypoint up on her handheld GPS, they cast off. She brought the inflatable up on a plane and swung the boat around what she told Blackie were "the balls of Sands Key." He turned back at her with a curious look. The dinghy shot out Sands Cut, with Bache Shoal a few miles to the east.

She steered the RIB toward the tripod marker poking out of the flat, almost oily water. Approaching, Dani throttled down, bringing the dinghy off its plane, and steered a long curve around the tall metal marker, "11BS." The dinghy scared away a few in the colony of cormorants that claimed it. The base of the marker was zebra-striped, caused by an alternating pattern of rust and bird shit. Nearby, five Park Service buoys bobbed in the water. She idled the outboard as they approached the first one.[9] She dipped her hand-held instrument in the water and checked the reading. Depth was 16 feet, and the water temperature a cool, but comfortable 73 degrees.

Blackie grabbed the buoy's line and looped the painter through its eye, checking and rechecking the knot. Dani killed the engine while he rigged up a "diver down" flag on an assembled oar.

---

[9] Moored at Bache Shoal, 25 29.03N, 80 08.84W.

"A perfect day!" he shouted into the water.

"It looks three-foot deep, but it says we're in sixteen!" Dani joyously replied. "I've never seen it so clear."

"Can you see the reef over there?"

The moorings were in white sand, but less than twenty yards away they could distinguish the brown silhouettes of the coral rising almost to the surface.

"I'd hate to hit that," she replied. Blackie shuddered as he envisioned kissing the keel of his Island Packet on it. The shoal sat in the middle of Hawk Channel, the heavily used route between Miami and the Lower Keys. The tripod marker was placed there to protect both the boats and the reef.

Within a minute they both were in their gear. Neither wore wetsuits or clothing of any kind. They both considered seventy-degree water bearable for a short swim. They went to their opposite tubes and sat down. On cue, they fell backward, fins in the air, over the side.

They saw nothing there. Just a flat, bright, sandy bottom. The moorings were buried in sand a short distance from the reefs to protect them. They swam over, approaching what looked like a forested mountain range rising up off the prairie. They were seeing the reefs on the perfect day. Blackie took three quick breaths and dove, scudding the sandy bottom, entering the forest of gently undulating soft coral. They swam between two lavender coral fans performing a slow motion hula-dance in the gentle surge. Blackie glided over a six-foot-wide dome of brain coral. He angled down, into a crevasse, frightening a big moray eel as it poked its head out from the razor-sharp coral. Blackie headed up, breaking the surface, searching it for the neon-pink ring on the tip of Dani's snorkel. She was nowhere to be found. He looked down, and there she was, following his path, surfacing beside him.

"See the eel?"

"Barely, I think you gave it a scare. What a mean-looking thing."

They dove again, swimming past and through every kind of coral. The longer they swam, the more fish appeared. Blue parrotfish, sergeant majors, and giant queen angelfish. Free diving, they could approach trumpetfish and puffers, following them in their wake. In such clear water, they could see an occasional jack or barracuda off in the distance. Clawless Florida lobsters, their antennae twitching, tried to hide under a ledge of coral facing Elliot Key.

After twenty minutes, they swam back to the dinghy and climbed over the tubes onboard. Dani grabbed a bottled water and a Ziplock bag of granola bars and shared, basking in the rays of the noon sun.

"Ready to try the hookahs?" she asked.

"Okay. But do we hold on by the mouthpiece?"

"What?"

"We hold onto them with our lips?"

"No," she answered, reaching into a net bag, "I saw a nylon belt that the hose hooks to at a store in Fort Lauderdale, so I made two copies for us – and one for Yul." She held them up with a proud look on her face.

"You made these?" Blackie asked as he inspected them.

"I'm trying to learn as many marine trades as I can, so I can be self-sufficient on an extended cruise. I bought a Sailright machine last month. It's in my dock box. I sewed that sock for the spinnaker, too."

"This is good work," he said, inspecting the harness. It had a quick-release clip for the hose in case it snagged on something. He was distracted by a thought. He wondered if she was planning on following Joshua Slocum or Tania Aebi and sailing alone around the world. Again he secretly hoped that she would take him with her.

She demonstrated the harness, and Blackie attached the hookahs to the tanks and tested each of the mouthpieces.

"You know we really should be careful around this coral," he said. "The whole point of these mooring balls is to keep anchor lines and chain from damaging the reefs. And here we're going to pull a hose over them."

"I was thinking the same thing. I thought we'd just go below the boat in the sand and try them out," she said, nodding in agreement.

Dani pulled a small flat jar from the bag and opened it. The smell of mangoes was overwhelming.

"What's that?"

"A waterproof body balm," she said mysteriously, as she stood and without the least bit of timidity rubbed it liberally on her perfect, naked body. "I found it in a little adult toy store between Washington and Collins Avenue. They had some really fun things in there."

"Um. Couldn't I – couldn't I do be doing that?" Blackie asked as he looked over the calm water in all directions. They were two on a big ocean, with only an old Hatteras and its smoke trail disappearing down Hawk Channel.

She handed him the jar. "Sure. But I get to rub some on you."

A minute later she pushed and pried herself away from him.

"Now sit over there and get on your gear," she ordered. "We need to try and keep our hoses from getting tangled up. Remember, safety first."

"Yeah, right," he answered, as he carefully, methodically coiled the hoses at their feet.

"Blackie?"

"Yeah?"

"Enough with the hoses."

He made a final loop as he squatted down. Before she sat on her tube she reached in her net bag and pulled out a Ziplock filled with crushed saltines.

"Crackers? Get them at that store, too?" he asked, while wondering what else he could learn from her.

"You'll see what they're for. Down there." She pulled the mask over her face, put the snorkel in her mouth, and with the regulator and cracker bag in hand, fell back off the dinghy. He mimicked her, plunging backward into the water.

Again they were suspended in the gin-clear liquid. The warm sun in the dinghy made the water feel colder, but Blackie noticed a strange, new sensation. Wherever Dani had rubbed him with the balm felt intensely warm, almost hot. Once over the shock, he realized the balm must have been spiked with a mild dose of cayenne pepper.

They swam and kicked and played below the surface, stopping to adjust the belts that held the hoses away from their waists. But both of them were buoyant; they found it impossible to stay down without constantly kicking their fins.

Dani gave him a hand signal to wait and pointed to herself and then up. She handed him the cracker bag. He gave her the okay, and she swam up toward the dinghy. Her body evolved into a perfect silhouette, with brilliant streams of sunlight radiating out from her. When she reached the boat she leapt up and disappeared. Angling down and kicking, Blackie was able to suspend himself a foot off the sand. Almost motionless, the only sound his mechanical breath in the regulator, he concentrated on the heat coming from the balm on his skin. It was a completely new and overwhelming sensation, not to mention a very pleasing one.

He was looking up the moment Dani dove back in, swimming fast down to him. In her hands were two pair of leg weights she used while exercising. They were mesh tubes filled with lead shot that could be velcroed to the ankles. She handed him the smaller of the two pairs and they put them on. Almost instantly they both became neutrally buoyant.

She swam to him and brushed against him, the friction and the balm working together to heat his skin. In their weightless space, fins rhythmically undulating, they felt, rubbed, caressed. With each stroke the heat from the balm and the deprivation of their remaining senses caused them to focus on the one sense, touch.

They swam together in a large circle skimming the furrows sculpted in the pale sand. Each caress, each kneading of the skin, produced warmth. Locked together in an embrace, they slowly revolved as they corkscrewed in slow motion on the sand. Blackie wondered if this sensation might have been what brought the sirenians back to the sea, or kept them from ever leaving it in the first place.

Blackie felt nibbles on his calves and knees and wondered what else was in that balm. He pulled out of his weightless trance long enough to see a school of grunts swarming around them. The greater their passion, the more the number of fish grew. As their movements became more intense and frenzied, the fish became more agitated, darting about in and out, as more crumbs poured from the small opening in the cracker bag. Finally Blackie slid inside her, and they slowly settled with a light thump on the sandy bottom. They rolled effortlessly over the dunes, surrounded by their cloud of yellow-striped grunts and an occasional sergeant major. The sensation of cool water against heated skin was both an anomaly and intense.

Dani grabbed his mouthpiece and pulled the regulator from him. He removed hers, and turning their heads, their lips met in a long kiss that seemed to last forever – until finally they came in a mutual aquatic climax. They kissed on and on, the life-giving air held at arms' length from each other. His back to the sand, his eyes closed, Blackie felt darkness coming over him. Was he blacking out? He opened his eyes, and through his mask he saw a shadow passing over near the surface. It was an Atlantic manta ray, seven feet across, gliding by in an arc around the dinghy.

As he slowly exhaled he grabbed Dani's arm and nodded up. She turned, breathing out, and watched the ray disappear into the expanse of aquamarine. When she turned back he put the mouthpiece to her lips, and she did the same for him. They both took a deep breath and slowly exhaled, the silver bubbles racing up to meet the sky.

Chapter 15:

Sands Key

Back on the cat after lunch, Blackie hung Dani's hammock between the headstay and the mast above the trampoline. Like kids in net bunks, the two reclined and read in the warm sun, she in the hammock and he sprawled out below on the trampoline. By mid-afternoon, looking for something to do, Blackie volunteered to go up the mast and replace the dead bulb in the steaming light, another job the Cabin Boy had volunteered to do. She fetched the bosun's chair from the forward port locker, and with the spinnaker halyard line around the electric windlass, she was ready to hoist him up. Blackie poked each leg into the contraption, a Sunbrella-canvas diaper with its ring attached to a snap shackle at the end of a line.

She tapped a few times on the footswitch, raising him a few inches up off the deck like a puppet with her the marionette.

"Wait. I've got one more toy for you," she said, tying off the line on the samson post. "Be right back."

"Hey, you can't leave me like this," he pleaded, his tattered Topsiders barely touching the deck. "You've got me by the balls here."

She ignored him and disappeared into the cabin. She returned with a very sinister-looking pair of high-tech binoculars and handed them to him.

"I completely forgot about these. I had my old ones in the holder."

"What are they, night-vision goggles?"

"Duh – it's rather bright out. Take them up and look around. Especially since you wasted your binos."

"I can't believe you're going to trust me up there with these."

"Just yell if you drop them 'cause I don't want to get knocked on the head."

"Aye, aye, Cap'n."

She undid the halyard and hit the foot switch. The soft-seated bosun's chair grabbed him by the crotch and sent him skyward. Just out of reach of the spreaders, his elevator stopped.

"What's wrong?" he shouted down at her.

"I've been meaning to ask you something. To discuss something with you," she replied, shielding her eyes with one hand as she held his life by the other.

"We have to talk about this now?"

"I can't think of a more appropriate time," she said cleating the line.

"So what's the question?"

"How come I found out eavesdropping on your conversations with complete strangers how you got the name Blackie?"

"Well, it's not something I normally bring up in casual conversation. Our savior was quizzing me and I was trying to expalin. And the ranger was questioning me in her investigation."

"You just never wanted to tell me, did you?"

"It just never came up."

"It's come up, I've watched it come up, and every time I've seen it in the light I've wanted to ask you about it."

"Well, it's embarrassing."

"What a strange reply for a fly boy. Most pilots would probably have a brief explanation printed on the back of their business card."

"So I break the pilot mold."

Well at least what you said to them explains one of the mysteries to me."

"And what's that?"

"That you didn't have like a 'dick-transplant' or something. It explains why your dick is black --."

"But not necessarily how I got one this size for a Scandinavian white boy," he interjected.

"You wish. You only wish. So again, how does it happen to be black?"

"You want to know the honest truth? It's been many years since I ran around naked in Hawaii, since it's been exposed for long periods to the sun, yet it's still got that ebony sheen."

"It *is* a transplant?"

"No. That summer in Oahu, I was a kid in college spending my vacation surfing on the North Shore. When I wasn't surfing I was playing nude volleyball or wandering around bare-assed. It got dark from all that sun – it had quite the tan and I was really proud of it.

"I was messing around with this local girl and that didn't sit well with some of the locals, so they pulled a prank on me. I had gone to a beach party just down the road from Pipeline. Had way too much to drink and passed out. And when I woke up my dick was – well, it was *really* black."

"They tattooed it?"

"I think I might have felt *that*. I went to a couple doctors – even to the clinic at the med school at college, but they had no explanation for it. Most think it was dyed. I was getting my annual physical a few years ago and the doctor, when he finally stopped laughing, said they used some tropical root. He had spent some time in New Guinea and said he had seen it there. And now it's been more than fifteen years and that ebony sheen refuses to fade away."

"That is one strange story. And since you're talking, I want you to tell me about your boat's name?"

"*Lille Sort Flise*? It's Danish."

"A woman's name?"

"No. It literally translates as 'Black Peter."

"'Black Peter?' You have the Danish words for black penis on your transom? You do fit the pilot mold."

"It means 'Small Black Flag' in Danish."

"Small? Okay, you really *don't* fit the pilot mold."

"No. A peter is a small triangular flag raised to the top of the aft mast to identify the rank of the captain or admiral onboard. You know, back in the 18th Century in the British Navy. I read about it in a Patrick O'Brian novel. Get it?"

"Yeah. Got it." She undid the line and sent him up the mast, stopping when he came to the steaming light at the spreaders. With his legs wrapped around the mast, he whipped out a Phillips screwdriver and quickly changed the bulb. Task accomplished, he grabbed the high-tech binos from around his neck and examined the horizon.

"Don't forget to turn them on," she shouted up at him.

He found the button and resumed his search. The breeze had returned, clocking around from northeast to just south of east and strengthened. Combined with the afternoon sea breeze there was a chop even on the bay. He focused on downtown Miami, a smudge on the horizon to the north that came into sharp focus.

"These are image-stabilization binos," he yelled down. "I don't think I've ever even held them before. They're great!"

"Typical pilot," she shouted, "loves the gizmos!"

He could see below the skyline a trimaran heading south, toward them, all sails up. Even from this distance Blackie could tell that it was tearing along.

The boat wasn't making the dog-leg through the eastern cut of the Featherbeds, but was obviously going to go right over the shallow bank. Blackie considered staying up the mast to watch it go aground, but decided to come down.

Back on the deck he told her, "Some idiot is heading straight for us right over the Featherbeds. Should be hearing the call for a tow any second on Channel 16."

Dani took her fancy binos and saw the trimaran, now hull up on the northern horizon from their vantage point on deck. "Wow, that boat is moving. What kind of engine can get it to motorsail at that speed?"

"I'm sure they don't even have the outboard running. The sails are making it go twelve, maybe 15 knots. That tri is planing. One of those Corsairs like Yul's. Wait a second! Let me see those."

Blackie watched as the boat sped toward them, its shallow draft allowing it to pass easily over the northern fork of the eastern bank of the Featherbeds.[10] He saw a large blob on the port amas through the binos before handing them over to Dani.

"Hell, I think that's *The King & I*."

"That's Yul? He never said anything yesterday about coming out." With the image stabilization, she was able to see the trimaran clearly. "First time I've ever seen him sailing. How can he get that trimaran to go so fast?"

"He seldom has a crew, except for his cat. He really knows how to get that boat to move. He said he once saw 22 knots, speed over ground, on his handheld GPS."

"Neither of us would even know what that felt like."

"He has to tack twice to get through the second set of markers. Watch him come about," he said, returning her the binos.

She saw Yul sitting Buddha-like on the port amas. Next to him was a smaller, obese statue in the same pose.

"What is that thing sitting there next to him?"

"That's his big fat tabby, Elvis."

"That's his cat? I've heard about it but never seen it, and I've been onboard his boat several times."

"The cat hates people except for Yul. I think it has some sort of phobia, because it hides whenever anyone comes onboard, and never ever leaves the cabin except when they sail.

---

[10] Yul over the Featherbeds, 25 32.39N, 80 11.57W.

I had to take care of it when Yul's aunt died back in New York. I fed it for a week and never saw it. I only knew from all those big stinking piles in the pan of kitty litter that it was definitely alive."

"What a huge, fat cat. It looks just like Yul – with hair."

"Yul's 'Mini-me,' but there's nothing mini about it."

At that moment Dani watched the jib sheet loosen and Yul scramble across to the other amas. Elvis followed and plopped down beside him. The boat swung across the wind and was flying toward them on the opposite tack.

"Blackie, what an incredible move! Those Olympics kids we saw practicing on those high-tech catamarans in the bay couldn't have done it better."

"Did you see Elvis?"

"For such an obese thing, he moves pretty quick. And he knows the spot for the crewman. "

"Yul said he trained him because he needs the ballast on the windward amas."

"Surprised Yul hasn't fitted him with a harness," she said. "If he can train him to drop the anchor he's got the perfect boat pet."

Yul tacked again, the two repeating the maneuver flawlessly, but for one glitch Dani couldn't help but spot through the binos. She saw he was wearing a life jacket, but only a life jacket.

"Please don't tell me Yul's naked."

"I do believe that is the method by which Yul likes to sail."

"Oh my god."

"You know a couple years ago he placed high in the multi-hull division at the Columbus Day Regatta. And that night he was given some award for being the Biggest Naked Fat Man."

"Were you there to see him?"

"No, never been to Columbus Day."

"Neither have I."

Both had always missed, by accident or design, the Columbus Day Regatta, what was the annual start of the Biscayne Bay cruising season. By that date the worst of the hurricane season was over and the temperature had fallen a few degrees below sweltering, so it was the perfect, long weekend for a wild party.

The racecourse was from near the Rickenbacher Causeway down to Elliot Key. Over the years it had gone from a sailing event to more of a drunken, on-the-water orgy. Hurricane Andrew had cancelled it for a year back in '92, but it rebounded and the wild scene became wilder.

The National Park Service, accused by some of being as spineless as a jellyfish, had tried to put a damper on the drunken revelry by forcing the race to be held the weekend *after* the holiday weekend. But the naked partiers said forget the race and showed up on Columbus Day weekend and raised their usual hell, so the race returned to its name-sake weekend.

A few years before some drunken idiots on a small open-bow powerboat, speeding through the hundreds of anchored boats, had plowed into the bullet-proof hull of an anchored blue-water cruiser. One of the six on the fishing boat didn't surface or survive.

The local Park Service was in a quandary: there weren't any booze-soaked bashes allowed at the foot of Bridal Veil Falls in Yosemite. No beer-can throwing parties on inflatables floating down the Grand Canyon. So how could they allow this event to occur in a National Park, even if Biscayne National Park was the red-headed stepchild of the NPS? Following the lead of any of the South Florida Law Enforcement Agencies when faced with enforcing laws passed to bring a modicum of decency to the locals, the park service did next to nothing. That was why they were racking up more fatalities on recent Columbus Day weekends. And why Dani and Blackie weren't sad that they had missed the regatta again.

With *The King & I* astern *Carpe Diem*, Yul made a final tack into their cove, racing by the port hull of the catamaran.

Blackie observed as the tri approached, "Quite the trio. You shave the cat and plaster walrus mustaches on it and Yul's dick, and you've got varying-sized, identical triplets."

"Some sort of perverse set of tropical babushka dolls," Dani added.

Yul, speeding past, shouted," I've got some news! After I anchor, come get me in the dinghy!"

A minute later the Corsair 31 was into the wind with all sails down, its anchor hooked in a patch of sand surrounded by turtle grass.

Riding back in the dinghy, Yul was intently talking to Blackie, and by the look on their faces, Dani could tell it wasn't good news. Yul came up first on the stern steps, wearing a pair of his size-46 boxer shorts that he was trying to pass off as a swimsuit, with Blackie right behind.

"So what's up Yul?" Dani asked.

"Some thieves broke into Blackie's boat," Yul said cautiously at the cockpit table. "Tore it up pretty good."

"Yul, it's okay. She knows about what happened at the grill. I told her everything. At least everything I know."

"So someone broke in to find that old report and the photos Blackie had," she said. "Did they get them?"

"I don't know, but I don't think so," Yul answered.

"I hid them in some gallon baggies down in the bilge, where I used to keep Yul's beer," Blackie added.

"So they might still be there?" she enquired.

"I would think so. Yul didn't check there, so they probably didn't either."

"How did they know you had that stuff?"

"We don't know."

"Yul, are you sure it wasn't just some kids?"

"They had to move the laptop so they could pull all the books off the shelf. No kids would do that – and then leave the laptop. No, they looked like they were after something."

"Nobody saw anything?"

"They must have come aboard after midnight. I noticed the lock was off on my walk this morning. I went aboard and saw what happened. But before I was to call the cops, I wanted to get ahold of Blackie. So I spent the next hour trying to get you two on your cellphones. What's up with that?"

"We made a pact on our first sail together to turn them off when we're out."

"That's smart – what happens if your mother slips and falls and goes to the hospital?"

"My mother's dead."

"I'm sorry, Dani. I knew that. You know what I mean."

"We've both decided to disconnect from the electronic tether, even if it's only for a sail. Do you really think cell phones have improved our lives? I don't think so."

"Well, I guess you're right, Dani. That's the point of getting away," Yul said. "I thought about calling the Park Service and having them get a message to you, but I didn't want to risk this being broadcast over the marine radio. And the fewer people involved in this right now, the better."

"So you didn't tell the police about what happened at the Barracuda Grill?"

"No. I never made the call. I figured it was Blackie's decision."

Blackie finally spoke. "We need to get back and I need to inventory the boat and clean it up."

Dani disappeared into the cabin and returned with a half-gallon jar of whole cashews for Yul. She also brought him an oil can of Fosters, the closest thing she had to *Old Grogham Light*.

"Like the size," Yul said, wrapping his fat hand around the can. "Just that there isn't much taste."

Blackie looked at Dani and shook his head.

Around the cockpit table of **Carpe Diem**, the three discussed their options, choosing none. Finally Yul stood and headed for the dinghy to prepare for his sail back. "We'll check your boat out before making any decisions," he concluded.

Chapter 16:

Harlis

Yul's trimaran was only a speck on the northern horizon when *Carpe Diem* passed through the eastern cut of the Featherbed Banks. They put the main and jib up, set the autopilot, and the boat headed north on a beam reach.

With the Miami skyline barely poking above the water ahead, the pair sat silently in the cockpit lost in their own thoughts. Finally Dani spoke.

"You're sure you don't want to go to the police? Might be safer."

"I'm still not ready. I've got nothing but the fact that I left the scene of the shooting. What a can of worms that could open up."

"Why don't I do a little investigative work for you?"

"How?"

"Ted doesn't know I'm involved. I've been on that Breakwater a time or two and know my way around. You and Yul could get Ted and his entourage off the boat, keep an eye out, and I could go onboard and have a look around."

"And if you get caught? The least that could happen is you'd be arrested for trespassing."

"Okay. So go to the police. Just do *something*."

"When were you on his boat?"

"When I still had my efficiency on Euclid. When I was young, wild and stupid."

"You're nothing like that now. Still young, though."

"I've completely purged that phase of my life from my memory - at least what I can remember of it."

"How well did you know Ted?"

"Superficially."

"What did you think of him?"

"A jerk with loads of cash. On South Beach those people tend to school in winter. They treat the models like they do maitre'd's or the valets for the Porsche. Throw enough cash at us and we'll do whatever they want."

"Did you?"

"Want a mineral water?" she asked, hopping off the chair at the helm and escaping into the cabin. She came back and sat in silence. Obviously she wasn't going to answer his question.

"Something else I wanted to ask you about," Blackie said, choosing his words carefully. "What was it with the guy that saved us last night? You acted strange, like you knew him?"

"How's that?"

"You got so quiet, then later you said that he saved you again."

"I was wondering if you caught that. I do know him. I'm almost sure I do."

"How?"

"He's been my protector - my guardian angel if you will - since I was a kid."

"You're kidding me."

"No."

"But you're not religious. You've said your parents never took you to church, either of them."

"True, but I can't change what has happened to me. The case is there for that man being my protector - that's the word I prefer to use."

"Have you ever talked to him?"

"Yes. And no."

"You've got some explaining to do. Check our course and give me the entire story."

Dani Parma wasn't sure when her guardian made his first appearance. Her mother had said that when Dani was six, about a year after the divorce, she had stuck her head into Dani's room to find her carrying on a long conversation with an invisible friend seated at the foot of her bed. She sat cross-legged on her pillows looking up at her friend and asking a question and listening attentively to the silent response. Her mother, on the advice of a psychologist friend, ignored Dani's fantasy; she was told it was a young girl's way of working through the trauma of the family break-up. Dani remembered none of it.

Dani's first recollection of the man was when she was 14. She had snuck off with friends to Texoma, a lake north of Dallas. When things turned too wild for her she left and started walking home – not exactly a safe thing to do since she was 30 miles from home. Two women in a fancy pickup were kind enough to stop and take her to a phone booth and loan her four quarters. She called both her parents and as usual got their voice mails. She hung up in disgust without leaving either a message.

A man in a big Cadillac drove by, circled, stopped and offered to help. But it soon became obvious that his main goal was to get her into his car. Despite his overly doting demeanor, she considered going with him since he was the only option. At that moment a beat-up Chevy pickup pulled up behind the Caddy. A huge black man in overalls got out and walked up to use the phone. He turned and said in an East Texas drawl, "Why don't you go first, darlin'?"

"I would, but I don't have any quarters," she said in dismay.

"I got two right here," he said as he handed her the coins. She spoke to her mother right after the first ring. She told her she was on State Highway 289 right outside the town of

Gunter. She hung up and looked from the big man to the one seated in his car.

"Darlin', I'm expecting somebody to call me on that pay phone, so I'm gonna stand over there by my truck till they call."

"Why don't you use your phone at home?"

"Ain't got one, baby," he said as he turned. He paused at the open passenger window of the Caddy, leaned over and said, "Hey mister, I see you got Oklahoma plates on this fancy car."

The words were barely from his mouth before the Caddy was in gear and tearing away down the two-lane blacktop. The big man loped over and leaned back on the rusty grill of the truck. Half an hour later the phone rang, and as the big man answered, her mother drove up. Dani hopped in the car and waved at him through the closed window, disappointed that she didn't have the chance to tell him goodbye.

"Blackie, I know this sounds like nothing. A chance encounter. Yet I really felt at the time that I knew him. The only image that stuck in my mind was that he was huge, of course, and that he had such a gentle, kind face and this bad scar under his right eye. They didn't go together at all."

"That's it?"

"Oh, no. I took to calling him Harlis. Don't know why. So many times I felt him near me, just not visible. His next appearance wasn't until I was out of college and back in Dallas. I was working late at the ad agency and driving home at close to twelve every night because of a big ad campaign we were working on. I made a nightly stop at a little convenience store near my home to buy an Amstel Light to wind down. One night I came out with my beer in its little brown paper bag and there is a note under my windshield wiper saying something like 'I want to meet you, call me,' and a phone number.

"I looked around and no one was there, so I pitched it. This happened again the next night, but the note was a little more, um, emphatic. On the third night I came out of the store not to find a note, but a man standing by my car door. He questioned me about why I hadn't called him and sounded really annoyed.

"I asked him to move so I could leave but he wouldn't budge. I was going to scream but no one was around. I froze in sheer panic.

"And suddenly, in a deep baritone, a voice over my shoulder says, 'I believe the lady has asked you to move.' The man looked over me – above me really – and froze. And then these two huge arms reach out around me, like they're my arms almost, and grab him and lift him off the ground and carry him to the sidewalk in front of the store. It's Harlis, of course, only he wasn't in those cotton-pickin' overalls but in what looked like a security guard outfit.

"He told me in this lilting North African accent, to leave while he held the man, and I drove off in a hurry.

"It took me a week but I finally got the courage to go by the store in the daytime, with a friend in tow, to find out who the man was so I could thank him. The manager said they never had a security guard on duty. This was North Dallas, not Miami."

"Couldn't he have been there because he just got off work like you?"

"Sure. But he did have that scar about two inches long under his right eye."

"And that's it?"

"No. One last meeting. And not too long ago."

Dani told about her recent altercation at a sub shop on Alton Road in South Beach. The condo-boom had turned traffic into a nightmare and a parking space into an endangered species. Returning from her gym, she had pulled into the tiny lot with its six spaces only to find three occupied by a Porsche parked at an obnoxious angle. She pulled up behind it and ran into the shop.

She announced that if whoever had the Carrera could please repark, she could take one of the spots. A man her age said that yes, it was his car, but he was about to order and didn't have time to mess with it, then turned and ignored her. She went out and parked directly behind his Carrera, to not block any of the other cars.

She took her place in line and watched the man grab his order and head out the door. He was back in a moment yelling for whoever was behind the silver Porsche to move it or else. She spoke up, as loud as she could muster, that it was her car and she would order first before she moved the car.

The man let loose with a tirade. "You goddamn bitch! You move that car or I'm gonna go out there and take a club to it."

She froze. She had seen a dozen of these scenes on the Beach, always shocking, always amusing, but never involving her. What had she gotten herself into? The jerk swung around and moved toward the door. A huge man with a shaved head seated at a table near the door rose and stepped forward, blocking the exit. The big man wore a Miami Beach sanitation worker's outfit.

He looked down and said, "You mess with her, mister, and you're messin' with me" in his best Florida cracker dialect.

The younger man stopped dead in his tracks and looked up to see that Dani's guardian was definitely not smiling. The jerk, lunch bag in hand, stepped around and barged out. He got in his car and sat there eating his sandwich. Dani casually gazed up at the menu, taking her time. When her order finally came she grabbed the bag and headed out. She stopped at the door and turned to her savior and said, "Thanks very much for being here."

But as she opened her car door her terror returned, since that ass might follow her while Harlis sat inside eating. She resigned herself to her fate and reached down to fasten her seatbelt. She looked up and there was Harlis standing at her hood, blocking in the Porsche. He had a smile on face and was waving. Her last glimpse of him was his giving her a wink with his left eye, not the eye with the scar under it.

"Dani, all I can say is to be thankful your protector wasn't some little old Cuban guy. You both might be dead by now."

"If he would have been, I don't know. Those guys can be pretty scrappy. They were the ones who had the balls to do the Watergate burglary."

"Okay, you're saying that those guys, with three different accents, were all the same person, or entity."

"I don't know . . . *yes, they were!* You don't believe me, do you?"

He reached over and put his open palm on her forehead. "Oh ah do believe you, dahlin'" he mocked, "And ah believe you have been saved."

Chapter 17:

José the Pirate

With *Carpe Diem* secured in her slip at Te Cuesta Isle, Blackie and Dani walked over to Pier Two to find Yul sprawled in his cockpit, sipping a cheap beer. The three headed over to the Island Packet to survey the damage. The cabin was a mess, with every locker emptied, all shelves cleared, the contents strewn about the sole. Blackie pushed away some of the mess and lifted a carpet runner, exposing the hidden hatch that opened down into the bilge.

He reached in and felt around, finally retrieving the cell phone and the packet of photos. The *Capn's* report was gone.

"They took the report about Ted," Blackie said.

"But left the phone and the photos?" Yul asked.

"They weren't looking for those. Probably didn't know I had them," Blackie said as he handed the items to Dani.

So this was what all the fuss was about, she thought to herself as she flipped through the files and then the photos. Unnoticed by her companions, she froze at one of the prints in her hand. She turned and walked forward toward the head, still clutching them. When she returned the three climbed the stairs up into the Island Packet's cockpit to discuss their next move.

"Obviously they've connected me with the *Skipper*," Blackie volunteered.

"You're a loose end to them, so you better be careful," Dani added.

"We'll stick together until this gets settled," Yul said. "I'm not letting you out of my sight in the daylight. And you ought to spend the next few nights on Dani's boat, if I can be allowed to make the invitation."

Blackie turned to Dani with a pleading look in his eyes.

"Of course you can."

"It might just be for tonight. A buddy left me a message on my cell. Wants me to pick up his trip to Port-au-Prince early tomorrow and I could end up stuck there tomorrow night."

"And you consider Port-au-Prince safer?" Yul quipped.

"The question still remains. What do we do about the mess you're in?" Dani asked. "I say we bring José in on it."

Yul let out a low groan. "What's your idea?" he asked. "Tell him about Ted and he'll go talk him to death. That would solve our problem."

"Why do you dislike him so much? He's just . . . opinionated."

"About everything," Yul said. "He's a victim of his own making. I mean, why would you move from LA back to Miami if you were a successful gay Cuban artist who idolized Ché?"

"To be a thorn in everyone's ass here?" Blackie volunteered.

"I heard his family had to move to Orlando from the harassment. Just because they conceived and raised him."

"They've even talked about renaming that street with his name in Little Havana," Blackie added.

"With his *namesake*," Dani clarified. "He was named after his uncle who died fighting Castro – well, preparing to fight Castro, in a training exercise out in the Glades with Alpha 66, I believe."

"So why exactly are we bringing José in on this?" Yul inquired.

"For a new perspective," Dani said as she pulled her cell out. "Let me get him over here."

"You've got his number and he has yours?" Yul asked. "Are you a masochist or have the million-minute plan?"

"Yul, you need to chill," she scolded.

A few minutes later, a pirate in silhouette sauntered down Blackie's pier.

"Ah, I see he has the puffy shirt on," Yul noted.

"I can't figure if he's trying to be Seinfeld in the puffy shirt, or Johnny Depp in the *Pirates of the Caribbean*," Blackie mused.

"He claims they both stole the idea from him," Dani said. "He said that he designed and sewed the prototype of that shirt back in the mid '90s. For a White Party in Miami when he was still in high school."

"Yul, you have to admit, we both want a shirt like that. Fulfill our fantasies of being a swashbuckling Errol Flynn and all."

"I'd look like I was wearing a parachute."

"Plus it doesn't fit in with your *au natural* look while sailing," Dani said.

"You'll never forgive me for that, will you?" Yul inquired.

"I certainly won't forget it. Seeing the three of you in my binos," she replied.

"Three?"

"You, the cat and your –. Never mind. You two just be nice."

On the finger pier José made his usual grand entrance with a flourish. He leapt up onto a stay, spun around and landed on the deck of the Island Packet in a graceful move that should have been recorded in Panavision.

"*Buenos tardes, mi amigos*," José said, reaching out and gently clasping Dani's hand. He leaned forward, looking into her eyes for that extra second before touching his lips to her skin. With the scarf wrapped and knotted on his head and his moustache twirled up on the ends, he did look like a '40s romanticized version of a Hollywood pirate. He did look uncannily like a Latino Errol Flynn. Blackie tried to repress the grin, thinking that despite his drawbacks, it was impossible not to love this guy.   Another of Blackie's favorite nautical neighbors.

"So am I the token *Cubano* invited to a secret-society meeting of the last liveaboard Anglos in Miami?" José chided, as he took a seat in the cockpit close to Dani. Blackie couldn't help but make the mental note that Dani and José, both about the same age and both with their perfect dark looks, made an incredibly beautiful couple. When he had first met José together with Dani, he thought they were a couple, and was happy to learn that they weren't. They were just good sailing buddies – and friends.

"We've gathered before we beat a retreat to decide if we should raze the town before we go," Yul joked.

"Despite the improvement that fire might bring, I'm afraid I won't be joining you, not with us living in a police state," he said.

"Hmm," Yul interjected. "Less than one minute before the conversation turns political."

"Political?" José asked with a genuine smile on his face.

"Police state?"

"You haven't noticed? This Homeland Security thing – I can't remember the German phrase Hitler had for it."

"You're saying we have a country run by Nazis?"

"I prefer 'Fascists,'" José mused. "Their presence in our lives is not meant to strike fear in terrorists, but in us."

"Explain."

"Those men in riot gear we are becoming so familiar with -- be it at the stadium for the Super Bowl, or at Times Square or even Bayside here at Miami on New Years Eve, are they really protecting us or serving as a reminder to us? Against whom have they used the men in black in their riot gear? American workers protesting the exportation of their jobs at those Free Trade meetings, or against Cuban Americans – whom I didn't agree with – protesting that kid being shipped back to Havana.   You can't find a single cop stopping the thousands running red lights in Miami, yet we can get an army of cops in high-tech riot gear to intimidate us from exercising our right of free speech."

"I think you're taking it a little overboard," Yul argued.

"And that's not why we're here," Dani interjected, trying desperately to get back to the matter at hand.

Dani told José a brief version of what had happened in the past week. Blackie followed along, but couldn't shake what José had proposed. It wasn't that hard to fall for José's brand of grandiose paranoia.

Blackie had met José the year before as they both passed through the figurative revolving door at the marina. Blackie had long ago espoused his belief that people at a marina fit into two basic categories: those who were either getting into boating – or out of it.

For many hoping to one day cruise, their dream of life on tropical waters was a flame that kept them warm and alive through those unbearable winters in the North. A sun lamp, a *Cruising World* and a reggae or Jimmy Buffett tape, and the escapism could turn into an obsession. That therapy did wonders in preventing severe depression in sailors up north.

A few did sell it all and buy the boat they hoped would be bound one day for the Exumas or Cane Garden Bay. Fewer held on to the boat for the manifestation of their dream. Many jumped ship before it ever left port, one of the principal reasons boat prices were lower in South Florida than the rest of the country: the abandoned dreams clogged the marinas and boatyards at the exit – the jumping-off point – from the comforts of home. Crew compatibility was a factor. Suddenly the captain and first mate weren't just crossing paths ashore in a palatial home in the suburbs, they were sharing a floating cell anchored off Watson Island. That was how José came to possess his beautiful sailing yacht.

José had found the perfect boat to fit his persona. He had bought a sailboat called a Gatsby from a couple that jumped ship after being driven ashore during one of Miami's infrequent but infamous winter storms. Anchored off the

Miami Yacht Club and Watson Island waiting to cross the Gulf Stream, the untested cruisers encountered their first bad weather. The pre-dawn gale had ripped a neighboring ferro-cement sailboat loose from its mooring. By the time the terrified couple had come on deck, a small flotilla, caught in the drift, bore down on them and pulled their anchor free.

Their Gatsby came ashore on a pier behind a fancy home on "Dan" Marino Island, one of the spoil islands on the Venetian Causeway. The island was actually San Marino Island, but a persistent fan had vandalized the street signs even long after the quarterback's retirement. Many suspected the same vandal of changing Dilido Island to "Dildo" Island on all the street signs, too.

When the news vultures arrived at dawn after the storm, the disheveled couple, suffering from shock, stood beside their beached boat in their matching Helly Hansen seagear. They were broadcast live on three local morning shows on another slow news day. The couple looked much like the rafters who came ashore escaping Fidel, only their half-sunk escape-vehicle cost a quarter-million dollars. Their boating life was over before they ever set sail.

José spotted the Gatsby in a boatyard and picked it up for a song from the insurance company. He went to work with his hired crew on its complete restoration. He was anxious to be free of the confines of the condo canyons of South Beach, no matter how much the value of his high-rise crackerbox had skyrocketed in only one year. He wanted mobility; he was sure he was on the crest of one of the cyclical boom-and-bust waves that had always washed over Miami Beach.

The Gatsby was a striking sailboat, so different from the fiberglass mold of her contemporaries. She had a bit of a Trumpy-yacht look and feel – a throwback to the 1920s, only the boat was made at the end of the 20th Century. José restored her to her original beauty and painted the name *Elena* on her stern, for Elena Burke, the Cuban diva of the '50s that took "filin" music to a new level. Despite her diminutive size compared to the motor yachts, *Elena* was hands down the classiest vessel at Te Cuesta Isle marina.

José recalled his dealings with their notorious neighbor and finally said, "I've met Ted a time or two, our circle of friends overlaps. As an artist, I have to suck up to the people with the money, no matter how repulsive they might be," José observed.

"Would Ché agree with you doing that?" Yul chided.

"I believe he did a little schmoozing when the ends justified the means. I'll make some inquiries about Ted and find out what he's been up to."

Blackie couldn't help but note that José's description of his relationship to Ted was almost identical to Dani's; they knew him, but didn't want to admit it.

The four sailors broke up their meeting with nothing resolved. José excused himself to head over to his gallery, and the rest drifted off to run their respective errands. Blackie flipped through the photos on the settee table one more time. One of the photos of Ted was missing. He guessed that either Dani or José had taken it to do their investigative work.

Chapter 18:

MIA – Missing In Action

Blackie crept out of the starboard-hull stateroom a little after four in the morning. A cold front had crept down the coast the evening before and brought another wave of cool, dry air into Miami. Dani and Blackie had shared in the dinner-prep while sipping a Colorado *Grand River Meritage Sauvignon Blanc.* She had brought the wine back from a photo shoot at the Book Cliffs near Grand Junction.

Dinner was vegetarian: a couscous salad followed by steamed asparagus and a creamed cauliflower soup, accompanied by fresh sourdough bread made in Dani's bread machine.

After dinner they retired to her cabin, the forward stateroom in the starboard hull. With the hatch cracked open over Dani's queen bed, the cool air poured in while the boat gently rocked in the breeze. They held onto each other under a down comforter and watched a '40s Bogart classic on the large LCD screen Dani had mounted on the bulkhead of the master cabin.

He had declined, but she sipped on a *Taylor-Fladgate Vintage Port* and munched on a half-cup of macadamia nuts. With the volume muted, they made love as Bogart and Bacall silently sparred in *To Have and Have Not* on the muted screen; they had both seen the movie before and fell asleep still entwined before the credits scrolled down the screen.

Walking the pier in the dark in his Alpha Airlines uniform, flight bag in tow, Blackie reflected on the previous night and the cruise with Dani. But that idyllic episode had come to an end; he was off to that nightmare called Miami International Airport.

MIA took a constant, but well-deserved public relations beating. A few years before on a Newark layover, he had taken a cab over to Manhattan and seen a rival airline's billboard in Spanish. It basically translated as, "Fly us from Newark to Latin America without having to go through Miami."

It was one thing to occasionally connect through Miami, but another to be based there. Blackie's only way to cope with the chaos was to look on it as one big joke, which it was.

Blackie had amused himself by trying to come up with the most absurd reason that there would be a disruption of service at the airport. He had come up with a few goods ones, and the best he called "The Wild Slice": A golfer teeing off at the Mel Reese golf course at the end of Runway 9R hit a high slice that pinged a low-flying DC-8 freighter. His shot was mistaken for a dud SAM, shutting down MIA. Yet fiction often paled to reality in Miami.

When he had first transferred his base to MIA, he was exiting the Flight Ops elevator on the way to his plane when pandemonium erupted at the ticket counter. A passenger had been dropped off by someone in an old jeep, and as the passenger and his bags were brought in through the open doors, the jeep sped off with a few loud backfires that sounded much too similar to gunfire.

Most of the passengers standing in line with their heaps of baggage were Miami residents. Conditioned to the sound, they gave a dog-like, Pavlovian response and hit the floor. Blackie stood there as the orchestrated scene unfolded. An elderly woman fainted, causing an FBI agent in line, there to pick up his armed-passenger form, to draw his service revolver and scan the scene for the shooter. Passengers screamed and ran, and a few dove behind the counter and hopped on the belt in their desperate attempt to escape. Before the screaming and confusion had ended, even the trinket and duty-free shops had pulled down their barred security gates. When order was finally restored, only a few hundred passengers missed their flights. Just another day at M-I-A.

About every day was a fiasco because the place was a fiasco. Built in the '40s, the original terminal had been added on to haphazardly for decades, as the county commissioners used the airport to steer pork-barrel construction projects to friends and financial supporters. Once, pulling up his paperwork for a flight, he had heard a senior gate agent explaining tongue-in-cheek to an exasperated passenger the reason for his half-hour walk through a labyrinth: that everything built after the original World War II-era structure had been designed by the architect Jed Clampett, renowned for the lean-to.

Even the newest concourse, built just a few years before, had cracks all over its façade, with chunks of stucco falling sporadically to the pavement below. During the summer monsoon season, Blackie had to dodge trashcans in the terminal, strategically placed to catch the roof leaks. The cans sat below plastic tarps fastened to the ceiling, with common green garden hose leading from the catchments to the cans.

MIA should have been razed and rebuilt anew, but that was impossible. There was no place to go with the Everglades to the west and the Gulf Stream to the east and an ever-rising sea of humanity in between. Moving would have been a good thing, because even the weather at MIA's location sucked. The airport was built where the ocean breeze met heated air from the Everglades, and starting on June 1st or so, Mother Nature turned on her tap over MIA each afternoon.

In summer, lightning and heavy rains often closed the airport in the afternoon, causing major diversions of planes to Fort Lauderdale, to Nassau, even to the Naval Air Station at Key West. Arriving at MIA after a surprise three-hour visit to Nassau (where they weren't allowed to deplane), the passengers, vacation over, scrambled through Immigration and

Customs, only to find that their flights north – the last of the day – had left an hour before. They were presented with the Act-of-God defense and were "on their own" for the night. On a busy summer night, hundreds slept on the floor.

Another pilot had even submitted a formal proposal to issue the stranded folks something more than a disposable toothbrush and tiny tube of toothpaste. He proposed renting them surplus military pup-tents, so they'd have a little privacy and something to insulate them from the many mice that scurried around the floors at MIA during the wee hours of the morning.

Blackie pulled the Beamer into the employee lot at MIA and strolled to the bus stop. He was on time despite the fact that he had been caught in a horrific traffic jam. A septic-tank truck had overturned on the Dolphin Expressway a mile from MIA, dumping a thousand gallons of liquid shit on the freeway. He was on time because he had factored in for that. He always factored in for the daily outrageous accident. He believed the copy writers for P. Rick Lopez probably had a prewritten script for their news show: "A *blank* (tanker-truck, septic truck, armored car) has overturned on the *blank* (Dolphin, I-95, Turnpike), spilling its contents and closing the road to all traffic until *blank* (noon, evening, midnight).

Blackie stopped in at Flight Ops prior to his flight to Port-au-Prince. He was First Officer on a 767 to the Haitian capital and then bringing it back, a supposed "quick turn." He pulled up the weather for the trip and at least that looked good. His only concern wasn't nature but the civil unrest he had heard about on NPR on the drive to MIA.

Over the years, Blackie had dealt with many weather situations flying international out of MIA. There was the mud at Caracas, the flood at Tegucigalpa, and the crud (volcanic ash) at San Salvador, Lima and the Caribbean airports downwind of Monserrat.

Sometimes the hazards were minute compared to a volcano but just as dangerous. He once had aborted a landing because a pack of wild dogs – lethargic, skinny mutts called Pot Licks – were sleeping on the runway at Providenciales in the Turks & Caicos Islands.

But the one wild card he still found unsettling wasn't weather or volcanoes or dogs but "civil unrest." And that was becoming more and more common in South and Central America. A flight crew departing their temporary hotel during "civil unrest" in Caracas was held-up stagecoach-style getting in their cab. The hotel security guard came out shooting, and the crew found that they were caught in the crossfire of an Old West gunfight, only these were real bullets from Glocks.

In Haiti "civil unrest" had become downright cyclical. Something expected – like the hurricane season.

He had heard the first-hand accounts of the tale of the Alpha Airlines DC-10 that had landed in Port-au-Prince during a period of civil unrest more than a decade earlier. After deplaning, the wide-body was hijacked ironically by one of the security guards hired to protect the plane. Without a crew, the plane was going nowhere, and when the man's demands weren't met, he shot at an engine, sending a bullet into the turbine and guaranteeing he wasn't leaving. The siege continued, with the desperado holed up inside, eating trays of airline food since the plane had been double catered for the trip back to Miami.

After a few days in Haiti's sweltering heat, the power turned off and the food gone bad, they still had no word from the perpetrator. Haitian officers stormed the plane. They found no one aboard despite having it surrounded throughout the ordeal. A new million-dollar engine had to be shipped to Port-au-Prince so the plane could finally leave. Flights were suspended for months until the Haitian government could come up with something resembling a security plan.

Now Blackie was flying to Port-au-Prince as another era of civil unrest swept Haiti. The latest in a long line of US-backed leaders had been ousted after being corrupted by power. The coupe came when he had resurrected the feared squad of secret police of his predecessor, brought back to keep his countrymen from questioning the looting of their country.

The flight was full, as were all others in and out of Miami, because of the upcoming President's Day weekend. Blackie and his Captain did their final preflight checks, with both commenting that things were going way too smooth.

They were almost ready for pushback when a call came from the company dispatcher that they were waiting on a bag pull. By federal decree, if a passenger didn't show up at the gate after checking bags, the airline was required to remove the bags before the international flight departed.

As with any Haiti flight, there was always a twist. They were missing four passengers, including one in a wheelchair. The four were found being detained at the security checkpoint. From what he could make of the situation, Blackie learned from the Captain that the security agent – the one who wanded the man in the wheelchair – was the person who determined the man was dead. And had been for some time.

Apparently the family had come from Haiti to Florida to see relatives in North Miami, taking advantage of a promotional $100-each-way local fare. The man, the family patriarch, had died of a heart attack two days before the return flight. Their calls to Alpha and an air cargo company determined that shipping human remains as cargo was almost eight times the "living" non-refundable fare. So the family had wrapped the man up in a blanket in his wheelchair and tried to get the body home in his assigned seat. They couldn't abandon him in Miami, and they couldn't afford to ship him home.

"This ain't the first time this has happened, Blackie," the Captain said in his southern drawl as he took off his headset. "Let me go see what I can do. You call the crew chief and have all their bags kept plane-side."

A half hour passed. Blackie was standing at the cockpit door talking to the Creole-speaking Flight Attendant when the Captain returned with two of the four missing passengers. The Captain was supporting an older woman – the sobbing widow,

Blackie presumed, down the jetbridge.   The Captain poked his head into the First Class cabin, empty but for three seats as it often was on the Haiti flights.   He turned and addressed the Number One.

"Put these two on the last row of First and be good to 'em. They've been through a lot."   He turned to the widow and to everyone's shock, spoke a consoling phrase in perfect Creole.

Blackie turned to the F/A and twisted his head quizzically.   She whispered to him, "He said in Creole, mind you, 'everything will be alright.'   I'm as shocked as you are."

The daughter, a middle-aged woman in the familiar Haiti travel outfit of a lace Easter dress and bonnet, grabbed the pilot by the arm and said, "Bless you, Captain.   Our family thanks you and we must repay.   My brother in North Miami will send you $20 every month."

"We'll talk about that when we get to Haiti. You better go sit down 'cause those folks in the back are pretty upset you made them late."   He turned and headed for the cockpit.   As he passed Blackie he muttered, "Let's get the hell outta here."

By the time they pulled out on the taxiway, they were stuck at the end of the next northbound complex.

"What did you do back there?" Blackie asked as he gazed at the long line of jets ahead of them on the taxiway. He realized that he was caught in traffic for the second time that day.

"Nothin'.   Just expedited things.   Lookin' out for my passengers.   That's why they made me a Captain."

"So I see. So what happened at the security checkpoint?"

"When I walked up it was a travesty.   Tons of TSA. Probably six levels of them.   They came out of their offices to view the spectacle.   Paramedics were there – but they knew he had been dead for more than a day.   Cops on bikes.   Hell, I was expecting to see that P. Rick news guy."

"What did you do?"

"Well, I was pissed.   Here was a man, probably a good man no longer living, with his loving wife and children doing what they thought best, trying to get him home, and yet all of 'us' were treating this like some big joke. I can't tell you the number of people that were laughing. What's wrong with us? It made me sick. So I took charge."

"I've heard you're a 'take-charge' kinda guy," Blackie said with a smile.

"Yeah? Who said that about me?"

"Never mind that. So what did you do?"

"I got the biggest Flight Ops bigwig to call the biggest Air Freight bigwig and expedite gettin' this man in a shipping casket and gettin' him on the afternoon flight home to Haiti. Had to give 'em my credit card number, though."

"Wow. I'm impressed."

"Been to Haiti?" the Captain asked.

"In and out. Never toured the countryside."

"What a place. A few filthy rich and a lotta dirt poor and little in between. That country is the job pool for every menial tourist-related job in South Florida. They keep the room rates low and the profits high."

"How'd you become an expert?"

The Captain pulled his wallet out of his uniform pants and opened it for Blackie. There was a photo, a stunning photo of a beautiful woman, probably Haitian.

"I've been dating her for about six months. She's a professor at Barry University. Teaches International Studies. Met her on a flight coming back from PAP."

"She's very attractive."

"Even more intelligent. Can you believe this good ole boy from Arkansas can fall head-over-heels in love with a woman from Haiti?"

"Will wonders never cease?"

"She's certainly been enlightening. Can you imagine me taking her home to my parents' retirement community in Hot Springs? I'm 53 and I don't have the balls to do that. At least not after what we went through meeting her parents in Haiti."

"She younger than you?"

"That picture was taken last year. How old do you think she is?"

"Thirty . . . two?"

"Forty six. The absolute most beautiful woman I have ever met."

"So back to our deal here, *Cap'n*. Somebody stayed behind with the corpse?"

"The son-in-law. He's coming with the body on the afternoon flight. I *will* be pissed if my own company charges me for his change fee."

The tower interrupted, telling them they were being sent over to Runway 9R, since a wind shift had switched the takeoff pattern back to the East.

Finally they were next in line to depart.

"Alpha Airlines Heavy 921 cleared for takeoff," the voice announced over their headsets.

The Captain throttled up and the 767 started its roll down the runway. They were only a few hundred yards into their takeoff when the Captain shouted, "What the hell is that?"

Ahead of them on the runway raced a vehicle, neither crash truck nor Aviation Department pickup, but an unmarked, speeding SUV, fortunately heading the same direction as their 767. Blackie could see emergency vehicles on the taxiways angling toward the car, but no word yet from the tower.

"Hang on, we gotta abort," the Captain yelled, as he throttled back on the engines and hit the brakes hard. They lunged forward in their restraints, and the giant wide-body skidded to a stop 200 feet behind the now-stopped SUV.

From their perch high up in the cockpit, Blackie and the Captain watched as the driver's door opened.

Terrorists?

A leg poked out, the foot in designer high heels, the slender leg in a pair of coral capri pants. An attractive woman in a tight-fitting, low-cut blouse hopped down from the oversized black SUV without missing a word on her cell call. She was waving her other arm wildly, spinning and jumping and obviously arguing with whoever was on the call, oblivious that she might be blocking a 767 from completing its takeoff.

Eventually the police arrived, guns drawn. They ordered her to drop her weapon or phone or whatever, but she kept screaming on the phone, stopping only to make an obscene gesture at the officers. They finally had enough and rushed the woman and subdued her, having to pry the phone from her hand, but not before she placed a strategic kick in the crotch of an officer, dropping him to the ground in pain.

An hour passed. The pilots watched the cops, now joined by feds in block-letter windbreakers, as they all milled around the 767 and the SUV. A couple of the feds had dogs in matching block-letter canine jackets. They seemed in no apparent hurry to end their chat, despite the Captain's pleas over the radio that the passengers on his plane were already three hours late departing.

The pilots conversed in the cockpit during the wait.

"Cap'n, what is that thing? An *Excursion*?"

"Nope."

"*Explorer? Expediton?* Blackie asked.

"Nope."

"*Escalade? Envoy?*

"Enough," the Captain replied.

"*Enough?* Never heard of that one."

"No, they gave that SUV a number, Blackie, but it's nickname is the *Escobar* – after that ole drug kingpin. Bigger than a Hummer, it's designed to be a cross between an SUV and a Bradley Fighting Vehicle. Big hit at the Chicago Auto Show and bought by trash with cash for protected trips to the mall. They love the stylin' but some of the buyers said it could have a little more armor in the side panels. Gets six miles to the gallon with the A/C on."

"See it's already a big hit in Miami," Blackie replied.

Over the radio, the Captain had been able to find out a few details from the ground controllers in Alpha's tower at MIA. The woman was apparently the mistress of the head of one of Colombia's big cut-flower importers at MIA. He was trying to set up a little afternoon liason with her, talking her in via cellphone to his airside office in that confusion of airfreight warehouses on the west side of MIA.

The woman, a Colombian national who neither spoke nor read English, was having trouble following directions via cellphone while traveling at 70 mph on side streets. She thought she had done as told and had sped through the southwest gate, snapping the flimsy arm at the guardhouse. Never slowing, she took a right and a left as he directed her that put her eastbound on the active runway. She told the FBI translator that when she first turned onto that big road she was happy to have finally found a quicker route home to her Brickell Avenue condo.

What was taking so long was what the dogs had found in the dozen boxes of roses in the back of the *Escobar*. Besides twenty dozen Colombian-grown American Beauties, they had found several kilos of very pure cocaine, and a Prada bag full of hundreds where the spare tire should have been.

The pilots were told that she admitted to the federal translator to having a little side thing going with the flower importer's warehouse manager. The Captain told Blackie that the importer's mistress was fucking him in more ways than one.

The two pilots laughed, and Blackie stated the obvious: "I can't believe she didn't know that you can't drive down an active runway in Miami with bags of coke and laundered money without taking a chance – albeit a small chance – of getting caught."

At noon, more than four hours after their scheduled 7 a.m. departure, the wheels finally went up on the Boeing 767 and they were headed for Haiti. That didn't bother Blackie, though, because he had already figured in a delay like this. He *always* figured in a delay like this. It helped him keep his sanity.

Chapter 19:

Over Rum Cay

Blackie emerged from the First Class lav and traded places with the Number One F/A waiting for him in the locked cockpit. With the door secured and the 767 on autopilot, the Captain and Blackie had a chance to look around and enjoy the flight. They were over Rum Cay in the southern Bahamas chain, streaking toward western Hispanola and PAP.

"So you said you're a sailor," the Captain observed, looking down at the near-deserted islands on a blue-sky day.

"Yeah, a liveaboard for years now," Blackie replied.

"You live in Miami?"

"Yeah, Te Cuesta Isle. You up north?"

"Lighthouse Point. Nice little house on a canal. Got a Glacier Bay cat with twin 250's. I can get to West End in under two hours. Go billfishin' mostly."

"From Te Cuesta Isle, I'm half a day from Bimini, but then I can only go maybe 7 knots."

"You need a stinkboat."

"No, I can't stand the sound of engines once I'm out of an airplane cockpit."

"You did say Te Cuesta Isle Marina? Over on The Beach?"

"Well, yeah, off South Beach."

"Did you know a guy named Spence? Spence Pritchard?"

"Sounds familiar."

"You might remember his boat, a really nice Viking. A motor yacht named *Amelie*."

"Yeah, I remember the name. The couple that bought it eventually changed it to *Grand Plan*."

"Yep, that was his boat. He flew for Uniform Airlines. Knew him since my Navy days. Not too long ago he shot himself."

"Jeez. Are you serious? Dead?"

"Yep."

"Sorry to hear it."

"You know that couple that got his boat?"

"Uh, Bobby and Belinda Burns. Not really."

"They didn't buy that Viking from him. They took it from him. They stole it from him."

"Stole it?"

"Yep. I tried to pull him out of his funk. Talked with him, tried to get him to seek help. No turning him around. He was in a fatal nosedive, and you can thank the Burns for it. I know the whole story, he told me all about it over a bottle of Scotch."

The Captain told Blackie one of the vilest tales yet to come out of The Land of the Second Chance, alias Miami Beach. It almost made Blackie airsick.

"Spence was only a few years from retirement. Flew the 747 for Uniform, mostly Miami to Buenos Aires, back when they were going great guns here. He had bought that Viking after his wife passed away from cancer. She was a landlubber and he had stayed landlocked up in Boca. But when she died, his goal was to tour the Caribbean in the Viking once he left Uniform.

"Everything was going fine. He was looking for something to do once he quit flying. So he decided to be a yacht broker, something he could do in St. Thomas if that was where he ended up. He found a part-time job at the SoBe office for a big yacht broker. Belinda was the manager. She hired him. Know anything about yacht brokers?"

"Not really."

"One of the most unregulated of professions. Anyone can do it, basically. Maybe twice-convicted felons are denied, and registered sex offenders since it's hard to get on and off boats with that thing strapped to your ankle – but not many others."

"Don't care for them, do you?"

"Nope. Well, if you knew Spence, you'd know he wasn't yacht broker material. He wore his heart on his sleeve. He was honest. He was always going to tell you what he thought, or what he thought was right."

"Refreshing attitude," Blackie said, remembering Dani's story about Belinda when she was searching for her sailboat. She had stopped at the broker's office to see if they had any used catamarans listed. Belinda first dismissed her as a bimbo model without the cash or credit needed to occupy her time. When Dani finally got through to Belinda that she had half a mil to spend, Belinda did an about face and pounced on her.

Belinda disparaged all catamarans, not having any to show, using innuendo and third-hand horror stories of their problems. She then took Dani aboard a custom steel ketch down a nearby pier, a boat with an eight-foot draft and 70-foot mast that smelled inside of rust. Dani was no fool, and she realized Belinda had an exclusive on the boat. In front of the gimballed stove, Belinda had looked Dani in the eye and in a confiding tone said, "Isn't this a wonderful kitchen? Let me show you the bedroom." Dani turned and walked off the boat, never looking back. Those two, despite ending up neighbors at Te Cuesta Isle, hadn't spoken since.

"Never believed in fate," The Captain said. "But how else could Spence have crossed paths with the Burns?"

"What happened?"

"They befriended him. Fawned over him, monopolized his time. He was at Te Cuesta Isle on that big, shiny Viking, and they were down the pier on their old '66 Pacemaker Sedan. Hell, I think the hull was wood. Guess Bobby thought it was time to replace the Pacemaker.

"Spence was working for Belinda and living in the same marina on a fancy Viking, and that obviously galled them. They coveted Spence's boat, and they got it."

"How?"

"They rendezvoused one weekend down at No Name Harbor on Key Biscayne, and after a few cocktails on the Viking, they talked Spence into putting in his overpowered Novurania tender and giving them a ride around Key Biscayne. So off they went.

"Spence said a guy on a jetski was dogging them, harassing them, really, and Bobby was goading him to try to outrun the guy. So he did, or thought he did. The jetski cut them off over by the Cape Florida Lighthouse, veering in front of them, and when he hit the wake, the next thing Spence knew Belinda was in the bottom of the inflatable crying out in agony, so he ran the boat up on the beach.

"Because of her relentless screaming and the heavy weekend traffic, they used the life-flight chopper to take her to Jackson Memorial. Bobby stayed behind with Spence, not for the fellowship, but to make sure the Marine Patrol gave Spence a breath test.

"They filed their lawsuit at the end of the next week. And what they were asking for was much more than the liability limit on Spence's insurance. Then things really got nasty. Spence's attorney could only shake his head. He put the numbers to it, and said it was better if Spence took early retirement, because Belinda and Bobby would end up with a big chunk of his salary anyway.

"Spence said he was at one of the Te Cuesta Isle parties and Belinda and Bobby had the temerity to walk up and tell him that they hoped there were no hard feelings. That they hoped the lawsuit didn't affect their friendship. That it was just business."

"Damn, that's cold," Blackie observed.

"Rather than hand over everything, Spence decided to fight back. He hired a pack of attorneys and ran up an outrageous legal tab to fight them. And his legal dogs dug up some pretty putrid bones in their past.

"The Burns own a duplex in North Bay Village. Way back when they were renting the apartment on the top floor when Bobby fell down the exterior stairway. They sued, and in the final settlement they got the place and rented it to one of the attorneys who represented them.

"Before that, they lived over in St. Pete. They had a three-year-old child. The kid had spinal bifida. One day the child disappears, and a year later her remains are discovered in a shallow grave up the coast. And in the meantime, the Burns have been busy setting up a non-profit corporation and appointing themselves its executives. They flew premium from coast to coast feeding those insatiable talk shows with their story: the heart-wrenching story of their missing daughter that turned into an even more morose story of losing their daughter to a sexual predator.

"You're not going to tell me they had anything to do with her disappearance?"

"No. Spence said there was no evidence to ever prove they had anything to do with it. But apparently their six-digit salaries at the foundation weren't enough. With a little creative accounting, the Burns were able to funnel a lot of money to an offshore account in Cayman *and* live a very opulent life on a waterfront place on Tampa Bay. But the accounting was a little too creative. When the forensic accountants were through, they had enough dirt on the Burns to have them quietly resign from their foundation, from the boards of half a dozen local charities, and skip town. They were an embarrassment, even for Florida. And sure enough, they resurfaced on Miami Beach."

"The Land of the Second Chance," Blackie added.

"That's a good name for it."

"Meyer Lansky might have been the first to apply it to Miami Beach. Or Capone, or one of our many local politicians in the last few decades. So what happened to Spence?"

"He went broke trying to take the offensive. He didn't stand a chance as the defendant in a civil trial in Miami. Juries dole out the doe, because they don't want to hex their chances one day on winning their own legal Lotto. The Burns got the insurance and the title to the Viking. Their duplex went to their attorneys for their fee."

"That's why I saw a 24/7 security guard at the finger pier of their slip when they got that boat."

"They were worried Spence might try to sink their happy ship."

"I would have."

"Spence was above that. Before he signed over the Viking, I told him to get behind the wheel and head out Government Cut and never look back. But he told me he wasn't going to run."

"So what did he do?"

"I told you he had retired – early – from Uniform, and as we all know they are in deep shit. He had already lost most of his pension. He decided to fly for a few more years. He was going to fly for a Guyana passenger airline. So he rode the jumpseat down to Georgetown to check it out. He called me after, told me that they had to buzz the runway to stop the pedestrians from crossing it so they could land. Nothing like buzzing a runway in an old 707. He shot himself three days after that trip."

"Not a happy ending."

"Time to start prepping this baby for touchdown."

Chapter 20:

Naughty, Nauti-Neighbors

In the afternoon, Dani headed over to *Elena*, José's boat, after having stopped by Blackie's Island Packet to gather what remained of the *Skipper's* evidence. José was gone, leaving her a note that he had to meet a client at his studio. She made herself a pot of tea and settled into the overstuffed cushions of the settee. José's boat was decorated in '30s period pieces, all Art Nouveau, not Art Deco, as he often reminded her. Awaiting his return, she sipped her tea as she examined the baggie of photos dredged from the bilge of Blackie's boat.

She couldn't help but question the absurdity of it. Why would Ted and his gang lure a homeless man to a public bar to execute him? Lure him into an alley at night on Biscayne Boulevard and stab him, now that was logical. No witnesses. No innocent bystanders. No manatee. Unless they were trying to make a statement. To tell someone something – and certainly not that poor old man.

She looked at the photos. She had also brought with her the photo she had lifted earlier. She knew that Blackie might realize that it was missing, and she couldn't live with herself if she destroyed it. She'd have to deal with the fallout when the discovery was made. She slid the photo in with the others, a joker in a deck of cards.

The only other item in the baggie was the old man's cell phone. She studied it. A cheap model, not a Nokia status symbol, just a functional piece of electronic equipment not often found in the possession of an elderly homeless man.

She powered it up and tried a simple 1-2-3 to get past the keyboard guard to his messages; he hadn't bothered to change it. She attempted to get to his mail but was denied. She tried to think of what the old man would have used for a passcode.

S-K-I-P. In on the first try.

Okay. She went to Messages and only one – a saved one – was there. It was brief, a woman's voice:

"Meet me at noon at the Barracuda Grill. And bring everything you've got with you."

Her voice was familiar, yet Dani couldn't put a name to it. She toggled over to the phone's address book but there wasn't a single name in the file. Either the Skipper had an incredible memory, or he had very few clients and friends.

She scrolled over to Recent Calls, and redialed the last number the old man would ever attempt on a cellphone – or any phone for that matter.

A woman's voice – a recording of the same voice – answered, gave the number and said to leave a message. Dani hung up. It was all beginning to connect.

She dialed the dockmaster's office at Te Cuesta Isle marina.

"Can you give me the number of Belinda Burns? It's Dani, I've got to talk to her about who they hired to adjust their compass." That was as good a line as any, Dani thought. Yul had said that for years a man trying to pass himself off as a certified compass adjuster frequently strolled down the docks memorizing the names and hailing ports at Te Cuesta Isle. Everyone figured that he was with the State of Florida Revenue Department, trying to nab out-of-state vessels that hadn't paid their Florida sales tax.

She scrolled to Recent Calls again, and the number the dockhand gave her matched the number on the cellphone. Fascinating.

How was that bitch Belinda Burns connected to this mess? She barely had time to pose the question when José stepped aboard.

"Why, *Daisy,* I see you've made yourself at home on the floating Gatsby mansion."

"Why *Jay,* come over here quick so I can put you in a pink cloud and push you around."

"Pink cloud? Was that in the novel?"

"Yes. Daisy said that in Gatsby's house the day they met again."

"Well, all I know is that when I sit in the cockpit of **Elena** staring across the water at your boat, all I see is a green light burning at the end of your dock."

"Touché."

"So tell me Dani, why do you look so worried?"

"Do you realize what's in this baggie? Do you realize what a mess Blackie is in?"

"From the look on your face, I believe you're about to tell me, *chica.*"

Dani held up the cellphone and explained.

José, trying to control his paranoia, exclaimed, "*Ay Dios Mio!* Who the hell is involved in this? Ted, The Twins *and* the Burns? Batten down the hatches!"

"Okay, okay. Calm down. We've got to come up with a plan here."

"Let's call Yul. He's a bigger target."

"Come on. Be real."

"Okay. You're right. We'll sit down and discuss this over dinner. I'll get in the galley and warm up a dish I have in the fridge that I made a couple days ago. What wine goes with *Ropa Vieja?*"

"José, I'm not that far along with my Spanish lessons, but you're going to serve old clothes?"

"Rags would be a better translation. It's cooked beef that you shred to look like rags in a tomato sauce. It's a very popular dish in Cuba."

"Sounds good. Why not serve it with that *Montes Alpha Malbec* I gave you? That's an incredible Chilean red wine."

"Sure. Retrieve it from my cellar."

Dani searched in a low compartment forward and found it in the third black sock she peeled. Like many wine-imbibing sailors, José kept his wines in a low locker and wrapped inside of old socks, dark for reds and pale socks for whites, wool condoms slipped over the bottles for protection.

"Do you have any idea, José, what The Twins do for Ted?" she asked as she studied the wine label. Grabbing her odd contraption from her daypack, she unsheathed its needle and rammed it into the cork. She pushed the small cylinder with her thumb and the cork popped out in one fluid motion.

José watched her ritual and commented, "Nice toy." Changing the subject, he asked, "Have you got those photos?"

Dani pulled out the stack and handed them to him. No need to hide.

José came upon The Twins in the third shot.

"Thank god they're naked. Otherwise they might have on those brown shirts of Hitler youth."

"I've never really met them. They showed up on the boat after I was long gone. So just who are they?"

"Ted's pets. I believe your *chico* called them the Pet Shop Boys. They're the Doublemint equivalent of the Filipino houseboy. With blonde hair. On steroids."

"They're gay?"

"No. They'll fuck anything that moves," Jose noted. "One night The Twins did try to get me to be in the middle of their whitebread sandwich."

"And you resisted?"

"I told you I don't care for fascists. But it would have been one hell of a *medianoche*."

"Well, it's obvious that Ted has them do all his dirty work."

"Such as kill old homeless men?"

"Probably," she said in dismay.

"That's something we need to find out. Are there any other shots of them?" José asked as he flipped through the remaining photos. He returned to one. The game was up. "And who have we here?"

"What?"

"Complete your question, Dani. More like 'What am I doing here?'"

"It's me."

"Nice ass. Haven't I seen this on the Internet?"

"You're a funny man, José."

"And you've got some explaining to do."

"I've been on that Breakwater, but it was a long time ago. One of many models to walk the gangplank."

"Gangplank — gangway - runway. It's all semantics."

"I guess the Skipper was keeping an eye on him, because his report is a decade old, but those photos were taken more than two years ago, one of the few times I was aboard."

"Did you know how Ted made his money?" José asked.

"I knew him after his viatical era. The insurance thing had dried up, and he was into importing X. He must have been the biggest importer of ecstacy on South Beach. And I might have been the biggest consumer."

"Ted. Into commodities markets. A true Renaissance Man."

"At one point I heard he had 300K of X a month coming in from Germany through Orlando. I did hear that the Twins got their start with him as a pair of his mules. Ted got out just before the feds got wise."

"And what's his newest venture?"

"When I finally straightened out, Ted was the last person I ever wanted to see. And of course we're neighbors now. Some of my old friends have told me that he made so much selling X that he was able to go legit."

"Legit? How?"

"He invested in SoBe real estate."

"Shit. Now I really hate the bastard."

The phone rang in Dani's backpack. It was Blackie, explaining how he was stranded in Port-au-Prince. Just as they were about to depart PAP, one of the ramp guys found a stowaway hiding in the wheel well of the 767. The resulting delay put the crew over the FAA-limit for flight time, causing them to go "illegal." Yet-another stranded crew from the day before was going to take Blackie's plane back later that evening, with Blackie deadheading home in a crew rest seat. But he wouldn't get back to the marina until the wee hours of the morning. Blackie hurriedly related The Captain's story about Spence and the Burns over a bad landline connection, since cellphones didn't work on that end of Hispanola. He asked her not to do anything until he returned.

"More developments?" José inquired, setting their plates down at the settee table.

"Blackie's stuck in Port au Prince. But the pieces of this puzzle are rapidly coming together," she said, telling him of the Burns' sordid past.

"So they were going to meet the old man at the grill?" José surmised.

"Yes. They must have somehow got wind of Ted's past and the *Skipper's* long-hidden report and were going to blackmail Ted with it. Their plan was probably to make that Breakwater *their* toy. Part of their grand plan."

"But Ted found out."

"Obviously."

"I don't think Ted is someone to mess with."

"Slime on slime. Like watching that video of the alligator and the anaconda battling it out in the Everglades."

"And our next move?"

"Eat dinner. Sit tight."

In silence they ate José's *Ropa Vieja* served with white rice and fried plantains, savoring it between sips of the Malbec.

"This is excellent, José."

"And a great wine to accompany it, Dani. So tell me. Exactly what went on over there on Ted's boat?"

"You don't want to know."

"Don't tell me you're afraid of shocking a gay arteest who hung out on Sunset Boulevard?"

"Hung out? No wonder you had to come back to Miami."

"Don't stray from the subject. And don't even think you can top me."

"Okay, it was decadent. Especially for a girl from a Dallas suburb. I look at myself – at my life now – and I feel as hypocritical as Madonna writing a children's book."

"The orgy thing?"

"What I can remember, yes."

"Only thing unique about that on South Beach is that you were on a $4-million waterbed."

"What was strange, or who was strange, was Ted. He had this powerful, magnetic attraction – "

"And a heaping crystal bowl of ecstacy."

"That helped. But he turned his magnetism into this power trip."

"S&M?"

"Yes, but even more than that. Fortunately it was a brief interlude in my life. I somehow survived intact."

"Dani, I think everyone – except maybe Mother Theresa and my great aunt over on Flagler Street – has experienced that foot-in-hell thing, even if it was only for a few moments."

"Part of life's experience," Dani surmised. "Although it's a regrettable part."

Dinner over, the dishes washed and drying in their teak rack, the two returned to the settee. José emptied his tin of dominoes and they played a couple rounds of the Cuban version of Mexican Train.

"You know I'm not letting you go back to your boat."

"I was hoping you'd say that."

"They certainly don't know I'm in your clique with Blackie and Yul. None of them. And I'm very happy you don't have a cat onboard that we have to go feed."

José changed the settee into a bed, his "Castro Convertible" as he called it, tucked Dani in and turned off the Tiffany sconce above her head.

"I'm in the master cabin if you need me."

"José, I'm lucky to have you as a friend."

"Same here, *chica*."

Chapter 21:

Bimini Bound

Someone was in the pitch-black cabin with her. She could hear the breathing, a rhythmic exhale. She tried to remain motionless, to not scream.

"It's me, *chica*," José whispered a few inches away.

"My God, José. You scared the shit out of me."

"Listen."

"What?"

"Can you hear that rumble? It's ***Ted's Toy***. They fired up the engines. We need to call the cops."

"And tell them what? That there's a curfew on million-dollar yachts starting their engines at Te Cuesta Isle Marina? What time is it?"

"Almost three. They're probably trying to escape."

"The cops can't do anything."

"Then call the Coast Guard. Homeland Security."

"Oh, so now they're your friends."

"Okay, then the Florida Marine Patrol."

"They'd never believe our story. What we should do is sneak over there and see what they're up to," Dani said.

"Sounds risky. But I'm willing to go with you."

José loaned Dani a black T-shirt and a pair of black cotton pants that she cinched up tight with a belt. He donned an identical outfit.

"We look like Viet Cong. When did this become fashionable?" she asked.

"I picked them up in Ho Chi Minh City on a vacation two years ago. Strange isn't it that we can visit there but we still can't go to Cuba?"

José handed her a pair of miniature binos and two small LED flashlights. She stuffed them into her daypack, put it on and said, "Let's go."

They crept off José's boat and up Pier Three toward the T-head. Ted had all the deck lights burning on the Breakwater, creating a curtain of light that would blind anyone onboard as a lookout.

"Let's get on that Scarab three slips down from *Ted's Toy* and watch," Dani proposed.

"That's someone's boat, Dani."

"It's *our* boat, you crazy – our government's. The DEA owns it. They seized it and keep it here to take DEA bigwigs out on junkets and such. No one's ever aboard."

"I'm going to end up on some watchlist."

"Come on."

They ran to the fingerpier and boarded, crawling to the opposite gunwale of the oversized speedboat.

"Gimme the binos," she ordered.

"When were you a Navy SEAL?"

"Get 'em. I see some movement on the bridge."

Dani focused on the high windows of the bridge and could see Ted and one of The Twins staring down at the chart table. Above them on the roof she saw the open-array radar slowly revolve.

"Does look like they're planning an imminent departure," Dani observed.

"So we can go to bed now?"

"No, let's go onboard."

"Onboard? Are you crazy, *chica*?"

"We have to find out what they're up to."

"Can't it wait till daylight?"

"They'll be gone. I know the layout of that Breakwater. There's lots of nooks and crannies we can hide in."

"So we just walk up the gangway?"

"No, we jump down on the swim platform while they're up front. At the top of the steps there's a door leading to the aft stateroom. Let's see what we can find in there."

"Probably whips, chains, maybe a captive or two. I'm not so sure."

"Come on. You've always wanted to be Errol Flynn, or at least act like him," Dani whispered. "Here's your big chance."

"Let me go put my pirate shirt on."

"No time for that."

Dani was about to crawl off the Scarab when a movement in the empty slip across the pier caught her eye. She grabbed José by the arm and pointed.

Two others in a dinghy motored up in the empty slip. They pulled alongside the finger pier and also surreptitiously watched *Ted's Toy*. She focused the binos on them.

"It's our friends Bobby and Belinda."

"Have they seen us?"

"No, I don't think so."

"Since when are they conspirators with Ted?"

"I don't know, but it looks like Bobby is getting out and heading over there."

They watched as Bobby walked up to the Breakwater and leaned out and passed an envelope to one of The Twins standing at the gunwale below the bridge. They watched Bobby come back and crawl down into the Burns' dinghy.

The couple departed, headed in the direction of *Grand Plan*. Their quiet four-stroke outboard couldn't be heard over the big diesels on the Breakwater.

"What were they up to, Dani?"

"I have a vague idea."

Dani turned her attention back to *Ted's Toy*. She counted three heads on the enclosed bridge, Ted and The Twins. She just hoped she wasn't seeing the image of one of Ted's boys in a mirror.

Dani crept out of the Scarab and José reluctantly followed. Fortunately it was a high tide, and they were able to lower themselves down onto the swim platform at the stern. They snuck up the winding steps and through a door into a passageway. They passed through another door to starboard and into the dark and expansive master stateroom. Danny stopped and retrieved a tiny LED flashlight from her pack and handed it to José.

He twisted it on and the tiny beam lit up the room.

"*Mira!* This cabin is as big as my boat," José exclaimed as he swept the beam from side to side. With all the walls and ceiling mirrored, the beam bounced back and forth to infinity.

"José, you keep a lookout. Anyone comes down that passageway, let me know. We can hide in the walk-in locker."

"Walk-in locker? *Ay Dios Mio!*"

Dani disappeared through a mirrored door. She reappeared moments later, her face ashen.

"There's two automatic weapons wrapped in beach towels in there. That's what Reggie told Blackie he saw smuggled aboard."

"That's it. We go to the police."

"I agree. This is way out of our league."

Before they could leave the stateroom there was a commotion on the stairs at the forward end of the passageway. Dani grabbed José and they ducked into the locker, closing the mirrored door. She cracked it open an inch to listen. One of The Twins passed by, talking on the handheld VHF. They heard him say he'd notify them when he pitched the aft lines on the dock.

"*Merda!* We're leaving," José whispered.

"I wonder where Ted would be going?" Dani calmly asked.

"We're about to find out. Are we going to stay in here? Is it safe?"

"Only one reason why I think so, José, and that's because we've got the guns."

Dani pulled the other flashlight out of the pack and turned it on.

José watched and then suddenly clutched her arm, a grin spreading across his face. "*Chica*, reach in there and get your phone out," José said. "We can call the Coast Guard."

"My phone's recharging on your settee."

"Oh."

"You got yours?"

"No. These pants were too tight for it to fit in my pocket."

"But we've got guns. Ever fired one of these?" Dani asked as she unwrapped the chrome-plated Mini Mac 10 from the towel.

"No. Be careful. The safety might not be on."

"Okay. We'll keep our fingers off the triggers. Unless absolutely necessary."

She handed José the other one, the AK-47, and they settled back in the corner of the locker, surrounded by Armani suits, Gucci loafers and an array of leather accessories, not for work, but for play. They were ready to make their final stand. They sat in silence, listening.

"Feel that?"

"That movement?"

"Hobby-horsing. We're heading out Government Cut. That's an inbound tide meeting a west wind. We're certainly not going up the Intercoastal," Dani surmised.

"You want to go commandeer this ship? We'll get them to surrender and call in a Mayday on the VHF."

"*Now* you want to be Errol Flynn. Does floating in the Gulf Stream always bring out the heroics in a *Cubano*?"

"Real funny. But this is something of a reverse migration. You don't think we're going to Cuba?"

"Who knows, José. Let's sit tight and not create a situation we can't get out of. When we dock we'll sneak off and call the authorities."

When the hobby-horsing subsided, the twin diesels were powered up and the Breakwater came out of the water onto a plane. The boat never made a turn, so Dani guessed out loud that they were headed east for the Bahamas.

José tried to get comfortable. As he fiddled with the cheap wood stock of the AK-47, he spoke, "To think that three years ago I was working at my studio in Laguna Beach. Getting ready for a show. And I was in what I thought was a long-term relationship."

"Meaning you're not enjoying our little adventure? Don't care for sharing a locker with me as a stowaway?"

"Sorry, *chica*, but no. I'm still trying to figure out why I ended up back in Miami. I gave it all up and came back here, of all places."

"Blackie and I have discussed it. He calls South Beach – Miami and all of South Florida, really – *The Land of the Second Chance*. Everyone's here escaping something."

"You're right. I was successful there in Orange County, successful beyond my wildest dreams. But I wasn't happy and escaped back here."

"Why? We've talked about many things, but never that. I didn't want to pry."

"I had a great thing going with someone there, but in the end our differences were too much to overcome."

"Tell me about it."

"He was rich. His name was Ron. He was a beautiful man, only a couple years older than me. Warm. Caring. Committed."

"Then what was the problem?"

"Somehow he was able to reconcile being gay and being a Young Republican. An *Orange County* Young Republican. Way up in the organization. One of the most conservative people I've ever met."

"He had no trouble reconciling his lifestyle with his politics?"

"No. He was born into wealth, and he loved his parents and they loved him unquestioningly. And they were – I don't know – *fiscally* conservative, too. When I first met him we discussed politics – argued would be the better word – all the time. But it was like trying to argue with one of the bow-tied neo-conservatives on the networks. You knew you weren't going to win an argument even if you saw him out with a Filipino diva in drag the night before."

"Was he open with everyone about you?"

"With his parents, yes. But I never went to any of the social functions with his conservative friends out of principle, which certainly avoided any problems for him."

"But I'd think the Young Republicans in Southern California are a little more liberal in their lifestyle than their counterparts in say, Dallas."

"Of course. Ron was a vegan. Yet I put oxtail in about every dish I make from beans to rice. To give it some flavor. We really didn't have much in common, did we?"

"You obviously did if you lived together."

José ignored the remark and plodded on. "His parents really are these warm, friendly people. They had an Oyster 66, a gorgeous cutter behind their home in Newport Beach. That's where I really got into sailing. They'd let us take it over to Catalina without them. And Ron sailed since he was a kid."

"So why did you leave?"

"I honestly don't know. Other than I was resisting being sucked into that two per cent of the population. The easy life of the elite."

"That's a strange but true statement, José. Considering that you gave that all up to be stuck on this boat with me."

José finally broke the silence with a question: "Ever wonder why we've both got boats?"

"Our escape vehicles from South Beach?" she replied.

"*Claro.* Exactly what I was thinking. For when it becomes unbearable. Face it, Dani, it *has* become unbearable. The pervasive rudeness, the shallowness, the megalomania.

The brief shelf-life of clubs, restaurants, residents. Only the sychophants sucking up to the next wave of the Nuevo-hip linger on. The place is so shallow it can never be anything more than ankle deep in trendy shit."

"You know that marine carpenter I hired to rework my nav station, José?" Dani asked. "He had his mobile shop in an old animal control truck he had repainted with a *faux*-Miami Beach seal on the doors that said 'South Beach Institute for the Criminally Trendy.' Under the screens in the back he had painted, 'Stay Back! Rabid Fashion Animals Inside!' It was hilarious."

"I remember that truck! I always thought it was for real, *chica*."

"You don't think this is a strange conversation for a SoBe model and a gay artist hiding on the yacht of a man who has never stood in line at a South Beach nightclub?"

"It is. I haven't told you, but when I went to my studio yesterday I had an appointment with yet another SoBe jerk interested in buying one of my paintings. He and his entourage arrived in three black Escalades. He's barely my age and he is a multi-millionaire. He lives in a palatial estate on a spoil island off the MacArthur Causeway. Know how he made his money?"

"Tell me."

He has a string of dot-coms pouring in the *dinero*. I did a little checking and hear he's worth close to $10 million."

"That's nothing new. He must have moved here from Seattle or San Jose."

"No. They're not that kind of dot.com. They're porn-based."

"Only in SoBe or LA," Dani replied.

"He got his break producing videos of women picked up in an SUV and banged by the video crew. Apparently all across America there is this insatiable desire by men who will pay online to see women degraded like that."

"I wasn't aware of it."

"After seeing the photo of you and Ted, I'm surprised you haven't."

"Not funny, José."

"God knows what that jerk paid those women for those little sex acts in the back seat of one of his Escalades – I only hope those Caddies have plastic seatcovers."

In LA they would have at least made scale, but probably not here in Miami," Dani observed.

"No, not much since most of them are – *como se dice* in English – I think the word is 'skanky.' He has expanded with more sites and more women willing to be forever recorded doing ever-more-degrading things. And he's apparently taken over the little mom-and-pop porn sites in most of Florida in what I think they'd call a 'hostile takeover,' *chica*."

"Muscled out the college co-eds and their web cams who were just trying to work their way through school?"

"He puts them under his umbrella for a percentage – or else. And the money that pours in goes to an offshore account in the Turks & Caicos."

"Another revered entrepreneur of the New Millenium."

"He's invested wisely back here in a SoBe restaurant. And become the new darling of the local late-night party scene."

"Only in South Beach do those types get their picture taken with the mayor, have streets named after them and treated with legitimacy – until their indictment. So who is this guy? Surely I've heard of him."

"William Buddho. But he goes by Billy Buddho. He's about to be our new neighbor at Te Cuesta Isle – at least that's what he told me yesterday at my studio."

"I saw him at PickAx and have seen his name on one of the local 'Celeb-Suck-Up' blogs. He's disgusting. How many cosmetic procedures do you think he's had?"

"Ten or twelve."

"What's up with that? Another phony bastard pumped full of plastic goo."

"Aren't we a little harsh there, *chica*? They're just trying to buy what God bestowed on you."

"They don't need to do that. Feeding an industry making millions off of their megalomania," Dani observed. "Why would anyone want to look like me? Do you realize the number of times I've been creeped out by somebody hitting on me at Starbucks? Having to deal with that. It bothers me and always will."

"It is a strange world, *chica*."

"So this Buddho, he's moving on a boat?"

"No, just parking his new toy on the outside pier. A 110-foot Diaship-Heesen named *A Fist Full of Dollars*. I won't even begin to tell you what genre of his porn videos that refers to."

"Even more disgusting. That yacht's bigger than Ted's. Maybe that's really why Ted is leaving."

"And with us as captives, *chica*. One of my moles told me that Ted actually invested some of the seed money in Billy Buddho's video venture."

"That figures. So did you sell this Buddho any of your paintings?"

"I don't have a price tag hanging from any of my works," José said with a wry smile. "And the thought of one of them hanging in his palm-lined villa was repulsive, so when I saw he was interested in one of my favorites, I doubled it."

"And?"

"After it's framed, we'll deliver it next week."

"You'll have to tell Blackie that one."

"Speaking of your pilot, what's up with you two? You have a good time on your mini-cruise?"

"It was – *interesting*. I don't know, José. He's fun to be around. But I'm just not sure we're meant for each other."

"What don't you like about him?"

"He's so here and now. He never talks about his past. When I try to prod him, he gives me snippets – like he's reading from his resumé. "

"Such as?"

"I know he's never been married and he has no kids. And that he's flown a plane for 15 years. But I know so little else about him."

"Do you really need to know?"

"He knows all about me. The situation with my parents. My escaping here –"

"Your party days on South Beach?"

"That really didn't last too long, thank god. I just don't know where he and I are headed, or if we're headed anywhere together."

They fell into silence and settled in for the passage. At 20 knots, the Breakwater would be at Bimini in less than three hours. They decided to try half-hour watches so each of them could get a little sleep. Neither captive on the Breakwater had any idea that a Viking motor yacht was heading out Government Cut on a course for an eventual rendezvous with the Breakwater.

Dani jerked awake the instant the steady rumble of the big Caterpillar diesels eased. She poked José, fast asleep on his watch. He mumbled something and looked at her.

"Good thing I'm not the master-at-arms, or you'd be flogged. You were snoring, José."

He embraced his AK-47 and sang that old song softly, trying to wake up, "'Hap-pi-ness is a warm gun.' We've slowed down?"

"Yes. It's about time to be at Bimini or West End."

"Dani, you have your passport?"

"Not something I walk around with in this pack, and not like I knew we were going to come here. But of course you're used to entering without documents – a cultural thing."

"I see you worked in the rafter bit again."

"You know I'm just kidding. Ever been to Bimini before?"

"No. Planned to do my first Bahamas cruise on *Elena* in May. And you?"

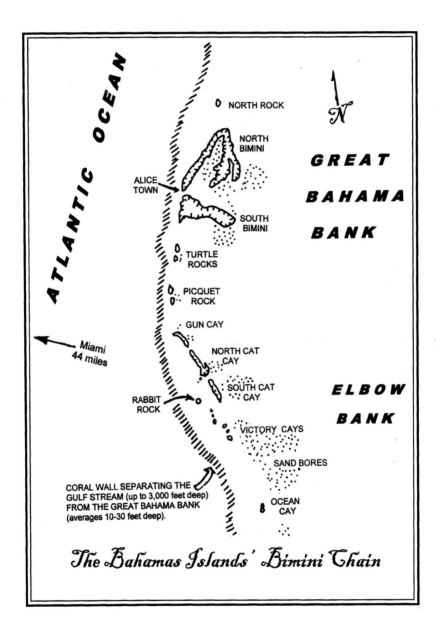

The Bahamas Islands' Bimini Chain

"Once, passing through. If this is Bimini and if Ted clears in, he'll do it at Alice Town. Only real town in Bimini."

"They have police?"

"They've got an Immigrations guy and a Customs guy, and a few young men in those snazzy, starched white uniforms that patrol the town on golf carts," she said.

"Could be a fun vacation."

"Let's peek out a porthole. Ted and his boys will be busy preparing to dock and won't be coming down here."

The pair crept out into the dark cabin. Dani searched for the hidden door handle to the master head. She finally found it and opened it, and the light of dawn poured into the room.

She peered out the porthole, adjusting her eyes to the light. She wasn't looking at South Bimini as she expected, but out toward the cobalt blue water of the Gulf Stream.

"We're heading south, right?" José volunteered.

"How'd you know?"

José held up the tiny LED flashlight. On the end of it was a miniature compass.

"You nauti-boy, you. I'm afraid we're heading away from Alice Town. We must be going into Cat Cay – what's technically North Cat Cay."

"To clear in?"

"There's a fancy marina there for the Cat Cay Club. They have one rotating bureaucrat who sits in a tiny cottage and does both Immigrations and Customs. The island is very exclusive."

Dani had sailed over on Blackie's Island Packet the year before on their way to the Berry Islands. Non-member boaters were permitted to clear into the Bahamas at North Cat's marina for a fee, but they were restricted to the adjacent bar and restaurant and couldn't wander around the island.

"Any police on North Cat?"

"A security guard. Only a few members are there at any given time. You wait here," Dani ordered, "I'm going to go look out the other side."

She tiptoed out of the master cabin and down the passageway before ducking into a portside guestroom. In a smaller head, she looked out the porthole and saw what was left of the crumpled tower built by the DEA on uninhabited Gun Cay. Next to it was the ruined shell of the Bahamian Defense Force barracks, also blasted by Andrew, and down from that the nicely painted and restored Gun Cay lighthouse.[11]

She waited for Ted to turn the yacht to port and head through the cut toward the marina on the eastern shore of North Cat Cay. The yacht motored past the cut, still heading south. She watched the expensive retreats pass by, all built in a low, hurricane-proof bunker-style. The vacation homes were tucked in dense stands of coconut palms and fronted by a golden beach. José joined her in the port-side head.

"We're not clearing in at Cat either," she told him.

"Where's he taking us?"

"If he has the tanks topped, probably wherever he wants to go."

The big Breakwater continued to glide down the coast. Dani and José decided to move themselves and their arsenal to the portside guestroom, so they could monitor their progress. There was also less chance of being discovered, since The Twins must have been quartered in the crew cabins forward.

Dani saw an outcropping of reddish rocks at the end of North Cat Cay pass abeam, and uninhabited South Cat Cay and its beautiful beach appear in the distance. After skirting a rock barely poking above the surface, the boat finally turned east. Clearing the tip of South Cat, the Breakwater rounded up to the north on the island's eastern shore.

The big diesels were idled. Dani didn't hear the splash of the stainless steel anchor forward, but she could hear the rumble of the heavy chain over the gypsy. Dani looked out at an empty anchorage, and told José that from the amount of scope let out on the chain, they were in fairly deep water for a

---

[11] Off Gun Cay light, Bimini Chain, 25 34.45N, 79 18.15W.

Bahamian anchorage – twenty feet at least.   The props, in reverse, gently pulled the yacht back, and they could feel the big boat tug on the hook, setting it.[12]

Finally silence. They were in the Bahamas, not officially, and anchored in a nice hidey-hole on the end of a deserted cay. On her own boat, Dani would have been thrilled. But under the current circumstances – being undiscovered stowaways on a yacht with some very nasty men – she knew this was not going to be a cruising vacation.

---

[12] Dollar Harbour anchorage, off South Cat Cay, 25 31.46N, 79 15.51W.

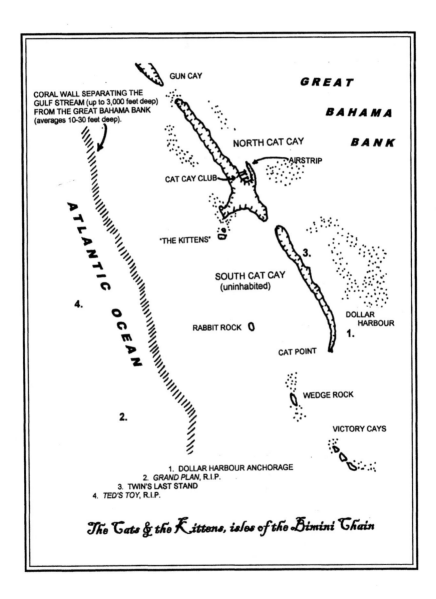

GUN CAY

CORAL WALL SEPARATING THE
GULF STREAM (up to 3,000 feet deep)
FROM THE GREAT BAHAMA BANK
(averages 10-30 feet deep).

GREAT

BAHAMA

BANK

NORTH CAT CAY

AIRSTRIP

CAT CAY CLUB

"THE KITTENS"

SOUTH CAT CAY
(uninhabited)

ATLANTIC OCEAN

4.

RABBIT ROCK O

3.

DOLLAR
HARBOUR

1.

CAT POINT

WEDGE ROCK

2.

VICTORY CAYS

1. DOLLAR HARBOUR ANCHORAGE
2. *GRAND PLAN*, R.I.P.
3. TWIN'S LAST STAND
4. *TED'S TOY*, R.I.P.

The Cats & the Kittens, isles of the Bimini Chain

Chapter 22:

Dollar Harbour Showdown

Dani and José took turns peeking out of the porthole while the other trained a gun on the locked door to the passageway.

"Inviting looking island, Ms. Crusoe. Perhaps we should dive in and swim ashore," José observed, scanning the part of South Cat visible through the oval of glass.

"It's uninhabited. Just a jungle of coconut palms and grapeleaf trees surrounded by a coral sand beach. We dinked over here for a picnic while berthed at the Cat Cay Club last year."

"We could live off the coconuts. Eventually someone would rescue us."

"I agree it'd be safer than here."

They heard a commotion in the passageway and muffled talking through the walls. The noise faded into the aft master stateroom. Dani put her ear to the guestroom door and could hear The Twins shouting.

"The guns are gone!"

"Those assholes got them!" added the other.

Louder, closer, Ted cursed, "Those fucking Burns have been aboard! They took them to even up the playing field when we meet. How did you two idiots let this happen?"

The Twins said nothing.

"We've still got the shotguns and the Glocks. They're under the bench on the bridge. We need to be ready for them, you fools."

Ted's berating of his crew faded down the passageway. Dani stepped back from what she realized was an unlocked door.

"Are they looking for us?" José asked.

"No. I think they're preparing for a rendezvous. With the Burns it sounds like."

"They're all in this together?"

"No, like I said, I think the Burns are trying to cut some deal with Ted. All part of the Burns' blackmail of Ted. Part of their grand plan."

"I still can't believe they'd mess with Ted."

"I don't think they care. Greed can blind you."

"And we're stuck in the middle of it."

"If they get involved in some meeting," Dani said, "We'll try to sneak off and swim ashore and get up to North Cat Cay for help. We can't let these bastards get away."

"Someone has to stop them."

"José, if we could get to the radio we could try to get some help."

"Storm the bridge?"

"No, Ted told The Twins he has another arsenal up there. So they're still armed."

"Any other options?"

"Let's check out the other guestroom. I think I remember Ted converted it to an office. Maybe he has a handheld VHF in there."

They crept forward to another stateroom and entered. Along the forward bulkhead was a built-in desk with an array of electronic gear. *Ted's Toy* had all the latest toys, including a multi-station electronics system, with its instruments neatly fitted into a teak cabinet above the desk. An LCD display combined the radar, sonar and chartplotter info all on one screen and was a duplicate of the screen on the bridge. Dani turned on the instrument and pointed at the full-color chart of South Cat Cay. A blinking boat showing *Ted's Toy* at anchor in Dollar Harbour, thanks to the GPS.

"Nice toy, Dani. At least now I have a fix on where we're at."

"If we get to shore, José, we can run up South Cat – that's less than two miles – and swim over to North Cat for help," she said, running her finger up the image on the screen.

"Sounds like our only option."

"Here's the thing I'm after," Dani said, pointing at a compact, but high-end, fixed-mount VHF radio tucked into the cabinet. "This is probably a stand-alone unit with it's own antennae, in case the one at the helm gets fried by lightning."

She opened another cabinet door and pointed at another VHF, a handheld plugged into its charger.

She turned on the fixed-mount unit, keeping the volume low.

"Don't you think they've got theirs on up on the bridge?" José asked.

"Probably. If we call out a Mayday or anything on 16, we'll have to get off of here fast."

Beside the VHF was another communications device, not nautical, with a small speaker built into it. Dani, without hesitating, reached over and turned it on.

"Be careful, *chica*, you're going to give us away."

She pushed a few buttons and adjusted the volume knob. The voice of Ted came over the speaker: " – we've still got a couple hours before those pricks show up. I want you two to be ready for them."

"An intercom?" José inquired.

"So the owner can eavesdrop on the bridge and listen in on the hired help, including the captain," Dani replied. "One of the perks of owning a $4-million vessel. I'm sure he has a mike in the crew quarters, too, so he can hear The Twins talk about how much they despise him."

"Right now this toy can really help us."

"José, you stand watch and let me know if there's movement out there. We need time to get this stuff turned off and hide before they come in."

"*Si*, sergeant."

Dani sat and listened. Ted was on a rampage.

"I pay you assholes to do one thing: provide me with a little security. And you can't even keep the Burns – a couple of scumbags – off my boat. You did wipe those guns clean with a wet wipe, didn't you?"

"Twice. And we wrapped them back in the towels like you said."

"I ought to make you stupid shits swim back to Miami."

Ted paused and then continued his verbal whipping.

"You fucking kill innocent bystanders. *And* a *manatee!* You fuck-ups blow up two boats, kill cops and some fools in robes, and let this pair of shitheads try to cheat me out of my boat! Damn, I don't know why I let you two hang around."

Dani heard a garbled transmission over the VHF speaker and turned up the volume.

"***Black Peter, Black Peter,*** this is ***Flying Fortress. Black Peter, Black Peter,*** this is ***Flying Fortress,***" the familiar voice hailed. It couldn't possibly be him, Dani thought.

No response.

"Roger, going to six-niner."

Dani was overjoyed in that moment before panic set in. She fumbled with the knob trying to get to channel 69.

"***Black Peter,*** this is ***Flying Fortress.***"

Another pause.

"Hey Blackie, headin' back north." Dani's mind raced. Cap'n Dick and Blackie were talking to each other on the VHF, but she could only hear Cap'n Dick overhead. She had to let them know where she was.

"***Flying Fortress, Flying Fortress,*** break for ***Carpe Diem.*** Break for ***Carpe Diem.***"

"*Black Peter*, standby, I've got someone breaking in. Go ahead *Carpe Diem*."

"Dick, it's Dani. We probably don't have much time. Just tell Blackie I'm on the big Breakwater over at Dollar Harbour, South Cat Cay."

"Dani, what are you doing over there? You two have a fight?"

"None of that. Please, just tell him before you lose him."

"Roger. Standby. *Black Peter*, Dani's on the big Breakwater over at Dollar Harbour, South Cat Cay, do you copy?"

A long pause.

"Roger that. He heard me Dani. He wants to know if you're alright and what he should do."

"Tell him I'm okay. Tell him I'll try to get to the marina on North Cat Cay."

Another pause.

"Cap'n Dick, did you copy?"

No answer.

"*Flying Fortress*, do you copy?"

Cap'n Dick and her connection to Blackie were gone.

Dani and José listened, but there was nothing from the radio or the intercom. She finally hit the button that put the VHF back on 16, the hailing channel. Not a word came from the bridge. Finally they heard Ted's voice growing louder as he returned to the helm. He was still reprimanding The Twins. They must have all gone out on deck before Cap'n Dick came over the radio. They obviously had missed the exchange.

"At least someone knows where we're at, *chica*."

"But what does Blackie really know? He doesn't know we're in trouble."

"He can probably figure that out and get us some help," José replied.

"And call the Coast Guard? We're in Bahamian waters. The Bahamians haven't had anyone here since Andrew other than a couple federal inspectors. No one with a fast boat and a gun."

"Blackie's bound to do something."

"We better sit tight. I'll monitor the intercom and you guard the door."

Dani could hear people moving around on the bridge, but there was little talking. Finally, Ted spoke.

"What I don't get is why these Burns dumbshits made me come all the way to Dollar Harbour for this little summit meeting. That stupid-ass Bobby Burns dropping off that letter last night was absurd. Those two have been watching way too much TV."

"We're sure in a secluded place, if that's what they wanted," one of The Twins volunteered.

"They're about to find out how secluded," Ted replied.

"When they come aboard why don't we just eliminate the problem?"

"You'll clean up the blood? No. One day they'd find a single, dried drop you missed, do a DNA test and that's it. Plus, I want to meet with them. See who else is involved."

"So you'll do lunch and they leave?"

"I'll find out what they want. And if we do any problem solving, we'll do it on their Viking. Understood?"

"Aye, aye, Capitan," The Twins replied in unison.

Dani wondered just how ruthless the competition was. Could those slimy Burns compete with Ted and The Twins? Like the anaconda and the alligator, this was to be a fight to the death.

Ted's demeanor changed as he planned the menu for their liason. "We'll have prawns, caviar and toast points accompanied by a little *Perrier Joet Fleur de Champagne*. The Brut Rose. The pink flower-bottle. Let them toast to the good life before their lives end."

"Assholes," one of Twins added.

"You two help me get the dinghy down, and then I'll go take a shower," Ted ordered.

José was peering out the guest head when an electric motor began to hum overhead. A rubber tube bumped against the porthole a few inches from José's face. He jumped back in a fright.

"*Ay Dios Mio!* What is that?"

"The dinghy, you dummy. They said they were putting it in the water. They're using the davit above us."

"Give me a heart attack!"

"We better get back in the locker. Ted said he is coming down to his stateroom for a shower."

Dani turned off the radios and motioned to José. She opened the bulkhead door and they squeezed into the smaller walk-in locker, still clutching their weapons.

"I'm really enjoying the Bahamas. Wonderful beaches," José chided inside their makeshift cell.

"Not exactly like they describe it in **Cruising World**."

They heard the door to the cabin open. They sat in silence, barely breathing, ready to shoot whoever opened the locker door. After a few moments the outer door to the passageway closed.

"Shit. I wasn't trained for this. I'm an artist, *chica*. I'm not sure my heart can handle much more."

"Close your eyes and imagine them dumping your body over the gunwale. That will give you some resolve."

"I haven't been this frightened since we came over from Cuba. Back in '89."

"You've never told me about your first Gulf Stream crossing before."

"My only trip on the Straits of Florida until now. I was only eight. We lived on Cayo Coco, an island on the northeast side of Cuba. I remember how beautiful the beaches were. So much better than Miami's. But my father just couldn't stay. He couldn't stand it anymore.

"Sixteen of us left on an old wooden sailboat and headed north. We had no motor and not much food. But we did pick a very good time to set out."

"Why?"

"It was a couple days before the Panama Invasion, December of '89. Our wind had died and we were drifting off the Cay Sal Bank when the largest ship we'd ever seen comes steaming right down on us," José recalled. "It was the United States Navy. One of those monstrous new troop ships out of Norfolk filled with tanks and buses and hundreds of soldiers, all in battle gear.

"They stopped dead in the water, and the ship opens up and a motorboat zooms over with food and water. They ended up taking us kids over to the ship until the Coast Guard cutter arrived."

"That must have been exciting."

"You wouldn't believe. I had always heard about America and here was this huge ship with bus loads of soldiers in high-tech gear picking us up and saving us. Welcome to the United States!"

"Different from home?"

"They had everything. They showered us with candy bars. They were really nice to us. Showed us around the ship. It was great. I almost hated getting on the Coast Guard boat for the ride to Key West."

"So after a story like that, how can you still be a communist, or a socialist? A follower of Ché?"

"From what I remember of our island, other than its beauty was the pace. It was a much simpler life. When we came here, we already had family here, and they were very successful. They were at the top of a home-products pyramid scheme that targeted Latinos. We went from poverty to working for – actually sponging off of – affluent relatives. But I just never fit in. I was the rebellious artist, even as a boy. And I just never bought into suburbia and the Greed-as-God, American-dream thing."

"That's not the opinion expected of a rafter."

"Those soldiers on that ship were so nice to me. But a couple days later they were invading a foreign country. They still don't have an accurate account of how many civilians were killed in Panama. As a kid I lived under oppression, but that's not going to make me embrace capitalism, imperialism and consumerism at all costs and without question."

"Two boatees living off South Beach saying they're fed up with hedonism – that's different."

"It is."

"I'm tired of this whole scene myself," Dani added. "You know I have a goal. This hedonistic place is just a passing phase."

"Your goal is to sail your boat to Chilé and make wine? Not that realistic, but a noble cause."

"And you?"

"I'll sail *Elena* to Cuba when it opens up. Do whatever I can to keep the island from being overrun with McDonalds and KFCs. Start a Sierra Club chapter. Do what I can to keep the exploitation in check. I have no doubt that within ten or fifteen years Cuba will be the fifty-first state, and they'll probably make Miami the state capital and rename Havana 'Little Miami.'"

"You said it, not me. And that's the power of a voting block. I'll try to remember your prediction. But we have to deal with this situation first."

Chapter 23:

Across The Stream

Back at Te Cuesta Isle, Blackie shouted into the VHF mike, but Cap'n Dick was heading north, out of range. The last words from him were that Dani was trying to make her way to Cat Cay Marina, and that she was okay.

He reviewed his options: Fly there. Go to Tamiami airport and rent a plane and fly to Cat Cay. But the airstrip on Cat was short, only VTOL aircraft could land there. He could land at South Bimini, but then he would still need to take a boat down to Cat and all that could take hours. He could fly on the Chalks seaplane to Alice Town, but even if they still had a flight, by the time he cleared in and took a boat over *Ted's Toy* could be long gone.

He could charter a floatplane out of Fort Lauderdale. But he had heard on the radio about a fatal accident on I-95 involving an animal control truck and a gasoline tanker. Although the fatalities were all crispy critters, they reported that the freeway was closed in both directions until noon when a forensic veterinarian and video crew from an Animal Planet reality-TV show arrived. Besides, what could he do when he got to Cat Cay? Land beside the Breakwater and swim over?

Powerboat? He poked his head out and looked across the marina. A weekday, all his powerboat neighbors were absent as usual. The only person stirring on the docks was Yul out on the T-head. He headed over for Yul's advice.

Yul was carrying aboard a cooler when Blackie walked up. "Hey, Blackie. See you made it back from Haiti in one piece."

"Yeah, a fun trip. Are you heading out again?"

"Great wind. I'm going to go troll out in the Stream. Kings are running."

"You're one of the few people I know who sail-fish. Yul, we've got to talk. I just found out that Dani's over off Cat Cay on *Ted's Toy*."

"Did she defect to the other side?"

"No, I think she was doing some investigative work for me and got caught. Or she's just a stowaway. She said she was alright and was heading to Cat Cay Marina. I need to go get her."

"Did she call you on Ted's satphone?"

"No, long story."

"You going to fly over?"

"I thought about it. But that doesn't look possible."

"Take your Island Packet over?"

"Too slow. I need a powerboat."

"I don't think anybody's here," Yul said, searching the marina for signs of life. "And there's nothing big enough at the rental place."

"I know. And my pilot buddies with their stinkboats are all up north of Lighthouse Point, so forget them."

"Why not take *The King & I*?"

"Sail over on your tri?"

"Why not? Winds are forecast to pick up out of the south at 15 to 20 knots. It would be a bit rough for a powerboat but perfect for this thing. We'd fly over there. We could be there in three hours."

"Is she ready to go?"

"Go get your passport, a light wetsuit and some dry clothes. And a change of underwear, 'cause you're gonna shit when I get this thing moving."

Less than a half-hour later, *The King & I* was motoring through the drawbridge on the east end of the Venetian Causeway. Yul stood and waved at the bridge tender, who came over Channel 13 and said, "Yul honey, you be careful out there today."

Instead of making the big circle around Watson Island near downtown, Yul made a beeline for the fixed bridge by the Coast Guard station.

"What are you doing, Yul? That bridge is only 25 feet high. You'll lose your mast."

"Where have you been? I've told you before about my little invention. You steer us toward that bridge."

Yul went forward and released the running forestay. The mast pivoted on a hinge on the deck and slowly lowered. At a predetermined point Yul stopped releasing the line and secured the stay.

They passed under the bridge with two feet to spare.

"That saved us an hour, Yul. Why did I not know you had a tabernacle mast?"

"You've never sailed with me before. I think I'm the only one with this boat to have it."

"It does come in handy."

"Pisses me off that I have to motor all the way down to the turning basin and back to get to the ocean. I have no idea why the bastards didn't make that bridge a 65-footer to begin with," Yul said, going forward to lead the running forestay back to a mast winch and crank the stick upright.

"I'll take back over. You go get on your wetsuit and put on a PFD. We're in for some fun."

Blackie went below and changed into the neoprene overalls and put on an unobtrusive inflatable life vest.

They motored out of Government Cut, passing a huge Maersk container ship in that narrow space between the jetties of South Beach and Fisher Island.

As soon as they cleared the point, Yul motored south out of the channel and pointed into the wind. They unfurled the jib and raised the main. Blackie turned the tiller and the boat fell off, pointing east-southeast, and the Corsair began to pick up speed.[13]

"Shit, Yul, we forgot about Elvis. You don't have the papers for him to enter the Bahamas."

"If we do clear in, they could come aboard and tear this boat apart and never find him."

"That blob of fat?"

"I guarantee you they'd never find him."

The wind freshened out of the south, and the Corsair shot forward on a plane. Blackie was tearing along at a speed he thought was impossible on a sailboat.

"We're going to get pretty wet," Yul shouted. "I have the GPS in a holder down there. Stick your head in and tell me what it says."

Blackie checked the GPS again for their speed over ground. "Yul, it says 18 knots! I've never seen that on a sailboat before! This is exhilarating!"

Blackie had spent his sailing life aboard displacement hulls, on boats that could make nine knots at best. A planing trimaran in the right conditions could do more than twice that.

"The seas are a little confused here, Blackie. We're in a reverse eddie, but when we get to the western wall of the Stream, you'll see what this boat can really do."

When they hit that river of saltwater, the ocean's hue turned a deep, cobalt blue. With the wind and water in sync, the waves evolved into a long, rolling swell. At the top of each swell, Blackie could look back and see the high-rise condos on South Beach barely poking above the horizon. The boat tore along, ripping through the water without an engine's roar.

"Now check our speed!" Yul shouted above the squeaks and groans of the tri as it flew over the water.

"Twenty two! Shit, I love this," Blackie yelled back.

---

[13] Out Government Cut, 25 45.35N, 80 70.54W.

"Scope that out!" Yul said as he nodded forward. An open-bow sportfish with a pair of 150s was up ahead, obviously on their way to Bimini. In the rough seas the powerboat had throttled back to keep from pounding the passengers. The trimaran was closing the gap.

"We're passing them, Yul! Why you crazy son-of-a-bitch!"

Alongside the sportfish, Blackie was able to see the shocked look on the face of the captain as they passed by. The captain tried in vain to throttle up, but the increased power only caused the powerboat to become more airborne.

"This is a damn first!" he shouted as a wave of spray covered him.

"Blackie, there's a new class of big trimarans that they water-ski behind. I've seen the video."

"I can't believe this is the first time I've ever been on this boat with you."

"Pisses Elvis off to give up his crew spot. He doesn't like company. But this is an emergency."

"You've got your shotgun onboard, don't you?"

"I'm an ex-cop with the typical love of weaponry. I've got enough firepower to invade South Cat and declare it a Banana Republic – a suburb of Miami!"

"Glad you do. I 've got nothing onboard as you know."

"I think you're the exception. I believe that's why there's a minimum of theft at marinas in Miami. They think us liveaboards are all armed to the teeth. And most of us are."

They lapsed into silence, the wind and its effects the only sound. Spray doused the cockpit as they hurtled easttward on top of the waves. What a beautiful way to cross the Stream, Blackie mused. As the boat crested a swell, he saw to the south a container ship heading up the Stream, only to disappear in the trough, then reappear closer off the starboard amas.

"Are we going to clear that thing, Yul?"

"No, I'll edge into the wind a little," he shouted back.

Eventually the ship rose like a giant wall ahead, the containers stacked on deck in a line ten long by six high. Blackie hoped that one didn't tumble off in the swell.

The tri cleared the stern of the giant vessel much too close for Blackie's comfort. When the ship's wake hit the boat, the tri went airborne for a few seconds before plunging down the wave. Yul's response was a big "whoop" and a laugh.

Blackie ducked below as they returned to course. He checked out the GPS; they were already a third of the way there, with an ETA of just under two hours. He prayed that Dani was still there.

Chapter 24:

A Symbiotic Relationship

After what José said seemed like a life sentence in a Cuban jail cell, the two crawled out of the locker. Dani turned on the intercom, while José crept into the head to look out.

"I see a dinghy coming this way. Off a big sportfish-boat that's just come in and anchored. Looks like the Burns," José announced.

Dani listened to the intercom as Ted gave instructions on the bridge.

"Okay you two, keep the guns out of sight. I'll find out what they want and tell them I'll think about it, and then you follow them back to their boat and solve the problem. Nothing happens until then. Got it?"

"Sure," one of The Twins responded.

"Who wants to do it?"

"Hans got to plant the bomb on the monks' boat. It's my turn," Klaus said with glee.

"After that fiasco, it most certainly is your turn."

"Bitchin'!"

"I'll be giving you all your orders over the radio on 72. Stay on low power. Just do what I say. No fuck-ups, and don't get creative."

"Yeah, yeah."

Dani and José heard the footsteps heading aft along the gunwale overhead. Then more steps heading forward, toward the dining area, or salon. Dani flipped the intercom knob to "SALON" to eavesdrop on the meeting.

Ted's voice: "Ah, the Burns. Welcome aboard."

Dani couldn't hear their answer.

"Hans, set out the prawns and the caviar and the toast points."

A cork popped, and over the intercom she heard the distinct clink of heavy lead-crystal flutes.

"To your landfall in the Bahamas. Have you cleared in yet?" Ted asked.

"No, we're flying our quarantine flag like you," Bobby Burns replied.

"Remember you've got 24 hours before you must clear in," Ted lectured in a condescending tone.

"We know that," Belinda replied testily.

"So let's cut the crap. What is it you want?"

"To be honest, Ted, it's your yacht," Belinda replied, taking charge of their side of the negotiations.

"You want my boat? But it's not for sale."

"We were hoping to barter, Ted. We trade you the Viking and some very incriminating information for the Breakwater. You'll still have a nice floating home and your real estate in South Beach."

"And just what info comes with the Viking?"

"How you made your seed-money in South Beach. By killing young men with big life insurance policies that they signed over to you."

"The money I made off my investments in the viaticals business is common knowledge. Old stuff. I've been out of it for years."

"People may have made 'legitimate' money off gambling on the deaths of AIDS victims, Ted, but there isn't a statute of limitations on murder, " Belinda replied.

From the silence Dani figured Ted had no reply.

"And what's that in your hand?" Ted finally asked.

"A report I believe you've been looking for – at least the original of this."

Dani heard nothing over the speaker for a long time. Finally she heard what she thought was a sheaf of papers slapping the table.

"There's nothing in there for me to worry about."

"Taken alone, probably not. But with this it's another story."

"You've brought movies," Ted said with measured sarcasm.

"And guess who's the director of this comedy," Belinda responded.

Dani was furious that Ted hadn't installed security cameras on the boat. She could only listen and deduce what cards Belinda was playing.

"Nice clip of the incident at the grill," Ted finally said. "So you bastards were there after all. I always figured you were in it with that goddamn pilot."

"These tiny digital recorders do a great job, don't they? Imagine what we could make just off the video sales of the execution to tabloid TV," Belinda said. "And of course what you're seeing here is a very good copy."

"Looks like the blooper reel. The Twins royally fucked up their mission, didn't they? It all would have worked if I had known the pilot was in with you on this blackmail thing."

"He wasn't."

"What do you mean he wasn't?"

"We figured out the pilot just happened to pick up the old man and take him to the grill. The old man must have given him the report and he hid it on his boat. We searched his boat and nabbed it when he was away."

"And you hid out and recorded this at the grill?" Ted inquired.

"We saw them drive up and waited to see what that pilot and the old man were up to. We don't know him. Bobby had brought the digital recorder to secretly tape my meeting with the old man, but ended up recording that mess your boys made out on the patio," Belinda said.

"I'm just glad one of them didn't shoot me by accident," Bobby interjected.

"Well, I'm not," Ted replied. "How did you two ever get wind of that report in the first place?"

"It's hard to keep a secret at a homeless shelter. That old man was sick and dying and had to tell somebody about what he knew but never acted on."

"Why didn't he give the info to the family?"

"Ten years ago the parents wanted to bury the secret that their son was terminally ill with AIDS. They dropped the ball, refused to pay him."

"And how did you find out?"

"We heard about it from the old man's cot-mate at the homeless shelter. He was working at a boatyard up the Miami River where we hauled the Viking. Connecting with that old man cost us a case of Bud."

"And what was he going to charge you?"

"He thought we were relatives belatedly seeking vindication. I believe he would have given it to us, if that pilot and your boys hadn't showed up."

"And the pilot had nothing to do with this?"

"Not a thing," Belinda answered emphatically. "But I have to ask you, how did you know we were to meet the old man at the grill?"

"Ask your husband, Mrs. Burns," Ted replied. "Loose lips . . . "

Silence.

"He was bragging a little too loud to one of the dockhands at the pool."

Finally Belinda spoke:

"So here's the proposal, Ted. You know of course we have copies of all this. But we're willing to make a deal. We follow you to George Town in the Caymans and we transfer the boats, since both of them are registered there. And we motor off into the sunset. French Polynesia to be exact. You lose about 30 feet of boat length but not everything. You go home and resume your life as a cog in the party wheel of South Beach."

"How in the world could you afford to maintain this thing? There's a reason they call it a Breakwallet," Ted pompously added in an increasingly anxious tone.

"We've got a few accounts earning interest over in the Caymans."

"What about the pilot?"

"If *Ted's Toy* never returns, we think the pilot will probably let the whole thing drop. Out of sight, out of mind. We heard rumors you were about to put this yacht up for sale and move to the top floor of a SoBe high-rise foreclosure."

"I'll admit that the yachting lifestyle has become somewhat tedious. And if the pilot doesn't let it drop?"

"It would be in your best interest to take care of him."

Dani shuddered as she listened to them plot the murder of Blackie for his simply being at the wrong place at the wrong time. These people would do anything to preserve their wealth. They were motivated soley by money. She thought that perhaps storming the salon with an AK-47 was a reasonable option.

Finally Ted responded. "Let me think on it for a while. I'll send one of The Twins over to the Viking with my answer."

"This is the best for all us," Belinda assured Ted. "We're out of your life, and you can run for mayor of Miami Beach or something."

"Let me think it over," Ted told her. He paused and addressed her husband. "Bobby, I think you've eaten that whole bowl of prawns without stopping."

"Very enjoyable. Must be a good-sized freezer aboard."

"Hans, escort our guests back to their dinghy."

Chapter 25:

Snuffing the Burns

The Burns sped away in their high-end dinghy, watched by José from the porthole. Ted and the Twins headed back up to the bridge to make their plans. "Do it simple, do it quick," was Ted's theme. "Klaus, take one of the Glocks and tuck it in your waistband. Scan the horizon for boats, and if it's clear, get it over fast."

To kill time, the three went in and had lunch, toasting with another bottle of *Perrier Jouet*. Finally, Ted went up on the bridge and hailed the Burns on the VHF. Switching to 72, a working channel, he told them that he was sending over one of The Twins with instructions on how to proceed to the Caymans, along with a few charts of their destination. Belinda, still acting as spokesperson, thanked Ted for making the right decision.

José watched out the porthole as one of The Twins sped by in the dinghy, two charts rolled up under his armpit. Dani had heard enough of the conversation to almost feel a little sympathy for the Burns; they were about to pay dearly for their greed.

José walked out of the head and said, "Chica, I think that now is the time for all ashore who are going ashore."

"Let Ted and the other Twin get back on the bridge. We don't want to meet the same fate as the Burns."

"How will we make our departure?" José asked.

"While they're up on the bridge on the radio with Klaus, we'll sneak off. We go one at a time. There's less chance of being spotted. You'll go first."

"Why aren't we going together?"

"I've got one last thing to do before I go."

"And that is?"

"I'm going to disable the boat."

"How?"

"In the engine room. Turn off the fuel to the Racor filters. Cut the fuel lines. Something."

"You've done this before?"

"Of course not. But I took a marine diesel mechanics class," Dani replied. "And all diesels have things in common."

"If it will get you off of here, then do it."

"I'll stay here at the nav station and listen in. You wait at the door. When it sounds clear, I'll wave you on. Get in the water quietly and swim for shore."

"Wait for you on the beach?"

"Get up in the bush. They'd never find us in there. Watch for me, and when I get to you we'll run up to the other end and swim and wade over to North Cat Cay."

They took up their positions and waited for the opportune moment. Dani reached down and tweaked up the volume knob on the intercom.

The silence was interrupted by Hans. "Ted, what's Klaus going to do if he gets there and the Burns have our guns pointed at him? They have our machine pistol and the AK-47."

"You're an idiot. They're both empty. You used up the clip on the AK-47, and I took out what was left in the Mac-10 before Klaus stowed them."

"José, come here," Dani whispered.

"What now?"

"Put the guns in the locker."

"Why?"

"There's no bullets in either of them," she said in dismay. "They emptied them before they wrapped them up."

"*Chinga!* I don't think we're very good at this," José said, opening the locker and placing them inside.

"Since we're not armed, you better get going. Now."

"We should go together, *chica.*"

"No. I've got to disable this thing. No way are they getting away with this. Go."

José stood at the door while Dani listened to the VHF on Ted's channel of choice, 72.

"Klaus, do you copy?" Ted asked.

"Copy."

Dani held up her hand for José to wait.

"You on low power?" Ted asked.

"Roger."

"What's going on?"

"Job is done."

"Good. Get back here and pick up Hans. Got it?"

"Copy."

Ted spoke to Hans: "Listen carefully. In the portside deck locker are some loops of half-inch chain. The ones we used on the dock cleats during the hurricane scare last year."

"I know where they're at."

"Take four and when you get over there wrap a pair around each of them. Take pliers and use the shackles to cinch them tight around their waists. Ditch them in at least 100 fathoms – that's 200 meters. I don't want them popping up later. And I don't want them anywhere near the boat. Use this handheld GPS and take the Viking to this waypoint I've plugged in and sink her. Don't torch it, right? We don't want to cause any attention. Just want it to slip below the surface."

"Okay. But how do I sink it?"

"Take the portable reciprocating saw and the shotgun and a box of shells. At the waypoint, go below and shut off the fuel filters. Hans, gather anything loose on deck and stow it inside to minimize flotsam. Cut the hoses at the seacocks with the saw. And open any portholes or hatches that you can.

Hans, you shoot as many holes into her as you can below the waterline. She needs to go down quick."

"This will be fun. What about their dinghy?"

"Take a dive knife and slice the tubes in all the chambers. She's got a four-stroke. The weight of the engine will pull her down. I see Klaus coming in.   Get your stuff and go."

Dani and José heard the tender zoom past toward the stern. She turned the intercom knob to "AFT."   Ted was at the stern rail shouting down to Klaus.

"How'd it go?   You've got blood all over you," Ted inquired.

"A breeze. Neither of them had the guns. I guess they trusted you. Were they stupid or what? They wanted me to be real careful with the tender against the swim platform, like the tender was already theirs."

"Assholes," Ted commented.

" I had the Glock on the sole, and when I held out the charts for Belinda, I was able to get her point blank in the forehead. And then Bobby maybe two seconds later. Greedy bastards only had a couple seconds to realize how bad they fucked up."

"You didn't let them fall overboard, did you?"

"Belinda swan-dived over on the swim platform, but I dragged her back up. The stern's a bloody mess. Like the time you got the big wahoo off Great Isaac. Want me to fillet them before we pitch them over?"

"No, you sick fuck. Do just as your brother tells you. He knows what to do. And wear gloves and try to wipe down anything you might have touched."

The stowaways heard the rattle of chain drop into the dinghy and the tender speed away. Dani switched back to the mike on the bridge.

Ted spoke on the radio on 72. "You there?"

"We're onboard. Engines are running, dinghies are tied on the stern," one of The Twins answered over the VHF.

"Make it fast. I want this over with as soon as you can – but don't forget anything!"

Dani ordered José to go. He still protested leaving her alone, even for the few minutes she promised before following him ashore. Reluctantly he headed for the door and the passageway, gripping in his hand a snorkel and mask he found in the locker.

"Go on," she ordered again.

"You be careful. When I see you coming, I'll run down to the beach for you."

"Good. Now go."

José headed down the passageway, and Dani resumed her post at the nav station.

"What's going on?" Ted asked The Twins over the VHF.

"Dumping the fish over. Heading for the last waypoint."

"Copy that," Ted replied.

Once outside, José crept down the spiral stairs, put on the mask and slipped into the water. He took a deep breath and swam as far as he could, as deep as he could. His only concern was that the water was so clear it didn't matter how deep he swam, he was visible from the bridge.

Over the intercom, Dani froze as she heard Ted say in almost a whisper, "I'll be damned. A stowaway. That fucking pilot! I knew he was in this with them."

José surfaced, took another breath and plunged deeper.

Dani listened to the commotion Ted was making on the bridge, then heard the boom of a shotgun firing overhead, methodical firing until it was obviously empty.

José heard a zipping sound through the water, and through his mask he saw the trails of bubbles as pellets zipped by. On his next surface he heard the pop of a handgun and knew he was in trouble. His only option was to continue on toward the beach. He took another breath and dove, the instant he felt the slug tear into his back. He dove again, his left arm useless, but he kept kicking for the beach.

Dani turned off the electronics and headed out the passageway for the engine room. She found the spiral stairs down and opened the watertight bulkhead and entered. She took off the daypack and retrieved the small LED flashlight and turned it on. In front of her was a giant Caterpillar diesel, one of a pair. They were giant 12-cylinder versions of the tiny diesels on her Venezia. She searched for a spot to hide in and found one behind an array of air conditioning units. Dani squirmed into the hole. She tried in vain to hold back the tears as she feared the worst for José.

Blinded by the pain, José didn't see the bottom coming up and scraped his chin on the coral sand. He surfaced and his feet ground into the furrows of sand. He trudged through the water to the beach, the golden sand warm on his bare feet, since both his Topsiders were lost kicking for shore. He tore off the mask, stopping for a few moments to catch his breath.

He looked down to see the blood soaking through his wet, black shirt, a darker sheen on the fabric at the spot where the excruciating pain radiated. The bullet had gone clear through the muscle of his left lat, barely missing his ribs. He turned to look back at the yacht, only to be knocked down by another bullet shot from *Ted's Toy*. He heard the bang a second later.

He felt more pain, this in the biceps of his left arm. Using his right, he pushed himself up and ran into the brush, diving behind a fallen palm for protection. Ted fired a few more rounds and stopped. José knew he was safe from Ted for now. His main concern was how long it would take to bleed to death.

Dani heard the second round of shots from her hiding place in the bowels of the Breakwater. Just as she realized the firing was over, the nearby diesels came to life with an incredible roar. And over that sound she could feel the rumble of the windlass bringing in the anchor chain. *Ted's Toy* was departing.

Chapter 26:

Swimming with Sharks

Ted throttled up, and the Breakwater lumbered out of Dollar Harbour and around Cat Point. He turned the boat southwest toward the waypoint he gave The Twins. Ted would need their help finding his prey before their stowaway made it across to North Cat Cay. Ted knew he had tagged the bastard twice with the Glock and figured they'd find a body curled up in the brush on the deserted island. Then it would only be a problem of disposal.

Ted steered the big yacht between the reefs surrounding Wedge Rocks and Victory Cay toward the deep waters of the Gulf Stream. Past the rocks, he throttled up and brought the boat on a plane, heading southwest. He watched the depth sounder hit 60 feet, then 100, and rapidly reach its limit. Ted checked the paper chart and saw the water was 400 meters – more than a thousand feet deep. Through his binoculars, Ted could see the Viking off in the distance, already settling in the water.[14]

Dani heard the engines throttle down and felt the Breakwater settle in the water. From the slight roll of the boat in the swell she could tell they were in deep water. Below, in her hiding place in the dark but noisy engine room, she turned on the handheld VHF and tried eavesdropping on the radio conversation between Ted and The Twins.

---

[14] Grave of **Grand Plan,** 25 30.48N, 79 18.51W.

"Hans, do you copy?" Ted asked on 72.

"Copy."

"I'm due east of you and within sight."

"We thought you said the plan was to wait for us?"

"Slight change. We have a little unfinished business back on South Cat. Is everything going as planned?"

"Right on schedule. I give it maybe five minutes, ten at the most to be gone."

"Do you still have their dinghy?"

"Tied to the stern. That's next to go."

"Hold off on that, we're going to need it. I'll wait here for you. Bring both the dinghies over as soon as it's done. Roger that?"

"Roger."

Dani decided that if she was going to do anything, now was the time to do it. She crawled out of her hiding place and directed the tiny beam of light around the room. She found a small workbench on the starboard side with a toolbox underneath. Inside she found a pair of large wire cutters – dykes, she had heard them called.

She scoped out the room with the light and finally found the two primary Racor fuel filters. They were just like the filters on her boat, a metal cylinder with a glass bowl filled with diesel underneath, only these were gargantuan. Without hesitating, she cut the fuel hoses, short pieces of black rubber that connected the copper lines to the filters. She figured that she only had a minute to escape the compartment before the engines sucked the bowls of the filters dry. She unlatched the watertight door, crept back up the stairs and into the cabin with the remote nav station. She turned back on the intercom and the fixed-mount VHF.

Nothing over the intercom but the omnipresent rumble of the big Cats. Finally one died, followed quickly by the other.

"Shit! What the fuck now?" Ted cursed to himself over the intercom.

She heard Ted trying to restart each of the engines to no avail, and then over the radio: "We're heading back, do you copy?"

Ted ignored The Twins while he continued to try and restart the engines.

"Heading back. Do you copy?"

"Shit, yes, I hear you!" he yelled over the VHF. "Get your asses back here."

She heard the dinghies approach, the only noise to disturb the deafening silence of *Ted's Toy* dead in the water.

She heard Ted's steps overhead carry down the port gunwale. She twisted the intercom knob and eavesdropped aft.

"Tie off and get up here!" Ted ordered.

At the stern Ted told his minions of the stowaway – the pilot he was almost sure. And that the prick had sabotaged the boat before he swam off. But Ted boasted that he got his revenge by clipping him with the Glock twice. He said their job was to take the dinghies back to South Cat and find the stowaway, insure that he was dead, and bring him back so they could dump him out in The Stream.

Ted was on a rampage: "I knew it all along. He's the leader of this gang. He's the one with the copies of all that shit they're trying to blackmail me with. We're rid of him and we're rid of our problem.

"Both of you take your guns and search the island. Start at each end and work to the middle. And keep in radio contact on 72. On low power. If you can't get me it's cause I'm down in the engine compartment."

"Ted, I'm starting to wonder where this will all end," Hans shouted up at him.

"Who the fuck told you that you could wonder'?" Ted shrieked back.

"You need to lighten up, Ted," the other Twin added.

"Get out of here! And don't come back without a body."

The hum of the two outboards faded into silence. She heard a commotion at the far end of the passageway, then Ted's steps as he headed down the stairs to the engine room.

*   *   *

Gun Cay Light had long ago poked its head above the horizon as the trimaran streaked east. They passed out of the cobalt blue waters into lighter shades of aquamarine. Yul and Blackie had decided to attempt the cut between Cat and South Cat Cay, to see if *Ted's Toy* was still in Dollar Harbour. If not, they could work their way up to Cat Cay Marina to look for Dani and to clear in.

Yul steered twenty degrees to starboard, and with the strong southwest wind pushing them on a beam reach, the tri flew toward the southern end of Cat Cay.

"Remember we've got to keep an eye out for the Kittens," Blackie shouted.

"Kittens?" Yul yelled back quizzically, as he scratched at the splotches of white on his deep-rust skin. The sleigh ride across the Stream had covered him and the boat with a film of dried salt.

"The Kittens off the southwest tip of Cat. They also call 'em Moxon Rocks. It shallows up fast after that."

"You're forgetting how shoal my draft is," Yul replied with a laugh.

They passed the reddish rocks to starboard, and Yul pointed out the waves from the southwest swells breaking over them; Blackie shouted that they were coming in on a high tide.

Ahead the gap between North and South Cat Cay slowly opened. A small breakwater had been constructed off North Cat, narrowing the space. They shot through the cut into the shallower waters of the Great Bahama Bank. Blackie watched the depth gauge hit 15 feet, then 8, then rise quickly up to 5.

They cleared a sandbar and turned south. Yul brought in the jib and main on a close reach. Yul turned the boat up into the wind, in irons, in the relatively calm waters on the east side of the empty island. Blackie scanned the horizon with the binos while Yul brought down the sails.[15]

"No boats in Dollar Harbour, Yul."

"We can only hope she made it to the marina."

"There's a dinghy on the beach. Over by those old pilings." Blackie said as he handed the binos over to Yul for a look. "Those pilings were for a beach house wiped out in Andrew. You can see what's left of a spiral roof hidden in the palms."

"I see that dink," Yul observed. "There's a couple people walking up the beach toward it."

"Yeah, great shelling on that island. Even some legal conch. Yul, check out the other dinghy coming through the cut behind us."

Yul turned and focused on the other tender.

"Oh shit! I think I'm seeing stereo trouble."

"What?"

"The blonde guy in the boat and the blonde guy on the beach are The Twins. And the other one on the beach is being led by gunpoint by one of those cloned clowns. I think it's José."

"José?"

"They've got José! Look."

Blackie took the glasses and focused on the scene on the beach. "That's him. You see the blood? He looks like he's hurt bad."

*   *   *

Back on the Breakwater, Dani turned the knob on the intercom to "ENGINE " and heard Ted cursing as he searched in vain for what caused the engines to die. From his ranting it was obvious that he didn't have a clue. She heard Ted snake up the stairs from the engine compartment to the bridge. Then she heard the

---

[15] *The King & I* off South Cat Cay, 25 32.31N, 79 15.77W.

distinct sound of an outboard approaching on the starboard side.

"Hey! Hey! Over here!" Ted yelled out the open door on the bridge.

Dani stepped into the head and peered out the porthole. Off the beam was a small, old, open-bow sportfish. On board was a huge barrel-chested man in a bleached white tank top, a sharp contrast to his shiny, ebony skin. Dani's heart leapt up. She was sure she recognized him. It was her Protector. It was Harlis.

"Meet me at the stern," Ted shouted down. Dani returned to the nav station and turned the knob to "AFT."

From the deck Ted hailed to the stranger. "Hey buddy, you know if there's a mechanic over at Cat Cay Marina? We've got engine problems."

"What kinda problems, mon?"

"I think its fuel."

"You a lucky mon, I *am* a mechanic. I fix de machinery over at Ocean Cay, mon."

"Ocean Cay? Where's that?"

"Over der. Look, mon, dat big mound o' sand on da horizon to da sout'. Da aragonite mine. Dis your first time to da Islands?"

"No. Usually head through Northwest Providence Channel on the way to Chub. What's aragonite?"

"Limestone. Bahamas' aragonite is pure calcium carbonate – best in de world, mon."

"You work on diesels?"

"On da big dredgers, mon. Twelve-cylinder Caterpillars."

"Hell, I probably got the same engines in this thing. If you get them running, I'll pay you a week's wages," Ted lied, knowing he'd never have to fulfill that promise. "Throw me a line and I'll tie you off."

Dani heard the heavy footsteps following Ted's down the companionway and the spiral stairs to the engine room. She had the urge to burst from the cabin and run into Harlis' arms, but held back. After a few minutes, Ted headed back up to the bridge and hailed The Twins on the VHF.

"Hans, what's up over there?"

"You winged that bird twice. He's walking, but barely. I don't want to have to drag him back to the dinghy so I'll finish your project on our way back in the tender."

"Where's Klaus?"

"He's coming 'round the northern point to meet us here on the beach. Something you need to know Ted."

"What?"

"He's not the pilot. He's our marina neighbor, José. The Cubano artist on that old sailboat."

"José?"

"That's what I said."

Ted paused before responding. "Any other boats around?"

"A sailboat offshore. Just some stupid cruisers on holiday, looks like."

"Proceed as planned. And make sure you get him out here before you finish it."

"Roger."

Dani used Ted's conversation with The Twins to sneak down to the engine room. She crept down the passageway to the stairs, pausing for a moment as she remembered that she had left the handheld VHF on the desk in the cabin. As she descended she could see the green glow of fluorescent light pouring through the crack in the engine room door. She was about to push open the hatch when Ted's voice boomed into the brightly-lit room. "Hey, Buddy! Can you hear me down there?"

She paused and realized for the first time that there was an intercom on the bridge, too, Ted just hadn't had it on.

"Yeah, mon, I hear ya!"

"You found the problem?"

"Yeah, mon, the fuel lines all been cut. You da only one aboard?"

"Now? Yeah, just me. Can you fix it?"

"Der's enough hose I can patch it, no problem, mon. Den we just bleed da system. Get ridda de air."

"Well hurry it up. We're drifting."

"I'm on it, mon."

Dani waited for what she thought was an eternity before slowly pushing open the heavy oval door. The big man knelt in the pose of a contortionist, a sheen of sweat covering his skin. He grimaced as he tightened a pair of stainless hose clamps with a socket driver. Even in the oversized engine room of the Breakwater, his immense size made him not quite fit. He looked up at her, startled, as she put a finger to her lips and then pointed up.

He understood her signal, and continued working on the line for the starboard engine. He attached the hose, filled the bowl and bled the air from the cylinders. Dani watched him work. She remained quiet, calm and reassured; she felt safe in the presence of her guardian.

"How's it going down there?" Ted inquired over the speaker.

"Starboard's almost ready, mon. Just lemme tighten de last two injectors."

"Tell me when."

A minute of silence passed.

"Okay, start her up, mon!"

Ted hit the switch and the big diesel cranked and cranked and eventually caught. Finally Dani felt it was safe to talk, but before she could speak, the big man grabbed her wrist and asked, "Dis your doin'?"

"Yes. I'm sort of a kidnapped stowaway."

"What you mean by dat? He de boyfriend? You two be fightin'? Mon, I don' need none o' dat."

"No. He's a damn evil bastard who'll kill me if he finds out I'm onboard."

The big man looked alarmed and ordered, "He might be headin' down here right now. Go get over der 'case he come below."

* * *

The Twins met up on the beach by the pilings. Hans prodded José toward the tender. Through the binoculars, Blackie watched José take a few faltering steps and collapse in the sand. The Twins tucked their guns in their pants and both grabbed José and dragged him to the dinghy.

Blackie knew time was running out. "We don't stop them now, they can outrun us in those dinghies."

"I'll start the engine and you steer us up that channel to them," Yul ordered. Hidden by the cabintop, he lowered the prop of the outboard mounted on the stern. "You take the tiller and try to cut them off. I'll break out the weapons."

The Twins rolled José's unconscious body over the tube into the sole of the tender, and looked up to see the trimaran bearing down on them at a creeping six knots. With their guns covered and tucked away, they rehearsed their story; they figured that there were already enough people involved in this mess. They slowly, deliberately moved apart from each other.

The shallow draft of the trimaran allowed Blackie to head close in to the beach, pulling parallel to the shore. In his wrap-around sunglasses and baseball cap they hadn't recognized him, and Blackie figured that to these two idiots, all sailboats looked alike. Yul stood crouched out of sight at the bottom of the companionway in the cabin, holding his pump-action stainless steel Mossberg shotgun. History was repeating itself, Blackie thought. Yul might finally get his revenge.

Blackie flipped the transmission to neutral, wanting to keep a safe distance from the two sociopaths in case they recognized him. He turned forward and shouted, "That guy have an accident? Need any help?"

"No. He's okay. A barracuda bit him while we were gigging for lobsters. Took a chunk of his arm off. We're taking him up to Alice Town to the clinic."

"Where's your yacht? Want us to go tell anyone what happened?"

The Twins didn't answer and slowly, in near synchronous movement, turned their heads and looked at one another.

Blackie glanced down and spoke softly to Yul, "I think the ruse is up."

"When I come up, you get down," Yul ordered. "There's a gun on the sole by your feet. You only stick your head up when I tell you. Got it?"

"Roger that."

"Go!"

Yul lifted his big frame up the ladder with surprising dexterity. He stood and held the shotgun at eye level, pointed at the right – the starboard – Twin.

"Okay, you fucking assholes! Get your weapons out and drop them on the sand. Now!"

Neither moved. Then slowly Hans stuck both hands under his shirt and pulled out the Glock in one and a small handheld VHF off a waistband clip in the other. His right-hand forefinger was on the trigger, his left-hand forefinger on the mike key of the VHF. He raised both to eye level in a definite show of something besides surrender.

"Okay, you other bleached-blonde asshole, get out your weapon and drop it."

Klaus slowly reached under his shirt and pulled out the Glock and held it head-high, his finger on the trigger.

"Come on, drop 'em!" Yul screamed.

"Listen, fat man. You can't take us both out from that distance and you know it," Hans said, making sure his words were heard on the VHF.

"Yeah, Manatee Man. What we have here is a standoff," the other replied. "Set down your shotgun and we'll work us out a deal."

"Where's Dani?" Yul asked, keeping the Mossberg trained on the one without the VHF.

"Dani? Who in the hell are you talking about?"

"Our neighbor. The woman who lives on the catamaran at Te Cuesta Isle. She was on your boat."

"She was on *Ted's Toy* with José? Then I think she was trespassing like your friend here. And you see what happened to him."

"You guys ever get tired of doing Ted's dirty work?"

"Not when we get a chance to fuck with a sea cow like you."

Blackie, lying flat on his stomach on the cockpit sole, felt something brush his leg dangling down into the cabin. He turned to see Elvis on the bottom step with one pissed-off look on his face. With alarming speed, the tabbie leapt up on Blackie, stepping heavily over him to the starboard amas and dove off the boat into the water.

The fat cat's swan dive off the amas distracted Yul for a split-second. Hans noticed Yul's head twitch, and in one quick movement he lowered the Glock and fired.

Chapter 27:

Rabbit Rock

On *Ted's Toy*, the big man worked feverishly to finish repairing the fuel lines on the port engine. Having bled the cylinders, he yelled out to the intercom to give it a try.

On the bridge, Ted pulled his attention from Hans' dramatic soliloquy on the VHF to turn the key and start the port engine. With both running, a smile returned to his face. He opened the drawer below the bridge's chart table and pulled out a handful of heavy black cable ties and his reloaded handgun. He shut down both engines and headed below to the engine room.

Ted paused at the bulkhead door, gathered his thoughts and stepped in.

"Okay, where is she?"

The big mechanic, in the midst of tidying up, stopped and looked quizzically at Ted holding the Glock on him in the doorway.

"Mon, you crazy? Who she?"

"That whore. That bitch. You been down here fucking her, haven't you, buddy?"

"Mon, *you* called *me* over here. *You* got *me* onboard to fix da engines. You all mixed up, mon."

"She cut those lines just so you'd come aboard and fuck her. Then you two were going to steal this boat from me."

Dani, clutching her pack in front of her, squirmed further back in her hiding place. She believed that either Ted was losing it completely, or he had a very perverse plan. She vainly searched the near-empty pack for anything to defend herself.

Ted reached down and pulled a half-dozen of the heavy ties sticking out of his pocket and threw them at his captive. "Put your wrist up to that post there, wrap one of these around it and cinch it tight. Now! We'll let the police at Alice Town sort this out," Ted lied again, knowing he wasn't about to do something stupid like forcing The Twins to have to carry close to 270 pounds of dead weight up the spiral stairs.

Dani heard the heavy zip as the big mechanics cuffed his left hand to the post.

"The other one. Do the other one."

"Mon, an' just how I do that?" the mechanic said, involuntarily glancing over in Dani's direction.

Ted paused, took a few steps into the engine room and stopped. From her hiding spot behind the big water heater on the starboard side she could clearly see the profile of Ted's face.

Ted turned and looked right at her. "Well, there you are. Another of my nautical neighbors. Get your ass out here!"

Dejectedly, Dani pulled herself out of the confines of her hiding place. As she stood, she slid the only weapon she had found from the palm of her hand into the pocket of her black pajama-outfit, the outfit José had lent her the night before.

"Dani, right? I fuck you and years later you fuck me back," Ted said with a laugh. "Why you SoBe slime. You whores are all alike. Sucking the sharks. You're a world-class remora fish."

"Ted, I'm surprised you even remember me. You've fucked a thousand women – and men – since me. Everybody gets fucked by Ted," she replied defiantly.

"Put one of those ties on your buddy's wrist. Now!" Ted ordered.

"Ted, he has nothing to do with this. Let him get on his boat and get out of here," she pleaded.

"The police in Alice Town can figure it out. Strap him up."

The big man was standing, yet still having to crouch over because of the limited headroom in the engine compartment. She approached and held up the tie.

"He has no plans to take us to the police," she whispered. "He's going to kill both of us when his boys get back."

"Shut up and put it on him!" Ted shouted.

She fed the end through the loop and pulled slowly, the tick, tick, tick of the notches slowed as she tried to leave her Harlis room to squeeze his hand out of the plastic loop.

"Tight!" Ted screamed at her, banging the handgun on the cylinder head cover of an engine. She jumped, jerking on the tie and pulling it tight against the big man's wrist.

"I'm sorry. I'm sorry for all of this," she whispered.

"Dani, I've got a little time here," Ted said with a smirk. "Why don't you give me a little thrill and pull down his pants and perform a little oral sex on him. Do it for me. I could get off on that. Just like one of our old parties on this boat."

She turned and glared at Ted, unable to speak.

"I see how you look at him, you fucking SoBe whore," Ted said with a sneer.

Dani turned and looked up at her Harlis. He shook his head and stared at Ted. "You are one messed up mon."

The tinny bang of a gunshot over the VHF filtered down from the bridge, followed by shouting on the radio for Ted.

"Get over here," Ted ordered to Dani. "Strap yourself on this post here. Now!"

Dani stepped over and took the tie and wrapped it around a vertical pole. She threaded the end through the insert and pulled tentatively. Ted reached over and yanked it tight, digging the sharp plastic edge into her skin.

"I'm not through with you two fuckers yet," Ted said as he disappeared up the spiral stairs.

Hans was still screaming over the VHF when Ted reached the bridge.

"Shit, Ted! They shot Klaus. They shot his face off. Goddamn them!"

"Where are you?" Ted calmly asked in reply.

"On the beach at Dollar Harbour behind the tender. They've got me pinned down, but I think I hit one of them."

"How many?"

"Two I think. They're from the marina. The pilot and the fat man."

"I'm bringing the big boat in. I've got a sportfish on the stern. I'll come in from the water and we'll finish this."

"What about Klaus?"

Ted ignored him.

Down in the engine compartment, the two captives tried vainly to free themselves. Despite the Herculean strength of the big man, he was only succeeding in making the ties tighter on his wrists. Dani watched the blood ooze from the cuts on his wrists and down his monstrous forearms, dripping onto the spotless engine room sole.

"Harlis, you've got to forgive me for getting you into this," she said softly in apology.

"Harlis? Girl, my name is Trevor."

"But you know me. You came to get me."

"Girl, I never seen you before in me life! I came onboard to fix de engines and now I'm only trying to get out of dis nightmare alive. Dis nightmare you made for me."

"You've never seen me before in your life," Dani repeated, dropping her head dejectedly, the words cut off as both engines roared to life. Over the din Trevor shouted, "You got anyt'ing to cut dat tie with?"

Dani patted her pockets with her free hand and shouted back in reply, "No, just a flashlight and a wine opener. I lost the wire cutters I used on the fuel lines."

"Got to be something we can do."

The roar of the engines consumed their words as Ted brought the motor yacht up on a plane.

"You reach dat electric panel behind you?" Trevor shouted over the roar.

Dani turned to see an elaborate electrical panel for some of the yacht's 12- and 24-volt systems. She reached over and could barely touch the latch on the plexiglass cover. With all her strength she reached out, the tie cutting deeper into her skin, as she tapped the latch down and the panel door swung open.

"Turn off what you can, girl," Trevor shouted out over the engines.

She slapped at the breakers, and the first one she hit was the engine room lights, pitching the room into darkness, but for the glow of the panel and a few gauges with lights.

She slapped again and again, turning off a few more, with no apparent effect. Then she saw a shadow caused by a figure heading down the stairs. Ted must have put the boat on autopilot and was returning. She had switched off something important.

She slapped at the breakers one more time and flipped off two more switches. As he stepped down to the landing she crouched in the darkness, hiding her face, trying to make herself invisible in her black outfit.

"You fucking bitch!" Ted shouted from the doorway, standing there in silhouette.

Dani gathered herself in a ball in an attempt to make herself smaller.

"I know what you did. You turned most of my electronics off. Afraid you'll have to pay for that, bitch."

With the Glock in his outstretched hand in front of him, Ted stepped blindly into the dark room.

Dani reached into her pocket and grabbed the wine opener and using her thumb and forefinger removed the plastic sheath.

Ted stepped forward, almost touching her with his overpriced deck shoes as his eyes began to adjust to the dark.

"Stand up, Dani. You know what I ought to do? For someone who lives off her looks – which is why I ever fucked you in the first place – I should disfigure that face, like your fat friend did to Klaus. Make you go through the last moments of your life with nothing."

Dani leapt up, her thumb on the end of the nitrogen can and her hand wrapped around the hard-plastic tool. She held it as a weapon, nothing like a cork popper, and in one swift move brought it down on Ted's chest. Like an ice-pick, the needle slid through the thin muscle layers between the fifth and sixth rib, jamming through the sack of fluid lubricating his beating heart. The tip of the spike pierced the heart muscle, causing it to momentarily fibrillate and Ted to shudder involuntarily.

The point of her weapon drove in through the thin heart muscle and into Ted's left ventricular chamber just as her thumb pushed down on the end of the nitrogen cylinder, propelling the deadly gas into the blood-filled compartment. The ball of gas moved out of the heart with the next contraction, causing a squeezing sensation in his chest. Ted shuddered, breaking out in a sweat and instantly overcome with a sense of doom. The gas quickly moved up the ascending aorta and into his main carotid artery heading up to his brain.

The bolus of nitrogen split in two. One pocket of air reached his retinas causing temporary blindness, with the rest of the air hitting the motor center of his brain and causing him to jerk his arm that held the Glock. He tried to grab her in a bear hug in a feeble attempt to keep control of his own body.

She kept pressing the tool against his chest, all the while shooting a steady burst of nitrogen into Ted's evil heart.

He made a final attempt to turn the gun's muzzle in toward her, but was stopped by the quaking of the muscles in his arms. In a spasm he jerked his hand and the gun flew backward through the door onto the bottom step of the stairs.

Dani held the device against him, pushing it with all her strength on his chest, her thumb locked down on the nitrogen cylinder. She held it there until finally she believed – until she was sure – it was empty. She pulled away from Ted, trying to distance herself from him but was stopped by the tie wrapped around her left wrist. She jerked the needle from his chest.

Grimacing, Ted forced his head down.   He shook violently, yet was able to raise his hands and tear open his ruined Helmut Lang shirt. In the faint light from the panel, all three could see frothing, bubbling blood squirting out of the hole in Ted's chest.

Terror on his face, Ted made a futile lunge toward Dani. With all her might she reared back and landed a hard kick in his crotch. Ted fell over in agony, violently twitching, his limbs curling up as the nitrogen spread through his arteries and veins.

As if in response to the demise of her captain, *Ted's Toy* lurched violently to port. A loud squealing sound, of the hull against rock, ran down the starboard side of the yacht. Dani fell to her knees, her arm suspended above her by the tie around her wrist. Like a ragdoll, Ted's body tumbled away on the engine-room sole.

"My god, Trevor! What was that?"

"Shit! We hit Rabbit Rock!"[16]

The engines continued to roar, the yacht still on its plane, yet even over that din they could hear the gurgle of water in the compartment, then saw it pouring in around their feet.

"Check de panel, Dani. Is de autopilot breaker off?" Trevor shouted at her.

She stood and stared and found the tiny backlit sign for AUTOPILOT, and saw the tiny LED light was off. She tried vainly to flip it back on, but the toggle was just out of reach.

"It's off," she yelled back, dejectedly, "And I can't reach it."

"We're probably headin' out in de Stream," Trevor yelled, head down, watching the water swirl at his feet. "She sinkin' fast."

---

[16] Rabbit Rock, 25 31.50N, 79 16.70W.

Dani stood and faced him. They were only ten feet apart, but a chasm separated them. She reached in her pocket with her free hand and brought out the tiny flashlight and twisted it on. She held the flashlight up and shined it in the big man's face. He squinted but didn't look away.

"You don't have a scar."

"What?"

"You don't have a scar under your eye. Harlis did. There's no hope, is there?"

"No, I got no scar!" Trevor shouted. "You people are nuts! You ever realize how bad you folks mess us Bahamians up?"

"What?" Dani asked as she stood there looking at him, dumbfounded.

"For hundreds of years you been sendin' us your problems. I should hate you people. But I just feel sorry for you."

Dani looked down; the water was half-way up her calves. She had nothing to say as she thought about what he had said.

"Tink about it. You ship your Loyalists here, t'anks from de King for der loyalty. Deh come here wit' der slaves, til most give up and go back to England, settin' my ancestors free – free to die of starvation.

"Den deh run guns during de civil war, rum in Prohibition, den de drugs and now crazy damn tourists like you and dat evil man at your feet. A crazy boom & bust cycle dat has done nuttin' but hurt deh Bahamians."

"I agree with what you say, Trevor. I'm just not sure how talking about that now is going to help us," she shouted back, alarmed that the water was already up to her knees.

With their blocks half submerged, the twin Cat diesels continued to roar.

Trevor paused in his history lesson. "Dani, take dat little flashlight and see if you can flip dat breaker with it."

"Trevor! I never thought of that." She stretched out and holding the flashlight by the end was able to knock the autopilot breaker back on. Slowly the yacht turned, the water in the engine room rising on the port side as the yacht swung around to its original course.

"Tink da man had it set for Alice Town?" Trevor shouted.

"No. He had no intention of going there. He was probably heading back to South Cat to get his boys. They did most of his killing for him."

"Dat's good. Dat's closer," Trevor said with a measure of relief in his voice. "If we head east, we'll hit de beach or a sandbar." He paused, then asked, "So tell me, who you tink I am?"

"You look a lot like a man who's protected me since I was young."

"Strange ting, girl. Years ago de boss at de aragonite mine was an American. An back den deh have some labour problems der. I kept an eye on 'im and he took to callin' me 'De Bodyguard.'"

"Well, without that scar under your eye, you're not my Harlis."

The words were barely out of her mouth when the boat slowed, coming off its plane. The water ballast was too much for the diesels to keep all that weight above the surface of the water.

"No, girl, I'm sure not your Harlis."

The water was above her waist, reaching the tops of the diesels. When the water reached the air intakes, the port engine died, followed quickly by the starboard.

*   *   *

Hans' shot hit the trimaran's mast with a loud ding. And a split second later Yul fired a deadly round from his shotgun, hitting Klaus full in the face, knocking him off his feet. Hans dove onto the sand and scrambled behind the tender for cover. Yul leveled the shotgun and was about to flush Hans out from behind his flimsy hypalon and fiberglass shield when he stopped.

"José's in the dinghy. I can't take the chance of hitting him."

"At least you've got him pinned down. You see what the other one had in his hands?"

"A gun and a VHF radio," Yul replied.

"Ted's probably on his way back here right now. And Dani's probably still onboard."

"We're drifting out," Yul observed. "There's a sandbar behind us. You need to go off the stern and lift the rudders and pull us on it, to keep our bow and cabin between us and him.

Blackie did as he was told, then clambered back in the cockpit. On shore, Hans reached his arm over and grabbed José by the collar and pulled his head up on the tube as a shield. He poked his head up beside José's.

"Hey Manatee Man! We need to talk about a deal or you can say so long to your friend here."

"If you don't do your best to keep José alive, I'd have no reason to not start blastin' away! Man, you are one stupid shit! You got less brains than what's left of your brother's over there!"

"You damn asshole! I will get you for that! If it takes the rest of my life, I'll make you pay for what you did to him!"

Keeping a bead on Hans, Yul spoke to Blackie beside him. "That was a worn-out thing to say. This guy's seen way too many movies. And like he's got much of a life left."

"Yul, the other dinghy," Blackie said.

They saw the Novurania up the beach floating away from the shoreline. When he'd beached it, the dead twin hadn't had the sense to throw the dinghy anchor in the sand. In the tidal current, the inflatable was heading right for them.

With the dinghy bobbing in the current, it blocked their view of Hans and José. Hans realized that this was his only chance. He stood up and took off at an angle up the beach, heading for the protection of the bush and grapeleaf trees inland. As he stepped through the heavy sand, he twisted to face them, both hands around the butt of the Glock, firing at them in an attempt to provide his own cover.

Yul tracked him, whispered "Stupid shit," and fired. Hans stumbled and fell face down in the sand only a few yards from his faceless brother.

"They picked the wrong line of work being Ted's cabin boys," Yul commented as he rose up in the cockpit.

Blackie jumped overboard and swam to the passing dinghy, grabbing the painter and dragging it ashore. He ran over to José in the other tender to see if he was still alive. His fingers on José's neck, he found a pulse, a very weak one.

Yul jumped into the water and pushed the tri off the sandbar. He lowered the engine and started it, running the trimaran up on the beach beside the Novurania. After chucking an anchor in the sand, Yul ran past José and Blackie over to Hans, lying in the sand. Hans still clutched the Glock. Yul pried it from his hand and tucked the gun in his shorts. He turned Hans over and checked for vital signs. There were none. He headed back to Blackie and José.

As they worked to clean up José, the two heard the drone of an airplane engine and saw the VTOL aircraft circling in from the north to land on the tiny runway up at the Cat Cay Club.

"Blackie, let's get him over there. He can be at a hospital in Fort Lauderdale in less than an hour."

"I'll shove you off, but I'm staying. I've got to find Dani. Have them call the Defense Force. Call somebody!"

"Ted might come around that point any minute," Yul said. "If he does, make sure you've got a gun."

"I'll get your shotgun out of the tri."

"If Ted heard much of what just happened over that VHF, he might have hightailed it out of here. He could be heading for Cayman or Haiti right now."

"It's possible. But I have to find out. Get going, you can't miss that flight."

They spread José out in the sole of the dinghy to make him as comfortable as possible for the short ride over to the airstrip. Yul fired up the outboard and pointed the inflatable north toward the runway at Cat Cay.[17]

*   *   *

The water was up to her neck and to the bottom of Trevor's chest. The big Breakwater was listing to port, judging by the angle of the water to the ceiling of the engine room. Neither had broken the eerie silence with words, both lost in their own thoughts as they prepared to embrace the inevitable.

Dani felt around with her feet and found the cowling on the closest engine and pushed up, raising her head to the ceiling like Trevor. She let out a sudden scream, as she felt something brush past her hip. She still had the LED flashlight in her hand and pointed it into the clear water, illuminating the pale face of Ted, two feet below the surface, looking up at her with a blank stare.

"What's dat?"

"It's Ted."

"You okay?"

"Ted just touched me," she replied, kicking at the corpse until it floated away.

"He's an evil man, but he's still dead. So don' worry."

"You have a family, Trevor?"

"Yeah. My wife died a few years ago, but I got two kids. Girls, both in private school over in Nassau."

"I'm sorry."

"I'm not, girl, not for having what time I had with her. And you? You have a family?"

"No one."

---

[17] Cat Cay Club runway, 25 33.24N, 79 16.60W.

"I'm surprised. I tink a beautiful woman like you have a family by now."

"Wasn't meant to be," she replied as her tears flowed.

"Girl, I know I'm not your Harlis, but in dese last few minutes I might not offer you protection, but I can give you some peace."

"Are you a minister or something?"

"No. But many of us Bahamians are still God-fearin' people. I know you may not believe, an' it not my place to try and make you. But I am at peace with whatever happens."

"Whatever happens," Dani repeated in reply. She pointed the light into the water, giving their tiny bit of airspace an eerie aquamarine glow. Her head was pressed to the ceiling, and the water touched the bottom of her chin.

*   *   *

Blackie boarded the tri and retrieved the shotgun and some binos. He reset the Danforth anchor for Yul's tri in the sand, all the while expecting the big Breakwater to appear off Cat Point. Racked by the anxiety of inaction, he hopped into the dingy, fired up the outboard and headed down the channel.

He cleared the tip of South Cat Cay and headed west. With Victory Cay on the port beam, he throttled down and scanned the horizon for *Ted's Toy*. He spotted a bit of superstructure on the western horizon. The boat was quite a distance off, judging by what he could see of it above the water. He punched the throttle down and headed out into the deep blue waters of The Stream.

The closer he approached the Breakwater, the more he knew something was terribly, terribly wrong. He realized that the curvature of the earth made objects disappear over the horizon, but as he motored toward the Breakwater, he concluded that the big motor yacht was never going to be "hull-up" on the horizon. The Breakwater was sinking.

At full throttle there was little more that he could do. The big yacht was beginning to settle fast, stern first, the water already up to the sheer line. The last two miles were taking an eternity. He shouted a Mayday on the VHF over Channel 16, repeating it again and again.

Blackie saw no movement onboard the Breakwater. By the time he was close enough to throttle down, the bow was rising rapidly skyward.

With gathering speed, the Breakwater eased ass-end into the indigo-blue sea. Blackie rammed the controls into neutral as he watched the length of the yacht begin to slowly disappear into the sea.

The tender settled to a stop in the swells. Blackie watched the Breakwater's radome disappear, followed by the bridge. He ticked off the stanchions for the bow rail as one by one they slipped below the surface. The final piece to vanish was the small pennant atop the bowrail.

Blackie drove the dinghy over the site and watched the bleached white hull slowly shrinking in the crystal-clear, blue-black water. Finally the image faded into the darkness and was gone. Blackie searched the area, spotting only a few cushions and other bits of flotsam making their way to the surface. He looked at the depth sounder on the inflatable; it was off the scale. The Breakwater was descending to the bottom in at least a thousand feet of water.[18]

Blackie finally had time to ponder the obvious. If Dani was still aboard the Breakwater, then surely she was gone. He picked up the mike of the VHF and reluctantly cancelled his Mayday over 16.

---

[18] Grave of *Ted's Toy*, 25 31.97N, 79.18.72W.

Chapter 28:

Epitaph as Epilogue

Word spread through the marina, spoken in low voices on the fingerpiers and in the dockmaster's office. Those who wished to attend the service for Dani were to meet aboard Blackie's Island Packet at eleven that morning. They were told to keep it to themselves, or there might be the whoop-whoop-whoop of the news buzzards overhead, providing live shots at noon to fill the gap between home-equity-loan commercials and promos for the news at 5.

Filing aboard was a small contingent of mourners, including Yul, José, Reggie and Tina and a half dozen other marina neighbors, a couple of friends from her modeling agency, the dockmaster and one of the dockhands Dani had befriended. All were dressed in tropical black. They all found a place in the cabin or cockpit as Blackie untied the lines.

José, looking pale and thin but dressed nattily in black shorts and black guyabara, was the last to board. He was helped onto the cutter with the doting assistance of Yul. A month had passed since the events at South Cat, but José was still recovering from his wounds.

That José had lived was a miracle. After the shooting, Yul had ferried José in the dinghy to the fuel dock at Cat Cay, where the dockmaster helped him load José into a commandeered golf cart. Yul sped to the airstrip where he literally hijacked the plane back to the states. The final bags were being loaded and the passengers already onboard when he pulled up in front of the VTOL craft.

The passengers refused to deplane the full aircraft, shouting indignantly that neither Yul nor José were members of the private island, and that the delay was buggering up their connections back in the US. Convinced that no one was going to budge, Yul pulled the Glock out of his shorts and grabbed the nearest passenger by the collar of his silk Hawaiian shirt, a man who indignantly protested that he was a Lord. The Lord was followed by Lady Anne, who disembarked while screaming threats that Yul would rot in the Queen's prison, despite the fact the Bahamas had been free of England since 1971. Having commandeered his two seats, Yul gave the rest a choice of staying onboard or deplaning. Seeing the bloody state of José, the other passengers leapt out without a protest.

Once in Fort Lauderdale, Yul considered pulling out the Glock again when an Immigrations Officer, in a classic bureaucratic pose, was going to refuse the comatose José entry without a passport. Yul screamed that José was a US citizen, and even if he was a Cuban, he had a dry foot on American soil. Cooler heads prevailed and José was rushed off on a stretcher for the ride to the nearest emergency room. Job done, Yul surrendered himself to the feds.

In the days that followed, the events came close to being an international incident between the Bahamas and the US, with all the bloodshed and loss of life. The Bahamas hadn't tried to extradite Yul to Nassau to face charges, but they had made it clear that he had best never surface there again. Only because no Bahamian casualties were reported did the House of Assembly in Nassau not push through another tripling of the US boaters' entry tax to stem the crime epidemic.

The authorities were still on the lookout for the owners of the dinghy Yul had delivered to Cat Cay. The Burns were considered to be Ted's accomplices, and the Viking was being searched for throughout the Bahamas and the Caribbean, but it seemed to have vanished without a trace.

With everyone assembled for the service, Yul raised a small, triangular pennant on the line up to the starboard spreader. It was the Island Packet's black peter. Yul felt it was the appropriate flag for the service.

With all onboard, Blackie brought the boat out of Te Cuesta Isle Marina and mimicked the first part of the route that he and Dani had taken on their sail just five weeks earlier.

The service was to honor her written wishes, to have her ashes scattered over the sea in the event of her death. But there were no ashes, because her body had not been recovered from the Breakwater, now settled on the floor of the Florida Straits 200 fathoms (1,200 feet) below the surface. Deep water and jurisdictional problems had nixed any attempt at salvaging or raising the vessel, and the Bahamians were reluctant to allow any Americans to try and profit from the tragedy. They addressed the problem by miring the salvage proposals in bureaucratic red tape.

Back in Florida, Blackie and Yul had dealt with the loss of Dani by trying to tie up lose ends. Yul found her will on board, and both he and Blackie were shocked to learn that Blackie was the sole beneficiary of her estate. She had left everything, in her own words in her will, to "her tight-assed pilot."

But just as Dani had felt that her inheritance was tainted, so did Blackie. Her legacy was to be tied up in the courts for some time, until she was declared legally dead. Blackie made sure that the payments were made on the slip rental, and he made routine visits to wash the grime off the Venezia's decks. His plan was to let the boat sit there as a memory to her. He realized the perverseness of that, and where the idea had come from. As a kid in a San Diego suburb, he had often passed an elderly couple's home in Mission Beach with a pristine classic Corvette drydocked under the carport. Several times he drove by while the old man was out waxing it. The summer he was off to college he stopped by to see if the old man had thought of selling it. The man was friendly enough, but in a weary voice, as if he had told the tale to an endless string of prospective buyers, he told Blackie that the car had belonged to his son. The boy was the big loser in the draft lottery – picked as number one. He had been killed in Viet Nam just before his twentieth birthday. And for fifteen years the car had sat there, keeping alive the memory of his son.

In the turning basin, Blackie headed the Island Packet up Government Cut, since no cruise ships were at dock on a Thursday. In the absence of ships, the Homeland Security contractors in their tiny inflatable boats weren't there to divert them.

Passing the jetties between South Beach and Fisher Island, he turned the boat to the south after unfurling the jib and main. The boat beat south in a 10-knot sea breeze out of the east. He steered for a mythical spot a couple miles off Cape Florida. Dani's resting place was to be 25-40 N 80-05 W, a spot on the charts in about 150 feet of water off Key Biscayne. Without her remains in an urn, their plan was to cast flowers into the sea in her memory.

When the GPS beeped its "approaching waypoint" alarm, Blackie turned the boat into the wind and furled all sails. There was no need to try and anchor in that deep of water with an onshore chop.

The Island Packet drifted slowly southward, caught in a reverse eddy of the Gulf Stream, as they gathered on the foredeck for the brief ceremony. The swells were too much for Dani's model-friends, both landlubbers, who ducked below to the heads. The rolling horizon gave them an acute case of melancholy *mal du mer*. Only the SoBe boatees hung out topside.

Yul began the eulogy, but a deep pulsing roar coming off the horizon drowned out his words. Yul paused, and the mourners looked to the south, where three large rooster-tails of white water gushed up off the horizon. The three dark specks below the plumes appeared motionless but grew in size, meaning that whatever they were, they were bearing down on the service.

The roar intensified, and the boatees looked at each other in wonder. Blackie considered running back to the cockpit and turning the boat toward them so as not to be hit broadside, but at the last moment the three craft turned tightly in unison to starboard. They roared past the Island Packet at 60 knots, three unmarked battleship-gray cigarette boats, all with a crew of four standing rigidly at the helm in full black battle gear, including helmets. Over their heads were three identical stern arches, each holding an array of radomes.

No sooner had the mourners taken in the sight than the boats were gone.

Blackie finally spoke. "Some things we just aren't meant to comprehend."

Yul resumed his eulogy. "We spend a brief time here on this planet. For some, the time is so much briefer than for others. What we do with that time is what matters. Dani took control of her life. Like her boat's name, she 'seized the day.' The people here on this deck were all touched by her. We knew her. We loved her. We will miss her."

Blackie wiped the tears away and looked down. He saw on Yul's feet a pair of black Topsiders, a ratty old pair that Yul appeared to have spray-painted gloss black just for the occasion.

"Blackie. Blackie, it's time. Did you want to say anything?" Yul asked softly.

Blackie turned and addressed the small crowd of boatee friends.

"She – she was very independent. I occupied only a tiny sliver of her life. Too often, we were like two ships in the Stream, crossing paths in the night.

"Just a few days before she – she died – we had sailed down to Elliot Key on her boat. There were times on that trip that I thought we had really connected. That there was hope for us. That I was tapping a tiny chink in that façade, that barrier of hers that she had created.

"But I guess – I guess that it wasn't meant to be.

"She could do anything she put her mind to. She didn't need me. She never really needed anyone. I wouldn't call her a loner, or aloof. But I think with the cards life dealt her she was most comfortable alone. For a naïve pilot who loved her as much as I did that isn't easy to admit, yet it was what I admired most about her. God, I'll miss her."

Blackie gathered the long, waxy stems of the tropical flowers and handed one to each of those onboard. One by one they went to the port lifeline and tossed their flower, a Bird of Paradise, off the deck. Blackie had bought the dozen stems from a vendor selling in the shade of the overpass near the Key Biscayne tollbooths. The flowers were a rare strain of stelitzia called Mandella's Gold, hand pollinated in a nursery in South Africa and flown by 747 freighter to Miami.

Blackie was last. He walked to the rail and held up the stem to examine it. The yellow flower emerged from the blue spathe, a beak-like sheath that made it look like an exotic bird's head. He admired its perfection. And he pitched it into the deep, blue sea.

*   *   *

The school of bonefish boiled the water on the opposite bank, the light reflecting off an occasional dorsal fin piercing the surface. Their flats boat slid across the surface of the shallow water. Trevor nodded his okay, and Dani fell into her routine, holding the line in one hand while flicking her fly rod methodically with the other. The weightless fly darted back and forth, finally landing just outside the percolating water. A solitary bonefish darted out of the crowd, snapped up the fly and shot away toward the mangroves.

The short but intense fight was over before she knew it, but the thrill was exhilarating. She once thought that fly-fishing was a just a guy-thing, but under Trevor's tutelage she was quickly mastering the sport.   Despite her success, she hadn't forgotten his observation that it was much easier to teach someone who had never done much spin or bait casting.   She certainly hadn't, and she was able to perfect her technique for a couple hours each day.

"Trevor, let's trade so you can continue our lesson."

"If dat is what you want, girl."

Dani wiped the sweat from her brow, the shallow flats reflecting the sun's rays on her tanned face. She ran her hand through her bleach-blonde, bristle-length hair. After cutting her hair, Trevor had found a bottle of platinum dye in a dusty box at the general store in Alice Town. Dani was surprised to find that one extra benefit of being a blonde was that it was at least a dozen degrees cooler when fishing hatless.

She truly believed that she was better off in exile. The whole Ted situation aside, just being free of things – cars, clothes, boats, bills – was an unexpected benefit to living life on the lam.   No more being hit on at the wine department at Epicure, no more grounding in the shallowness of South Beach, no more rudeness.   Yet she still looked over her shoulder constantly, expecting at any minute for a RIB-full of Coasties to come storming into her cove and snatch her back to "civilization." That she had gone this long undiscovered she believed was a miracle. That she had found Trevor – or that Trevor had found her – was another. And that they were both alive was the most unbelievable miracle of all. She recalled the day on Ted's yacht and the exact moment when she had witnessed the ending of that chapter in her life.

She had stood on the engine block, the water to her chin. She held the tiny LED flashlight at arm's length and pointed it up, the ice-blue beam reflecting off the ceiling. Less than ten feet away was Trevor staring at her, not with a look of hatred or malevolence, but a look of sadness, even pity.

Neither spoke. And then it floated by between them. The cork popper. She let go the little flashlight still tethered to her wrist and grabbed the utensil, its shiny 2-inch needle washed clean of Ted's blood. She jammed the needle between the heavy cable tie and her wrist. The tie was so tight she was forced to jab the sharp spike through the plastic box with the tab, poking her tendons and veins. She pulled with all her might but the tie didn't budge. She turned her head toward the ceiling and gathered in what she knew would be one of her final breaths. She would try a different tack. With the needle against her fingertip she led it to the tab and slowly wiggled it in. She made a tentative tug with her arm and felt a click. She repeated the procedure, feeling a tick-tick-tick and then a welcome zip. She was free.

Dani swam the few feet over to Trevor. Stopping to press her nose against the ceiling she gasped for the precious air. She poked the barrel of the tiny flashlight in her mouth. She grabbed his wrist with one hand while jabbing in the needle of the cork popper with the other.

She nodded her head and Trevor pulled. A few ticks. She pried the needle in again, tearing into his ebony skin. He pulled and the plastic ribbon ran free. One left.

Trevor reached out and with one hand gently held her up by her waist in the water. He turned and leaned back, his mouth an inch from the ceiling, and took a deep breath. Dani grabbed his other wrist, found the tie and jammed the needle in. Trevor tugged and the tie unzipped on the first pull; practice made perfect.

They both swam for the light filtering in from the stairway. On the fourth step they emerged from the sea. After clambering up, they both stopped at the landing and filled their lungs with the welcome ocean air.

They ran through the salon to the aft deck and once outside scanned the horizon. Not a single vessel was in sight.

"Girl, what you want to do?" Trevor asked.

"I want to get out of here. I want to start over," Dani said without hesitation.

"No Defense Force? No Coast Guard?"

"No murder charge. No publicity. No pleading self-defense. And no looking over my shoulder for one of Ted's henchmen."

"So get in da boat girl. Let's go."

She untied the painter that held his old sportfish to the sinking megayacht while Trevor fired up the outboard. A few minutes later the settling Breakwater was a bump on the southern horizon.

Trevor kept well off shore as they headed north for Bimini. Dani heard the familiar voice of Blackie shouting a Mayday over the boat's VHS. The two looked at each other and Dani shook her head. Finally she spoke.

"No. I want to start over, Trevor. I don't want to ever have to explain what I just did. Not to anyone."

"Den I'll take you to a place I got on East Wells for awhile. Til we work tings out."

Trevor ran up the coast of North Bimini, looping around the upper end before heading east, then south through a narrow channel between two curtains of mangroves.

"I got dis ole fishin' shack you can stay at for awhile. Hide out til tings calm down," Trevor said. They rounded a few bends in the mangroves and eventually pulled up to a one-room weathered-wood building on stilts tucked into a side channel.[19]

Trevor told Dani that during the frequent down times at the mine he earned extra income as a fishing guide. He had two places, one on East Wells and another fishing shack up Fresh Creek on Andros. He often made as much guiding rich Americans for a day or two than a week at the aragonite mine.

Dani hid out in the old shack and never stepped outside, with Trevor making a daily visit to bring food and water and to check on her. He finally admitted to her that

---

[19] Trevor's North Bimini fishing shack. 25.44.50N, 79.14.53W.

things were looking bad. An influx of entrepreneurs attempting to capitalize off the tragedy had invaded Alice Town. Some had great plans to raise *Ted's Toy*. Others were there with a Betacam and cameraman, trying to eke a living off the tragedy, which was entirely possible since there was a SoBe model involved.

A week into exile, Trevor showed up with his boat loaded with gear. The aragonite mine had closed for a month while they dredged the channel, and his daughters were with relatives in Nassau for the rest of the school term. So he had decided to gather up Dani and head for the safety and solitude of his other fishing camp over on Andros.

At dusk they headed across the Elbow Bank for the big island. They ran down inside the barrier reef on the east side of Andros, past Paw Paw Cay and Hard Bargain to the outlet of Fresh Creek. At Coakley Town, with Dani staying out of sight, he transferred the gear at the empty dock into his flats boat, and the pair headed up into the shallow labrynth to the west. Trevor's fishing shack was on a small island in the brackish waters far up Fresh Creek.[20]   The place was so remote that Trevor was able to take her out on his flats boat the next morning, giving her the first of many fly-fishing lessons.

And she settled into an idyllic routine. She ate fruit from the Mennonites grown in their orchards and fields in northern Andros. Trevor caught lobster or a grouper or snapper for dinner, and Dani learned the native skill of cleaning fresh conch.

As she poled the shallow-draft skiff, she watched Trevor casting the rod. With incredible ease he presented the fly, leader and line to his target, a tarpon. She watched him effortlessly complete his forward power stroke, the back muscles rippling as he completed his cast. She and Trevor were more than just friends. They had returned from the abyss, both realizing they had saved one another.

---

[20] Trevor's Fresh Creek fishing shack on Andros. 24.42.06N, 77.61.54W.

She felt a sudden sadness as she thought of Blackie back in Miami, unaware that at that moment he was doing his best at closure, standing on the deck of his boat and pitching an exotic flower into the water off Key Biscayne. The moment passed. She handed Trevor a pair of pliers so he could release the tarpon he had hooked, giving the silver fish another chance. This was her new life, and it was exactly as she wanted it to be.

Glossary of Nautical Terms

(note: nautical terms often have multiple meanings. Definitions here are as the words are used in the novel.)

Aft – toward the back of the boat. Opposite of fore.
Amas – pontoons or outriggers on each side of the center hull on a trimaran.

Bahamian Moor – anchoring with two anchors in a confined creek or space that minimizes the swing of the boat.
Batten – fiberglass slat(s) that fit in the mainsail to strengthen it.
Bilge – lowest part inside the boat below the sole (floor).
Bimini (top) – canvas or vinyl cover over the cockpit for rain and sun protection.
Bosun's chair – canvas sling chair on a halyard used to go up the mast.
Bow – forward part of the boat. Opposite of stern.
Bowsprit – Platform forward of the bow securing the jibstay.
Bridge – or helm, where the steering station is, usually high up on big boats.

Coaming – raised edge around a cockpit to keep water from running below.
Cleat – anvil-shaped fitting on which lines (ropes) are made fast.
Close Reach – sailing close to the direction from which the wind is coming.
Cockpit –steering and seating area on sailboats.
Cutter – sailboat with two sails forward (versus one for a sloop).
Cutwater – the forward edge of the stem or bow at the waterline.

Davits – supported arms used to suspend the dinghy at the boat's stern.
Dinghy – or tender or dink. Small boat (often inflatable) carried or towed by the bigger boat. Used to ferry the crew ashore.
Draft – depth below the waterline of a vessel. An important factor when sailing in the shallow waters of Florida and the Bahamas.

Fathom – traditional measure of water depth (one fathom is 6 feet).
Falling Off – steering the boat further off the wind.

Halyard – line (rope) to a block (or pulley) at the mast top to raise up the sail.
Head – toilet, or room with the toilet on a boat.

In Irons – having the sailboat pointed into the wind, sails flapping, going nowhere.

Jib – or headsail. Forward sail.
Jibe – altering course to bring a following wind on the opposite side.

Knot – measurement of speed on a boat. 1 knot equals one nautical mile per hour (or 1.1 MPH).

Lanyard – short line on a tool to wrap around one's wrist to keep it from going overboard if dropped.
Lazarrette – locker for sails usually under the cockpit seats.
Leeward – the opposite direction from which the wind is coming. Opposite of windward.
Lifelines – plastic-coated wire that creates a protective fence around the sailboat to prevent going overboard.

Main – primary sail attached behind the mast.
Masthead – top of the mast to which blocks or pulleys are attached for halyards; location of wind instruments, windex and lightning dissipator.

Painter – line for towing a dinghy behind the mother ship.
Pennant – small triangular flag flown from a line up to the spreader (in modern days), flown from the mizzen mast in olden days.
Port – to the left; left side of the boat (looking forward.)

Sheet – line (rope) that attaches to a sail to control its trim.
Shoal – a shallow patch in the water.
Snapshackle – sail hardware similar to a carbiner used for attaching line.
Sole – floor of the boat, usually in the cabin or cockpit.
Spinnaker – Balloon-like (and often colorful) headsail for running downwind.
Spreader – horizontal projections from the mast that spread the shrouds, the wire rigging that supports the mast side-to-side.
Stanchion – the waist-high pole that support the lifelines.
Starboard – to the right; right side of the boat (looking forward.)
Sundowner – any drink quaffed onboard during the sunset-spectacle ritual.
Stay – the wire rigging fore and aft that supports the mast.

Tack - altering course to bring a headwind to the opposite side of the boat.

Winch – drum-shaped sail hardware that uses mechanical advantage to tighten sheets (lines to sails) to control them.
Windex – arrow-shaped wind-directon indicator at the mast top.
Windlass – drum-shaped anchoring hardware that uses mechanical advantage (and often an electric motor) to bring the anchor up.

256

About the author:

Kevon Andersen has been a liveaboard sailor with his wife, Debbie, for more than 17 years. They sail in the Florida Keys, Bahamas and the Caribbean. This is his third book, second novel. A nonfiction work, **Prisoners of the Deep**, co-authored with his brother Brian David Andersen, was published by Harper & Row in 1985. In addition to sailing and writing, he has worked parttime for two decades for an airline, with most of those years at MIA. He is also an avid UL hiker.

SoBe Boatees was written onboard a sailboat, a Pearson 390 sloop, where the author continues working on the second and third installments in the Blackie Petersen trilogy.

Ordering copies of this book:

- Visit your local bookseller and ask for a copy of *SoBe Boatees.*
- Visit an online bookseller and order a copy.
- Go to the author's website, vonniebooks.com and order a copy (and for more information.)